I0550572

Life Is Hell and Suburbia Is a Lie
or, the slow-speed come apart.

A story in three parts by Ken Carter

Uppity Negro Publishing
Lakewood, Co

Uppity Negro Publishing
Lakewood CO 80215
http://www.uppitynegro.net (come visit us, and read Ken's blog!)
'Life is Hell and Suburbia is a Lie' Copyright © Ken Carter
Cover design by Ken Carter
Back Cover images by Michal Zacharzewski SXC
First Edition (finally!)

ISBN-10: 0615479162
ISBN-13: 978-0615479163

A special thank you to my wife who has supported me in all my dreams. Without her standing behind me with unending encouragement, this book would have never been finished. Thank you.

Author's Note:

This book was written over a period spanning ten years. Parts of it may offend you, and indeed I hope they do. I hope this book causes you to question something, anything, that you believe and forces you to examine it. Within that examination you will find what you believe proven true or false. Either way, you're welcome.

Chapter One: Who peed in your Wheaties?

<u>Now</u>

Her mother had been right. It felt like warmth on the wind. She really hadn't expected it to; She had expected it to hurt somehow.

<u>6 Months Prior</u>

Walter Betha lived on Oak Street. There are a great many Oak streets throughout the United States and possibly the world, but none like his. See, on Walter Betha's Oak Street, he's the local paperboy. Each morning, around 4 a.m., the bundles of newspaper arrived outside his door. He's never met the magical beings that drop those bundles off, but he knows that each morning, they will be there. It was as sure as the sun rising; As sure as the world turned, those papers would appear. Once, and only once they had not been there, but that was due to an error at the printers. The newspaper's office in charge of supply had called Walter's mother early that morning so that she could tell him there would be no deliveries that day. That was a very dark day for Walter Betha. When you are the paperboy and you have no papers to deliver your emptiness is epic and vast.

Each morning at 4:13, his Spider-Man alarm clock would wake Walter up without fail. It was an exact time that Walter had found worked best through trial and error. For many years he had found that getting up at 4:15 was adequate, but later found that by getting up 2 minutes earlier, he was able to take a few more minutes to wake up as he brushed his teeth and dressed. Saving those two minutes allowed him to get out into the world two minutes earlier and his papers were delivered two minutes earlier. He was extremely proud of finding this time saving breakthrough. He was amazed no one had thought of it before: the earlier he woke up, the earlier he was able to deliver his papers. If one followed this simple plan, Walter theorized, one could avoid being late. His parents secretly wondered with joyous anticipation when Walter would discover that if he woke up just before the papers were dropped off and got himself ready before they got there, just how efficient he could be.

When that alarm rang at 4:13, Walter would scramble from underneath his sheets and throw on his old pair of sweatpants. They were his unofficial uniform required to be worn at all times while tending to his paper route. He washed them once a week, just after finishing the Sunday route. The comic section's wet ink had left many a stain on those old sweats. He wore a matching zip-up sweatshirt. Both came in the once standard, now forgotten sweat-suit gray. Walter wasn't big on other colors for his work clothes. He was all about his routines. Gray was what he was used to; gray was what he wanted. Once, many years before, Walter's mother had made the foolish mistake of replacing his worn gray suit with a red one. Walter was irate, and disappointed. Seeing his wrath, and pain, his mother never made that mistake again. Walter liked gray, so Walter got gray.

As he prepared each morning, Walter thought of Oak Street. Oak Street was special to Walter because out of the four streets on his route, Oak Street had the worst tippers. Normally, this would be a bad thing, but to Walter, it was heaven. See, on Oak street he could let loose. He could aim for cars and lawn ornaments. In his day he'd taken out more than a few windows. Sure, he had to reimburse the owners but, *boy, was it fun*. To the average person this would seem like a menial bit of entertainment. To Walter Betha, the 22-year old mentally retarded neighborhood newsboy, it was to die for.

On this particular Thursday morning, Walter finally finished rolling the papers at about 5 a.m. He performed this duty under the hawk-like eye of his mother. She sat patiently, offering no help. This was one task Walter did on his own, because he could. She wouldn't dare injure his pride by offering her help. He didn't have to ask his mother, father or brothers for any kind of help. Truth be told, Walter's mother was glad he had something he could do on his own. Much of Walter's life was spent being told what to do, and watched over. He couldn't live the life of other children, due to his mental retardation. The world was always viewed through a ten year-old's eyes, where Walter was concerned. He would always be a child. His mother would always be a mommy, and never a grandmother. She would watch over him until she died, and secretly, she hoped he would not live to see that day. Mrs. Betha's worst fears were constantly shadowing her daily thoughts. Who would take care of Walter when she was dead and gone? Her husband, while a good man, would be woefully incompetent at such a task. He worked in an office wearing expensive suits and talking in paragraphs of twenty dollar words that when spoken before intelligent men made it painfully obvious that Mr. Betha was full of it. That, of course, was his job. Lording over the modern slave pits, now called cubicles, he didn't have much to say. He sat around drinking coffee and spending expense account money on lunches with other executives who did the same amount of nothing for a career. They talked numbers and strategy and didn't really do anything. Mrs. Betha had no doubts that the man would be a complete failure as a single parent. He'd end up frustrated and Walter would end up in a home somewhere. Walter would never deliver another paper, and he'd die old and lonely with the mind of a boy who'd never reached adolescence. These very thoughts made their rounds through the halls of her mind every day. Each day, when she ran through this scenario mentally, her heart broke the same. While she was here and could make sure that Walter had a good life, Mrs. Betha was content to watch and let him have what little glories he could. Delivering papers fulfilled him. In turn, it fulfilled her.

By the time 6 o' clock rolled around, Walter was on his way down Oak Street. He had been down the other three avenues that he delivered to. The saddlebag satchel that had started the morning teeming with all the news fit to print was now hanging doggedly to one side, it's load lightened almost completely.

Walter always saved Oak street for the end of his run. It was the conclusion of his workday. His long trek each morning culminated with a victory run down Oak Street. The street of bad tippers and overdue bills. Oak Street wasn't like the surrounding neighborhoods. Oak Street wasn't a group of prefabricated homes made of shoddy materials all painted white to off white with trim in tan to light brown. No, Oak Street was "old" suburbia. Oak Street, unlike the other streets on Wally's route, was made up of separate, distinct homes. These weren't just houses. They had been lived in and built around the families who owned them, instead of the family trying to fit in a box that had been created based on weak interpretations of modern design dressed up in cheap stucco.

As he turned on to Oak Street he noticed a bonus prize in the distance. It was Mr. Kirkland. Mr. Jack Kirkland was head of the local Homeowner's Association. He hated Walter, and Walter in all his innocence, hated Mr. Kirkland right back. It was more than oil and vinegar. It was good versus evil. Walter was youth, innocence and joy. Mr. Kirkland was a bitter old man who hated life simply because he had to live it. He clipped coupons and tried to use them past their due date. He kept his porch light on through Halloween night, and never answered the door or gave out a single candy. He used his dead mother's Handicap parking sticker, and when he parked in the spaces, often took up two of them. If the Grinch had ever come to life from the pages of the old Dr. Seuss classic, he would have slithered out of his cave and into the liver spot mottled skin of Jack Kirkland.

This morning, Jack was ambling about his front porch checking the various rose bushes his wife had waiting there to be planted. Jack had been forced to take the day off of work to tend these flowers. His wife wanted some of the plants moved to the backyard but complained that she didn't have the personal strength to do the job. Jack had been recruited against his will, due to a threat of the withholding of adult relations by his wife. Jack waited on his porch now for "that damned retard with the news," sipping a cup of excessively strong coffee. It was beyond bitter mud, likening itself more to salt-flavored pudding. Thick with caffeine and bereft of sugar or cream, the concoction was how Jack Kirkland enjoyed a cup of joe. The only thing he was missing was his fresh Marlboro but the wife had made him quit ten years ago after he underwent surgery for colon cancer.

Walter raced down the street, being careful to bombard the familial cluster of gnomes at the O'Leary household. Nicole O'Leary, the daughter, was always nice to him. Mr. O'Leary was always mean. Mr. O'Leary often "forgot" to pay the full amount for his newspaper subscription. Walter never forgot. He remembered each time he passed the O'Leary household.

His aim was dead on as he whizzed past Mr. and Mrs. McGuire's cat. The feline scampered away over the wooden fence and into the jungles of the backyard to safety. Walter came upon Mr. Kirkland, standing in his front yard with a cup of coffee in his hands. Suddenly, a dream of heaven entered Walter's mind. Walter visualized it all like a professional baseball pitcher. With a raising of the arm and a closing of the eyes, he watched it all play out in his mind. With eyes shut, he released the paper and it flew with laser guided accuracy. There was no wind to flaw it's flight. There was no rain or snow to beat the paper to the ground before it found it's target. The morning was clear, save for a slight bit of fog holding dearly to the ground, becoming little more than a dying gray as the sun rose in the morning sky. Jack Kirkland was caught by surprise by this blatant assault. Jack had seen Walter coming down the street. He watched the boy throw a newspaper deliberately into the O'Leary's gnomes. Not that Jack really cared about the gnomes. He hated the O'Leary's and their spiteful brat of a daughter, not to mention the hooligan they called a son. No, Jack could not have cared less for the gnomes or the O'Leary's. Seeing Walter destroy the gnomes reinforced Jack's belief that Walter was a miscreant and a vandal. If there were any other way to get his morning paper delivered to his door, Jack would have taken it immediately. He had known the boy despised him, but he never expected an all-out drive-by-newspapering.

Jack's early morning reflexes betrayed his move for safety. His mind told him it was moving his sluggish limbs, but in reality nothing was happening. Jack was forced to watch as Walter humiliated him. The paper slammed into the coffee cup. It flew from his hands, spraying molten morning java on his chest. The thick concoction stuck to him like melted plastic, barely running down his torso. Chest hair singed and curled back in fear of the immediate assault of heat. Jack let out a feminine scream of pain as the glass fell, breaking on his foot. It was a cup given to him by a vendor competing for his company's services. The cup had been one of many; free, worthless swag that Jack had piles of, but now this one meant something. Any other day, it would have just been a coffee cup. Today, having it broken by Walter Betha, Jack suddenly realized just how much he liked that particular cup. Walter laughed.

He laughed so hard he crashed right into a parked car across the street. As he scrambled to his feet he noticed the raging Mr. Kirkland looking dead at him. Walter threw his bike up and hopped on. Jack Kirkland walked across his own lawn toward the boy. When he did, the morning sprinklers came on as they were timed to, and he was frozen by the grip of an icy morning shower. Jack's muscles tightened with spasms, and his body went tense. His skin became rigid as his teeth ground themselves nearly to dust. Walter rode away to freedom. Jack Kirkland shuffled with a sigh and a mind to murder the mentally handicapped. He snatched up his soaking paper and as he did, his eye caught the O'Leary lawn next door. It was a full half-inch shorter than his own. Jack knew that couldn't be right. He had just cut his grass three days prior. What it meant, was that the O'Leary's had cut their own lawn a full quarter inch below the acceptable HOA standards, and in doing so had made Jack look like he wasn't maintaining his own yard. It was contemptuous. Jack walked through the sprinklers and put his face at eye level with the grass. Gritting his teeth, he plucked a handful of O'Leary grass in his hand, in case they needed proof and stormed into his house. They would be receiving a letter about this. They could count on that. He had no idea what was about to begin in the house next to his and how little they would ever care about his suburban, mini-fairway.

You see, that morning, Nicole O'Leary's parents had told her the news. They called her down from her room in her Hello Kitty nightshirt, and cooked her breakfast. This was not a regular occurrence, so she was a bit taken aback by the entire situation. Normally, her father was off to work at this hour. Her mother slept in until at least 10 a.m. Today though, was different. Today, Nicole sat in the kitchen at 7:00 a.m. Her mother had made her favorite breakfast: French toast. Two months prior, her father had allowed them to finally stop calling it "Freedom Toast". She preferred the meal just as it was being prepared: Cinnamon and a nice jar of syrup would help her complete the sugar bomb that would have her nerves on edge for hours. It wasn't the healthiest, and she knew time in the gym would be needed to take it off, but it tasted so damn good.

Her father, remembering that it was a Thursday in November, called her in sick to school. The breakfast had piqued her curiosity. The phone call increased the weird. Nicole, being an 18-year old honor roll student, was by no means stupid or ignorant. Being book smart isn't where it ended for her. Besides her academic excellence and intellect, Nicole was well versed in the ways of the world. She had known this day was coming but had not expected it to come so soon. She could have called them out, right there in the kitchen that day. Maybe she should have. It probably wouldn't have changed anything, but you never know. Nicole would look back to this day over the next few months several times. This was the day everything changed, she was sure of that. She wasn't sure that given a second chance, she would react any differently.

Nicole's auburn hair was cropped short with blonde highlights. It hugged her head like a swimming cap. She ran her hands through it, but it still appeared slept on. She rubbed the smudged mascara from her eyes, carrying with it yellow crusts of sleep. She felt awkward at the table. Her long nightshirt fell only to her mid-thigh. She was uncomfortable with her parents getting any sight of her matching panties. Especially her dad. That would just be disgusting. Her parents would probably feel the same way about the hickeys on her inner thigh, had they seen them. Jeremy Bloom, head of the chess club had given them to her two nights prior.

Nicole didn't know why she had deflowered him. Being an extremely popular girl (vice-president of her class, head of the business club and debate team, co-captain of the pep squad, ex captain of the varsity cheer squad by choice), something about the intelligent outcast appealed to her. He weathered the experience rather well for a virgin. Jeremy lasted a full ten minutes longer than her current boyfriend (Chad Walters, head of the ski and swim teams). Plus, Jeremy had serviced her before they began and that was always a bonus. Sure, she had to coach him most of the way, but he was a great student and that made it worth her while. Afterward, he thanked her with tears in his eyes, which she supposed she was owed. After all, how many uber-geeks get laid by one of the best looking girls in town in the Wal-Mart men's room? Nicole and Jeremy had retained a weird friendship after that. "Friends with Benefits" was what her friends called them. She and Jeremy would steal looks at one another in the hallways before and after class. Jeremy was afraid of Chad, but desperately attracted to Nicole. Nicole felt something from Jeremy that just might be love, but she didn't know it yet. Nicole was glad that Chad hadn't found about any of it. Otherwise he and his ski team buddies would be scouring the Chicago suburbs they inhabited, looking to, "beat that faggot's ass," never minding the fact that Jeremy had committed what were obviously heterosexual acts with Chad's girlfriend.

Nicole, at the breakfast table, smirked at the irony. Six of the thirteen members of his ski-team were in the closet. In fact, they were most often in the closet with each other. If not that, then it was with the married men in their thirties who patrolled Mead Park looking for a little experimental action after hours. Nicole was pretty sure Chad had "experimented" with some of his teammates at one time or another, but she looked past it, and the other rumors. Chad was the most popular boy in school. That meant Nicole had to have him. She had to have the best, at all times, and settling for anything less was beneath her. Being with Nicole helped Chad avoid most of the homosexual rumors surrounding him. After all, if he was sleeping with a girl that beautiful, who everyone wanted to be, how gay could he be? The relationship worked because they were both vultures feeding on the same carcass of a relationship.

Nicole left her wandering thoughts of Chad behind, focusing instead on the surreal meal before her. Her mother had placed a full plate on the table while trying to hide her puffed eyes. Elaine O'Leary had been crying, and would again soon. In recent months the Prozac, Xanax, and other brand name medications had failed. The tearful episodes had increased not only in frequency, but in intensity as well. So had Nicole's mom(Elaine) and pop's(Harold) late night arguments that began as barely audible whispers and matured into full blown shouting matches that pained her heart as well as her ears. The constant yelling and screaming kept Nicole up many-a-night. The arguments usually began with something small, perhaps the choice for dinner, and wound up as battle royales, full of thrown dishes, holes punched in the wall, and a few times, physical violence on the part of both parties. During these twilight hours of spewing hate-speech and violence, Nicole usually reviewed her trigonometry or homework from her other honors classes. It was a waste of time waiting for her parents to finally give up and go to bed. Most nights, if her homework was light, she would go out and get drunk with Chad and his buddies. He rarely ever took her out alone. Nicole wondered how often he lied to her about being busy with something else when he was really patrolling Mead Park with his teammates. All in all, he did provide her with an inebriated distraction from her abysmal family life, which served all the purpose she had hoped to get from him.

Her parent's fighting never bothered her older brother, Jackson (Captain of the dip-shit team, Co-Captain of the Losers of America). When he wasn't out with his girlfriend (Queen of the stoners, sluts and dropouts), he was passed out in his room. He was the average 24-year old failure. He had no clue. About anything. Nicole had known about their parent's issues from the start. Jackson never cared about anybody but himself. He and his friends thought they could do whatever they wanted to whomever they wanted. They thought they could hurt anyone who got in the way of their next good time, and no one would care. Jackson inherited many of these traits from his father. Nicole hated her brother, and his friends. No part of her heart cared for him, in the slightest. She'd often wished that on one of his weekend binges, that he'd just die in a ditch somewhere and never be found.

Her father stood across the room from her now. Leaning against the doorjamb, he watched her eat. Watching things was his specialty. Harold preferred the term, "observing". He was the a prominent employee of a large bioengineering research facility funded by the leading pharmaceutical company in the world. The company had begun as his own, but with a need to finance several profitable patents and breakthroughs, he needed true financial muscle and backing. Selling out to the pharmaceutical was the only option he was left with in order to protect his company and his work. In turn, he gained more power in the industry, but lost much of the control of his company. He still sat on the board of directors along with two of his original board members. However, they were outnumbered two-to-one by the new arrivals that had come from the drug pharmaceutical. It was one of the few cases where great power did not end with great responsibility, but an actual loss of capability. At the end of the day, the company ran him and his research, no matter what he believed. They would squeeze him for all that they could get and in the end he would be voted out of the boardroom, and removed from the payroll. He was expendable, and when his research finally stopped providing the company with enough financial blessings, he would be lucky to be terminated unceremoniously by some corporate headhunter who would be paid a sizable sum just to tell him he had be let go.

Conversations with Harold O'Leary revolved mainly around the cold facts in life. He didn't know much about feelings, and considered them more weaknesses and lies than anything else. This was the foremost reason he had been no good to his family for years. If you couldn't see a sample of something under a microscope or find it at the end of an equation, it meant it did not exist as far as he was concerned. Or at the very least that it didn't matter. He was a fifth generation conservative and as such was a dedicated subscriber to the American conservative movement. He would kill if Rush Limbaugh told him it was the American thing to do. He'd strangle Michael Moore or Hillary Clinton on general principle. Nicole wasn't sure how many times she'd heard his tired rant about "them Mex-ee-cans" taking American jobs, and the need to keep the "true" America a "clean" culture. He would often end the speech with proclamations of love for all of mankind if they'd all just vote Republican. Any disagreement with him tended to get one branded as a socialist or even worse, a traitor. Harold loved his country, so long as things went his way. His detest for anything liberal ran deep. It took very little to send him on a politically charged tirade. Nicole avoided all conversation with him, as much as possible.

He was a bigot and a pervert. He loved Nicole because she could bring her friends over, giving him a chance to ogle them up close. He thought Nicole and her friends had no idea. *Nicole knew*. She knew where in the garage he kept his stash of dirty magazines or pictures of her friends he'd secreted out of her room for whatever twisted personal uses he had for them. She knew he muttered her friend's names when he was masturbating in the bathroom. Nicole wasn't sure if her mother was aware of the inner pervert her father fostered, but she wasn't sure how Mrs. O'Leary couldn't know. It seemed most often that she and her mother were the only ones who did pay attention to anything going on in their home. For someone who spent his time "observing", Harold O'Leary ignored everything. He didn't understand that wrongs just didn't go away. They had to be dealt with, and sometimes the way to deal with them was never forgetting. Nicole would never forget. *He had watched, and she knew it.*

Her mother was more aware of her surroundings, or had been, though not by much. She wasn't overbearing or mean or oppressive or overprotective. She was just... average. She went to church every Sunday at the local Catholic Church for the morning service. She went to Wednesday bible study at the local Lutheran church. Each Sunday, she would pack at least one dish to church. This was to share with the parishioners as they entertained themselves with un-Christian gossip in the pews after the service. Mrs. O'Leary wasn't sure if she was going to heaven, but she would be damned if she wouldn't try. Nicole had gone with her mom every weekend. It was one of the few things that they had together for many years, until recently. It hadn't been so much a bonding experience as it was Nicole making sure her mother got to smile at least once a week. Nicole knew her mother was suicidal and had been severely depressed for years. Of course, lately, there had been no church. Her mother had been too drunk or doped up to do anything but drool on herself in front of the television. Nicole had stopped trying to encourage her mother to return to their usual routine. After feeling defeat after so many weeks of suggesting and prompting to return to what had been the status-*quo*, Nicole had given up. Her mother was on a downward spiral, and Nicole didn't know how to stop it. She stood back, and merely tried to slow the descent, hoping that she'd at least finish college before her mother killed herself. To complicate these matters further, there was the strange relationship that Nicole and her mother had.

No amount of church could amend some sins. Nicole's mother had been jealous of Nicole since Nicole reached puberty. Nicole became the apple of her father's eye then. Mrs. O'Leary knew why, but she couldn't deprive her daughter of friends because her father was a goddamned pervert. At least he had never tried to touch any of the girls, so much as Elaine knew. This was another reason for the wedge dividing the Mr. and Mrs. Because of this, Mrs. O'Leary would often tell herself it was Nicole's fault. Thankfully, praise the Lord, she never acted or showed that she felt this way in front of anyone other than her husband. For all their faults, Nicole had loved each of them once, although in vastly different degrees. Her mother was still dear to her. Her father was nothing in her eyes, but a bank account.

The current situation was beginning to get out of hand. Nicole had little to no idea what the morning was going to bring about, exactly. She had the gist of it, but the Saturday Morning Special breakfast that her parents had cooked up was getting to be a bit too strange for her. Mrs. O'Leary sat on the table, admiring the beauty of god's creation in her daughter. Nicole could have avoided her gaze to help things along, but she was tired of helping things along. Everything Nicole was supposed to be in life, she was. Why couldn't life, just this once, be everything it was supposed to be for her? It was a completely rational thought to her. In reality, Nicole had been afforded more opportunities than most ever dreamt of. It was a selfish idea, but to such a spoiled brat, only something so heinous could be considered rational. She stared at her mother with false expectations of joy through a chewing grin. The food tasted sweeter than ever. Already, it was working away her hangover from the previous night's drinking binge with her friends.

Her mother clasped her hands together on the table.

"Sweetheart..." Mrs. O'Leary started, only to trail off in a breath. Her voice had begun to crack already. Nicole continued to stare, even venturing to raise her eyebrows in question, daring her mother to say it. Nicole had to hold back laughter when she caught a glimpse of how stupid she looked in the reflection on the fork. The look on her face could not have been a simpler expression of joy. A small upward turn to the lips, and wide doe-like eyes did wonders to make her look like a total moron.

Her father cleared his throat, leaning forward. He felt control of the situation slipping away, and from his observation, someone had to step in and keep them on track.

"What your mother is trying to say-" he began but Mrs. O'Leary didn't allow him to finish.

"I can handle this Harold." Her mother was sterner than Nicole had ever heard. She hadn't even looked at her husband when she addressed him. Her eyes remained on the floor the entire time but the whip had been cracked. Harold visibly recoiled, furrowing his eyebrows and turning his face so fast, he may as well have been physically slapped.

"Nicole, sweetie," her mother was back to the soft tone Nicole had always known. "Your father and I have been having problems for some time now. And... well... we've decided to separate." It was as if once she opened her lips, Elaine wasn't able to contain herself and had to just spit it all out. Mrs. O'Leary had been holding this dark secret in and could finally release the beast onto the world, like the Seventh biblical seal had been broken.

Nicole lost her grin, but kept eating. Mrs. O'Leary planted her face on the table and began to bawl. Her father tried to console his soon to be estranged wife. He put his hands on her shoulders and began to rub them, despite her rebuff seconds ago. She shrugged him off. He would have cried, if he knew how. Instead, he figured the sexless streak he had been on was going to last another night. Defeat washed over his face and weighed down his soul dragging his shoulders with it. Mrs. O'Leary left the room in a disheveled hurry. Nicole took it all in with her grin returning. She looked at her father, smacking on the French toast with obnoxious exaggeration. This was it then. She knew it was coming, but didn't know it would feel like this. Her father stared back at her for a second, and then looked away, unable to hold her idiot's gaze. Nicole blinked slowly and snorted trying to hold back laughter. Somewhere in the distance of some unknown point in the darkest area of herself, Nicole heard a snap, like a dry twig breaking. It echoed around the emptiness she felt, growing into a tumultuous thunder that silenced itself when she finally blinked her eyes. She swallowed the toast slowly. Her mouth was dry and it felt like she was swallowing dirt. Nicole took a deep breath, and moved on to the next bite. It was what she was supposed to do.

Her father eventually snagged a beer from the refrigerator and left the room. It wasn't his normal routine, but he had been drinking a little more lately. He hadn't reached the level of alcoholism that her mother had delved down to, yet. Harold O'Leary was just having an extra beer or two a week, with this being one of those. He had waited a good two minutes after her mother had run off, to make a hasty retreat himself. He didn't bother saying another word to Nicole, or even looking in her direction. Nicole sat in the kitchen alone. There was no point in letting a perfectly good breakfast go to waste. Nicole ate slowly enough to try and enjoy it, but also with a sense of haste. She felt as if time was running out for her, but she didn't know why. Her parents were separating, but not divorcing, right? Still, that dreaded proverbial sense of impending doom began to crawl over her. When she finished eating, she washed the dishes she had used and set to drying them.

Suddenly, her mind was reeling. She stared back at her face in the reflection in her now clean plate as she dried it. Time and time again she had played this morning out in her head long before it happened. None of her ideas on how this day would unfold were anywhere near to the truth. She thought she knew exactly how she'd react. She didn't know anything. In her dreams, or nightmares rather, she knew everything she would say to both of her parents. Her words would make them see the error of their ways, and they'd talk it out and get back together. Her mom would stop drinking and her father would apologize for all his wrongs and become a decent man. In reality, she hadn't a clue what to say or do. Just breathing was a struggle at the moment.

Denial perched on the nape of her neck, pecking away at her reality. She knew it was ignorant, but she wondered if it was all a joke. She wondered if her parents would both come bursting back in. They would yell, "Surprise!", revealing the hidden video camera who's tape would be sent off in an attempt to win the grand prize from some "Funniest Videos" show. In truth, she knew none of that would happen. She knew this morning had been all too real, and that's why her reality was crumbling.

Nicole dropped her plate in the sink, where it broke into several pieces. She marched to the nearest bathroom and opened the medicine cabinet. Near the front was a year-old Percocet prescription she been given for a root canal. Nicole took two and looked under the sink. Her mother's stashed vodka bottle was waiting with open arms behind the trashcan. Nicole took three long swigs. She could do it. She could take more pills and a few drinks and get it over with. It wouldn't hurt, and then she wouldn't have to deal with any of these feelings that were raging through her.

She couldn't do it. Nicole fled the bathroom and ran smack into her older brother. His beer belly made for nice padding and saved her from major injury. She did fall softly to the floor.

"Whoa, spaz." Jackson was hung over and filthy. He reeked of marijuana and day old whiskey-sweat. He hadn't changed clothes in three days and hadn't showered in twice as long. His stench was augmented by his alcohol tinged breath and his body sweating to recover from a long night of drinking in the abandoned Drive-In. His bristled face left him in permanent shadow. His grungy Pantera shirt felt slimy to the touch. He knelt, Nicole thought, to help her. He extended his right arm, and she reached out to him. Jackson batted her hands away and picked up the half-smoked joint she had dislodged from behind his ear. His face sneered at her lame attempt to receive assistance.

"Ass." Nicole sighed, standing on her feet with her own power. She brushed her hands off on her shirt, not bothering to hide her disgust.

"You look like shit." Jackson grinned. "And you almost ruined my morning blaze. If I don't smoke I don't go to my classes. Me not in class means dad's a little unhappy, you dig?" Jackson accented his point by poking his half-smoked joint, pinched between his fingers, into her chest.

He stank. He stank like a homeless drunkard who's been wallowing in waste from a meat processing plant. His odor, Nicole guessed, seemed to be a mix of spoiled lunch meat and vomit. The sweat from his pores was like pure manure. Burn marks coated his lips and fingers from smoking his joints too far down. He was exactly what he looked like: A stale burnout.

"You're on academic probation at a community college where you take 1 class. A remedial English course with all the exchange students. Unlike you, they'll all pass and contribute to society. Loser." Nicole pushed past him, staying far away from his visibly greasy hair.

"Hey, Nicky," he called after her. "Here's an idea: Don't be such a bitch! Not everyone can be perfect like you!"

She batted a hand behind her, giving him the bird and dismissing him from existence. Nicole had no idea what to do next. Idly, she moved to the living room and sat on the couch. The drugs were beginning to take a placebo type of effect. They were making her numb. It was ironic that after waiting her whole life to feel something real, she went out of her way to try and dull the pain away. But it never went all the way away, no matter how many pills she took, or how many bottles she drank. After her breakfast today, Nicole wasn't sure that she'd ever be free of pain. To her, it seemed her life was falling apart. Yes, she hated her father, but he was her father. She wanted her family to stay together, and just fix things. She wanted them to be what they always dreamt they'd be. Instead, her world was being disassembled one day at a time, and she wasn't sure where it would stop.

Nicole sat alone, staring at a blank television screen for nearly two hours. This is all she knew to do. She had been raised in front of the idiot box and now it sat with her, feeling as dull and gray as she did. Her mind slowly moved away from the breakfast. As she began to reach the peak of her intoxication, she wanted someone to talk to. Anyone would do. Well, anyone besides Jackson.

He wasn't an option anyhow, even if he weren't off at school. Her father, who was useless in these situations, had left for work almost as soon as he had finished his beer when he had left her in the kitchen. Her mother was no doubt in her bedroom, down the hall, self medicated into submission. Nicole wondered where her mother's mind went that was so much better than here. What did she see when she dreamt? Was she happy? Nicole hoped so. Even if she couldn't be the parent she should be, Nicole hoped her mother was happy. She hoped because she knew that same life was her future. Not only did it depress her, but also it managed to scare the laziness from her. Every day she had fought to make sure she wasn't her mother. That wasn't the future she had dreamt of and worked for. Her goals never had and never would include home economics. Now, as she sat drunken and inebriated she realized she had to get up and move. Sitting here was only bringing her closer to that future she dreaded. It took the fear and a massive draw from the well of willpower to bring her to her feet.

She stumbled through her room and began to ready herself. Nicole was a spoiled girl. When she reached her 13th birthday, her parent's had not only given her an extravagant party; one of her gifts was the master bedroom of the house. The walk in closet and full bathroom were all hers and hers alone. Her father reconciled this by saying it cut down on the time she spent occupying the main restroom. No one believed him. He had been obviously bitter, but it kept Nicole happy, and she wasn't one who her parents liked to upset. Nicole had never known boundaries or true discipline. Any sort of attempt at discipline often left with Nicole crying tears and her parents giving her more than she had originally requested. When she had wanted a bigger room, there were two options, give her the master bedroom, or add on another room for Nicole. Both were options her parents could afford, but just switching rooms with her was easier. They had tried to offer her the chance to remodel a room in the finished basement, but that was where Nicole's gym equipment was kept, along with Jackson's room. Nicole refused to sleep anywhere near her brother. That was unacceptable. She was the quintessential spoiled little rich girl who got whatever she wanted... until today.

As she brushed the remainder of breakfast from her teeth, she searched for her wireless phone. Her cell phone was nearby, but it had terrible service from her room. Never mind that it was the latest, shiniest model that her carrier could provide. This was America, and having the fanciest phone most often sacrificed the actual telephone functionality first. But hey, she could connect to YouTube from anywhere in the world. That had to have its uses.

Nicole noticed a background sound she was quite used to. Elaine was awake. Her mother's crying was audible upstairs. It wasn't uncontrolled bawling, more of a soft sniffling and muffled whimpers. It was a regular occurrence in the home, akin to the creaks of the foundation and frame on a windy night. It was the soundtrack of the house.

Nicole turned the television across from her bed on and pumped the volume up. While she was used to the noise, she didn't like it. It not only made her uncomfortable, it made her angry. Nicole rinsed, spit and dialed. The first time she was directed to voice-mail. She left no message and hung up. Then she pressed redial. She would not be denied!

"Hello? Nicole? What's up. Where are you?" A voice answered on the second try. It was Natalie, Nicole's best friend.

"Hey, Natalie, come over please." Nicole put on her best voice, while not bothering to hide the tears. Her efforts were somewhat overcome, as her voice cracked slightly near the end.

"Nicole?" What's going on? You okay? Mr. Liebermann almost killed me for my phone going off in class. You know how he is." Natalie didn't realize how dire the situation was, but she knew Nicole. She knew by the tone of voice and could hear the tears over the phone. Natalie was acutely aware that Nicole wasn't often upset in this manner. While Nicole may have had a scathing rage when angered or upset, she was most often a cool customer, able to keep her emotions under control. If there was anything Natalie knew about Nicole, it was that her best friend was always in control. Nicole didn't have the average teenage girl's weekly breakdowns. Nicole O'Leary was cunning, and resilient. The emotions conveyed to Natalie through simple nuances in Nicole's current state spoke volumes to her.

"Natalie. Get over here. Please." Nicole sniffled, wiping tears from each cheek. She didn't want to have to beg, but at this point, she wasn't above it. Her pale cheeks flustered to a bright red, as did the tip of her nose.

"Sweetie?" Natalie asked. The size of the emergency had begun to break through her young adult haze of idiocy. "I'll be right over. Just let me fake some cramps. Give me twenty minutes, okay?" Nicole could hear Natalie scuffling back to her classroom. She too was aware of the huge pain in the ass that Mr. Liebermann could be.

"Okay..." Nicole hung up with no further words. She let her body fall back onto her bed with a near silent plunk.

Chapter Two: God Bless America

"Hey-ya, Harry!" That was David Stern. He was one of the security managers of Hallibush labs, Harold O'Leary's employer. They often chatted for Harold's first ten to fifteen minutes at the job. Harold enjoyed it because David was a man with common sense. He did use the name Harry instead of Harold when addressing him, but Harold forgave that. He never voiced his hatred of that nickname because David was a party man. If there was one thing everyone could have learned from the late, Great Ronald Reagan, it was that no Republican should ever speak ill of a fellow Republican. The idiocy and fascism of that idea never dawned on Harold. He believed he was being not only a good friend, but a patriot by behaving in this manner. Harold didn't realize that true friends, will not only tell you when you are wrong, but will stand against you, publicly if need be, to stop you from making a mistake. Later in life, Harold would look back and see that the people he thought were his friends, really weren't his friends. For now, Harry and David were boss/employee, and bowling team buddies.

Hallibush Labs had been built in the early nineties. It hadn't been a completely new building either. Previously, it was a much smaller lab that went by a much smaller name. Once they had designed a new antibiotic that could target several Penicillin resistant strains of bacteria, they were in the money. Hallibush bought them out and built a new lab around the old one. Along with the new lab came new, top-notch security. A large barbed wire, electrified fence surrounded the area. Motion sensors hugged the corners and weight detectors slept in shallow graves in the lawn. There was one way in and out of the area. It was a gated entryway that allowed one lane in, one lane out and never both at the same time. This gated entry required the scanning of an employee badge across an electronic reader. Harold's ID badge gave him access to all of Hallibush, not only entry through this first gate. Just before passing through the gate there sat a security office. The identity of anyone passing into or out of the grounds was verified here. Not only must they present valid ID, the security guard would scan the same ID Badge across his personal card reader in the security office.

"Hola, David. How goes it?" Harold greeted him with a smile.

"Smooth as ever. Runnin' a bit late, are you?" Dave quizzed.

"Unfortunately, yeah." Harold sighed and handed over his I.D. badge and driver's license.

"Trouble on the home front?" David asked. He took the badge and passed its bottom bar code through a scanner connected to his personal computer. He would now wait for the computer screen in front of him to bring up a personnel file that would show the picture and driver's license number of the employee tied to the badge. This was positively a waste of time. Dave and Harold had both worked together when Hallibush was... before it was Hallibush. However, the security was routine and without routine there was chaos. With chaos came liberalism and with liberalism came baby-killers and satanists and peace-mongers and race mixing and everything else that was a bane to society. So they stuck to the routine.

"Wife and I broke the news of our separation to the daughter today." Harold confessed. He watched his picture and file pop up on David's computer screen. With Harold and Dave's daily chats, Dave had been keenly aware of the current personal problems Harold was facing. This was their therapy: the morning talk. It was almost like a confessional for Harold, although he couldn't see that he had done anything wrong, so he had nothing to confess. He mostly told of the flaws he saw with his family while steadfastly remaining completely blind to his own.

"Oh. Sorry to hear that. Is little Nicole okay?" David had a hard time with age. Nicole hadn't been little since he had last seen her five years ago at a company picnic. She didn't come to the labs, ever. She hadn't attended any other company picnics in the past half of a decade. Neither had Nicole's mother. Dave hadn't seen any of Harold's family in some time, he realized. He had only been hearing about them when talking to Harold. That was too bad, in David's mind, because Elaine O'Leary was easy on the eyes.

"She seemed alright." Harold smiled. He believed himself because he was clueless to the truth. His daughter was devastated. Harold hadn't been able to see through the fake smiles she had presented at their terribly awkward breakfast.

"Well that's good. I'm sure you'll work through this," David was eager to move on. While he enjoyed his chats with Harold, he was getting tired of hearing about this downward spiral that the O'Leary's were on. David felt Harold just needed to get control of his family back by using a firm hand and some tough love. Harold also had a tendency to drag on about his wife if you let him. David tried to change the subject as fast as possible. "Jackson still in school?"

"Yep," Harold too was relieved to move forward with the conversation. Sometimes he felt that he revealed to much to David even though Dave was a good friend. Nothing that they talked about became company gossip, so he was a friend and a confidant. "He's catching on."

"Well that's certainly good news, Harry. You oughta get that boy in the service." David advised. Of course, for these two, the military could possibly fix all the world's ails. If there were something a good drill sergeant and an ass-kicking by a man in uniform couldn't fix, these two with their polar opposite intellects couldn't think of it; a true case of the blind leading the blind.

"I'm tryin,'" Harold laughed. "God knows our boys could use it." Despite what Harold said and felt, the last thing any soldier in service needed was Jackson O'Leary standing next to them on the field of battle. Jackson was irresponsible and nothing but trouble. The surest way to get any unit decimated by the enemy would be to stick them with Jackson. Harold knew that his son was an utter failure, but would never admit it. Jackson was his son and heir. He was the one who would carry on the family name. Harold would look past just about all of Jackson's faults, simply because of what Jackson could (but never would) be.

Every man on earth wants to leave a legacy, and he wants his son to inherit that legacy and carry it on. It's a genetic code that we as males have programmed and hardwired into our souls. We love our daughters and tend to protect them more, but nothing can give a man the same sense of achievement as naming his son, and knowing that his legacy will be carried on. Perhaps we don't feel this way with daughters simply due to societal constraints. We "give" our daughters away, and let another man brand them with his family name. Even when a woman refuses to take her husband's name, she still takes it, at least in her father's mind. But our sons, our sons are our legacy forever.

Harold's son was a douche bag in the truest sense of the word. Harold would have someone to leave a legacy to, but Jackson could only spoil and ruin said legacy. Jackson was a dimwit with nothing ahead of him but loose women out for his money and a bad liver from years of drinking. Harold's legacy that provided the money would be pissed away, literally, and finally, Jackson would sell his portion of it to the highest bidder, who would then make millions of dollars from it.

"Maybe you can get him interested in time for the vote this year." David speculated. He had slowly directed Harold away from the family talk to politics, where they were on safe ground. Harold and Dave both agreed on nearly every issue available, so it was the pot and the kettle calling each other black. Although, they were republican, so literally calling each other black would be an insult.

"Oh, he'll be in the booth," Harold assured him. "No way we'll let that jellyback in the big house." Lies. Jackson wasn't going to get out and vote. Harold knew it. Dave knew it, too. Jackson wouldn't vote until a president ran on the reefer platform and promised a pound of dope for each voter out there. Jackson would probably be arrested for voter fraud in that case, for trying to vote one too many times.

Harold took his badge back and placed his car in gear. He made a mental note to make sure that Jackson did go out and vote this year, and vote for the only party that knew what was good for America. Voting was a right that people had died for. Voting was the only way to make sure the liberals didn't sell the country out to any communist in the world. This was all ignoring the fact that the current Republican president had put the nation into record debt and allowed China, the world's largest communist, to buy it. Harold was tired of his son being a failure. It was time for Jackson to start growing up. Not voting was a crime. Harold vowed that from now on, that crime could possibly be the one failure that Harold would not forgive.

"See you at lunch." David waved him through.

"Yeah." Harold threw a hand over his shoulder as he pressed down on the gas. He calmly clipped his I.D. badge back onto his shirt, and slipped his driver's license into his wallet. Driving a route he'd driven for years, Harold sleepily moved toward his parking spot. It was closer to the front doors than the handicapped parking, which was illegal, but they had never in all their years had anyone use the handicapped parking.

Until they did, Harold was content to leave them two spaces stealing the 3rd for himself.

Harold had formed this company with his partners. His personal research had opened the doors for them to become something more than just another bio-med research company. Keeping his pristine spot, closest to the front door was Harold's way of preserving his feeling of ownership, even if he and everyone else knew that the company no longer belonged to him, he'd not give over his entire kingdom. He had to keep his this parking space, which was a metaphor for his throne, at the very least.

Beginning with the moment he sat in his car and started it in the morning until the moment he parked it, this had been Harold's life for years. Yes, the conversations with Dave varied, but each morning was this same boring routine. That's what suburbanites did. They lived the same stories over and over and over from the safety of covenant protected housing. Harold never ventured to live, because that was unsafe. Why drive across town to a new restaurant, unless said establishment was merely an addition to some other area of suburbia. Suburbia was a massive kingdom after all. Despite that massiveness, it was complacent. It was complacent to be boring and safe. Because that's what safety brings: boredom. Harold was okay with the safety and boredom. It was predictable. It was the end to the equation that was his life that he expected and could deal with. He got in his car each morning, drove the same route, drank the same cup of coffee from the same gas station, and parked here, in his spot. Had Harold lived an eternity, he would have dug a rut on his daily path, much the same that the Colorado river hollowed out the Grand Canyon. Makes you realize the canyon really isn't so grand, huh? Just a piece of water stuck in Mother Nature's version of suburbia, and happy with it.

Harold made his way past the metal detectors at the front door and past the lobby desk. He smiled at Berta, the receptionist, secretly wishing he could fire the old biddy. She had worked for his company since the buyout by the pharmaceutical. Apparently, she was the aunt of some kid who inherited a place in the pharmaceutical's higher ranks. He didn't earn his wealth or position, like Harold, had. The kid had it given to him. When the new facility was built, Berta was brought in to answer telephones, and greet guests. The only guests that Hallibush labs ever had were federal inspectors and deliverymen. The federal inspectors were Harold's bane. They constantly held back his research and reinforced his feelings that the federal government held too much control over private citizens and over businesses. Harold already paid them a ransom in taxes. That wasn't enough. They had to inspect his work and offices on a routine basis and tell him what he was allowed to do in the name of furthering mankind. It was selfish and fascist, in Harold's eyes. As was having to keep Berta on staff. Half the time, she was asleep, for all to see. That's because she had nothing to do. No one was calling every hour. People weren't stopping by this secure of a complex on a daily basis. There was no need for Berta. Having her there was a waste of money and inefficient. One day,

Harold would find a reason to fire her. Until then, he just hoped that she'd find a way to fall, break her hip, get pneumonia and die. He pictured her little white afro bouncing off of the concrete every time he walked into the office. 64 years was time enough on this earth for someone so lazy, Harold thought. One quick fall could end it all. Harold thought about cutting the budget for deicing the parking lot this winter as he made his way to his desk.

Harold had to pass through another card reading station that sat next to Berta's desk before he could move one. The guard here, Randall, was familiar to Harold. He was a younger black man. Harold was pretty sure that he was hired to fulfill some sort of federal Affirmative Action rules. Another example of government controlling private citizen's right to do what they wanted to. Not that Harold disliked black people. He just felt that being told to hire them was wrong. Harold, in all his conservative right wing zealotry, was actually probably right about that.

The affirmative action movement in America had grown into a beast all it's own, becoming a tool of "reverse racism". "Reverse racism,"... only a country that had been huddled into a corner of fear by something could stand to use the term "reverse racism". That country was the United States of America. "Reverse racism" in America means, to put it simply, being racist against Caucasian people. "Reverse racism" wasn't at all the reverse of racism, but actual, die-hard, American born and bred racism.

Unfortunately for much of white America, the reparations for slavery and the oppression of minorities came in the form of vast social changes. While most people were hesitant to give money or property for these reparations, time would show that these solutions would have been much simpler. As it stood, the social changes came to the front quickly, and then slowly infiltrated through society until they were overwhelming, and frankly, unfair. Suddenly even the misuse of the word, "Them", by someone of a paler complexion could end with the loss of a job, and a person being ostracized from society. Imagine being treated like an outcast not because you were a racist hate monger, but merely because you used what should have been a perfectly acceptable pronoun.

Suddenly, people were being forced to give away things like scholarships to college for students who weren't qualified. Granted, the country had to make-up for the wrongs of their past open oppression and continuing covert oppression, but the Affirmative Action movement began to go too far. Those who had earned something were denied it for others who had not earned it to make up for wrongs done to the latter's racial ancestor's by the prior's. Now we are in an era where the oxymoronic phrase "Reverse Racism" (which, don't forget, means actual racism), has become part of popular use. Today in America, people totally unqualified are given jobs based simply on skin color. Students are let into schools that they could not complete a remedial course in. People who were held back by racism and hate in this country do deserve a fair shot. However, the sins of the father shouldn't penalize the grandson. If he wants to fix it, the grandson should make a larger effort to fix and support inner city grade and middle schools instead. So, America is left with this fustercluck and no feasible way to end it in sight. Some schools and companies are still hiring/admitting based on racist beliefs. On the flip side, qualified white people are being passed over. Minorities have *carte blanche* as far as humor and pop culture to say whatever we wish. The last 20 or so pages you have read are proof of that. Whites are crucified for some of the most mundane and innocent comments. Allowing an "all-black college" is considered alright, as was someone expressing their belief in "Brown Pride" or even "Black Power". When a white person uses these same phrases, it is taboo. White people in America are stifled when attempting to celebrate themselves openly. Not that it matters. White America makes the laws, and holds the majority of the money and power. Just being them, and us just living in their country, is a celebration of who they are. The country needed to continue with it's reparations, but the reparations are dividing the country further, and making the majority slowly but surely the subjugated group.

As for Randall, the security guard, he was hired because he was qualified, despite what Harold believed. Harold may have been on the board for the company, but he had no idea about his ancillary employees that didn't share his voting habits. Dave was his buddy, but someone like Randall? Harold had no idea that Randall was studying to attend law school, and just like his job, he had earned that. Randall earned his full ride scholarship based on academics, and not athletics. Harold could care less, because his prejudice had already cemented who Randall was in his mind, and this is why Affirmative Action laws still have a place in America, flawed as they may be.

Harold swiped his ID badge as Randall waited for the machine to approve Harold's passing. Just as the first gate was a waste of time and payroll, so was this second checkpoint, as far as Harold went. Randall knew Harold. He didn't need the ID badge swipe or the 15 seconds of uncomfortable silence that they went through every day. To do anything else would have broken the routine though, and everyone knew how that would end.

His ID badge was accepted, of course, and Harold made his way to his office without ever saying a word. Harold's office was set at the corner of a brick of cubicles. It was an actual office, with all glass walls. His view, while not the best being that this was only a one story building if you did not count the basement, was better than any other. His space was actually four cubicles converted to one office, giving him a despotic amount of room. Two long brown desks graced two of the walls in an L formation. Along another wall was a table with a laser and ink printer. Harold was allowed his own fax/copier machine as well. His larger desk held his PC and monitor. The second desk held a backup PC that his assistant would often use. Pictures of his family littered the desks because they were supposed to. Harold couldn't remember when half of them were taken. What he could remember was the day he won each award that was hung around his walls. He knew the day, time and exact parameters of the project that had won them for him. He knew who held the patents to each of them, what his percentage of profit was on each patent, and when those patents would lapse. This was his work, the only thing in the world he truly loved. Harold wasn't an emotional man, so he didn't realize that the warm, fuzzy feeling he had for his inanimate creations was love.

The office area was generally empty in the morning, as everyone was in the lab physically checking the night's results that they had read on their computer reports when they first arrived. Today was no different. Each morning, when entering, Harold saw anyone who was working in this area, because he had to walk past all the other cubicles. Save for a few assistants running in and out gathering pages of data to compare, Harold was alone. He sat at his computer, and placed his designer briefcase alongside his desk. The animation on his computer screen caught his eye.

His screen saver was a model of a bacterial spore growing into a full-blown bacterial organism. It was an archetype of Harold's pet project. As of yet he couldn't prove it, but he knew the next great antibiotic leap lay within this spore. His thoughts drifted to the fame and fortune that lay ahead. He could change the world. Incurable diseases would be at his mercy... maybe. If anything, it'd give doctors a better chance against routine bugs like Streptococcus, the common everyday cause of strep throat. Harold had been working on it with personal dedication for three years now. A breakthrough was close, he felt. They were on the cusp of utilizing the spore's antibiotic properties, and from there, they would have the rugged job of synthesizing the proper parts for mass production of medication. Even if the breakthrough came today, it'd be months to years before he'd have a working model to present for any kind of clinical testing on living animals or even humans. Hopefully, Hallibush would allow him to keep his usual .06 percent of the patent. At even that fraction he'd make millions overnight.

"Oh! Mr. O'Leary." Startled by his assistant and intern Rebecca, he turned to face her.

"Sorry Mr. O'Leary, I didn't mean to disturb you." She blushed. There were several things Harold wanted to say to her. Most of them would have ended in a sexual harassment lawsuit. He longed for his father's day when a man could take a woman over a desk and teach her some discipline. Nowadays the socialists had convinced women that a man teaching a woman respect in the office the old way was rape. Every day, the past Harold clung on to seemed to slip away a little more.

Rebecca was a pretty girl, by any standards. She had a well rounded figure at 5'3". Her auburn hair hung straight to her shoulders, held back from her face today with a white headband. Her body was mostly hidden by her white lab coat, but Harold could see through it to see a peach colored blouse, and her black slacks ending in low-heeled boots. It was a professional look, but the shoes were a bit expressive. Of course, in the cold sterile world where they worked each day, it didn't take much to stand out. Compared to Harold's white shirt, black slacks and black shoes, she was dressed for a ball. Her boots, though, caught his eye as he looked her up then down with a smile on his face. Her boots were a faux-rust design with hints of intermixed reds, browns and golds. It was a trendy, homey kind of look. Harold decided that they went well for some reason with her sensible hairstyle, and simple, black rimmed glasses.

"It's fine." Harold finally voiced. "I haven't even started for the day. I was running behind and just walked in actually. Could you possibly grab me a cup of coffee and we'll go over these results." Harold smiled while taking a stack of papers from her arms. His demand was an order, not a question.

"Sure thing, Mr. O'Leary. The culture's look like they've responded well to the treatment we tried, by the way." She smiled and whisked herself from the office. She was working hard not only at the office, but on her master's degree also. Impressing an influential company like Hallibush was something she intended to accomplish no matter what. A position working on a project like this one could be career making, possibly earning her enough to start a small research firm of her own. Harold leaned out of his office; Watching her go provided him as much entertainment as seeing her arrive.

Nicole didn't bother to move an inch when she heard the car arrive in front of her house. She had no inclination to move at all. The slight changes in her body due to breathing were more movement than she desired. She wanted to be still. More than that, she wanted to be silent. She wanted to be numb, and unavailable. She wanted to be dead. She had been lying there since she hung up the phone and intended to continue doing so until forced to stop. She was trying to figure how to make it all go away, but her brain refused to provide any sort of solution to that problem. Nicole was a master manipulator and a terrible force to reckon with when she wanted things to go her way, except in this case. She had no idea what to do. She was at a loss. She had figured life out, and then life went and threw her the proverbial curveball. Unfortunately, Nicole was never the best softball player, so that curveball had not only been a strike, but a perfect strike. It had backed Nicole off of the plate, and forced her to step out of the batter's box.

She knew by the sound of the car that it was Natalie outside. Nicole would recognize the buzz of that 1973 convertible Volkswagen Beetle. It had that neat little hum that almost made it sound like one of the flying spaceship-cars on the Jetson's cartoon. Natalie called it her Slug Bug. Nicole and Elizabeth teased her and called it the booger because Natalie had helped her father restore it and in the process had painted it a glowing lime green. It had probably been pretty cool in the seventies when the car came out to do such an atrocious thing. Not so much in today's world. There's no accounting for taste, but it is a stone cold fact that American teenagers have some of the worst taste of all.

Nicole hated the color, but loved the car. She herself had gone the easy and quite common route. As much as she would have hated to admit it, she too had been following the routine of suburbia most of her life. She allowed her parents to buy her a Mustang for her first car. While this wasn't regular practice for all teenagers in the country, it was pretty commonplace for that pretty little rich girl in town to own a Mustang of some sort. Despite challenges from all the competing auto makers, the Mustang held a certain mystique. It wasn't the best put together car. It wasn't the most fuel efficient. It wasn't the fastest and surely not the safest. It did have a flavor and history all it's own. For some reason, the Ford Mustang had staying power with the youth of America. Nicole didn't like the Mustang for any particular reason. She was just expected to get the car, so she did. Being the "it" girl in her school meant she had to fulfill certain expectations for the all the people looking at her every day. Having the Mustang was one way to do that. The Mustang was perhaps the only American car that you could purchase for under $50,000 that would impress high school kids just as much as a BMW or Mercedes. Even a used one.

Nicole heard two car doors slam. That meant that Natalie hadn't come alone. Nicole didn't expect her to. Nicole was the most popular girl in school, so just about everyone was her "friend". Her true friends, though, consisted of a small circle of two girls: Natalie and Elizabeth. Whilst Nicole was the queen of an elite inner circle at school, her confidants and trusted friends numbered only two. These two girls had been her support system for most of her life. Nicole knew Elizabeth was who Natalie had brought with her. Natalie would have brought no one else. She knew better. Even though they were best friends, she wasn't immune to Nicole's wrath. Natalie had been on the receiving end of Nicole's rage more than once, but not in a long while. We tend to hurt those closest to us the most, and it was no different for these two girls.

Once, Natalie had divulged one of Nicole's closest secrets to someone other than Elizabeth. She had told a classmate in junior high school that Nicole was having unprotected sex with a boy Nicole had vehemently denied any relationship. The story of course spread through school. Nicole was horrified, and humiliated. In retaliation, she had slyly let slip in a casual conversation that Natalie had an abortion. The conversation unfortunately had been with Natalie's mother, who had no idea that her daughter had traveled across two state lines to receive said outpatient treatment.

Natalie walked up to the front door of Nicole's house with Elizabeth, the last of these three amigos. Natalie had her shoulder length black hair in a laid back ponytail. She was the tallest of the group by nearly two inches. Her pale complexion was offset by small clusters of freckles, like galaxies of stars in a clear night sky. Most of these freckles were centered on her forearms and cheeks. They were most obvious when she smiled or blushed as blood rushed to the area and darkened these patches even further. Natalie held an athletic frame with androgynous features.

Elizabeth, on the other hand, was the shortest of the three. She had been blessed with straight, fiery, red hair that barely fell to her neck. She layered it out in waves with a hot iron so that it curled down and away from her face and neck. It was tipped with very subtle blond highlights. Unlike Natalie's freckles, Elizabeth's blended with her complexion. Her rosy cheeks hid her sunset orange freckles perfectly. She topped off today's look with a straw cowboy hat, curled up on the sides.

Elizabeth and Natalie wore matching outfits as they always did on any day when they, as the Pep

Squad, had official school business to attend to. Natalie wore pink jogging pants with a red North High Trojans hooded sweatshirt. Elizabeth sported purple jogging pants with a pink Trojans sweatshirt. Had Nicole attended school today, she would have worn a white version of the same shirt with blue pants. They had to coordinate, but not match exactly. While other squads, namely the cheerleaders, did tend to match outfits exactly when not in official uniform, but showing school spirit, Nicole thought it looked creepy, so the Pep Squad quit doing it as soon as she joined. She still thought that their matching attire made them look like clones or soldiers, but it was school policy that they wear clothing to increase school spirit. It was one rule that Nicole would not be able to change, no matter how popular she was.

Natalie and Elizabeth didn't bother knocking or ringing the doorbell. They were practically family. Natalie's mother had been BFF's (Best Friends Forever) with Nicole's mom from the 5th grade onward. Theda, Natalie's mother, had married Nicole's uncle Hank. Natalie was not Hank's daughter. Natalie had been born two days after Nicole. Hank had been in the service and overseas from before the time of conception through birth. He did not meet Theda until he returned home. Natalie's father was a drunkard and a hustler. He swindled his way into Theda's heart and then her wallet when she was still a college freshman. Then he got her pregnant and about the time he found out about it, he disappeared. Nicole and Natalie were celebrating their first birthdays together, as they always did, on a cool Saturday afternoon when Theda met Hank. A year later they married. Natalie had never known any other father. She had often wondered, as any adopted child does, about her birth father. Who was he? Where did he go? Did he ever think about her? These questions ran through Natalie's mind daily. She was happy with the parent's she had. The father she had known was all the father she'd ever need, but still, that nagging doubt ate at her constantly. The need to identify with someone who had abandoned her left her feeling incomplete.

Natalie entered Nicole's home and immediately heard the living room television. She walked toward the sound calling out Nicole's name. A television talk show greeted her. Someone was telling another someone that they had an affair with someone's brother. Nicole was nowhere in sight, which was odd. Any other time Nicole was sick or faking to be, she would have been right here, sitting or lying on the couch with her head at that funny angle she used when watching television. It always looked as if Nicole were actually living the show she was watching, rather than just viewing whatever was on. The reason Natalie knew this was because more often than not, Nicole was watching the television while Natalie was watching her. Natalie knew more of Nicole's subtle personality quirks and physical nuances than Nicole did. She always wondered what Nicole was thinking, hanging her head to the side and grinding her teeth. Natalie could see the tension that ran through her best friend 24 hours a day. It kept Nicole's body rigid, no matter how fluidly she seemed to move to the outside world. No one else saw it. They only saw what Nicole wanted them to see. Natalie had known Nicole all her life. She knew the girl who was lying under that public projection.

Natalie walked to the nearest bathroom and found the door open, the room empty. The bathroom cabinet was slightly ajar, which usually meant Nicole or her mother had been dipping in the alcohol stash under there. Natalie herself had used this same stash when she had been in the house and feeling in need of a drink. She proceeded to Nicole's room, eyebrows arched. It wasn't unusual for Nicole to drink this early. She lived a child's life of excess and knew nothing of consequences. It was unusual for her to call Natalie as upset as she had. That was something that had never happened before. Something had caused Nicole to dip into the bottle early as well. Natalie was dying to know what it was.

"Nicky?! You okay?" Natalie called. Being family, she had no regard for waking Nicole's mother. She wasn't even sure her mother was home. Even so, if she was, she wouldn't get mad at Natalie. She never did.

Natalie heard no answer. The riddle grew before Natalie's eyes. They found Nicole's room with the door shut. Natalie looked to Elizabeth. One shrugged and the other followed suit. All they could do was walk in. Natalie rapped softly on the door. The car keys in her hand jingled like Christmas bells.

"Nicky?" Natalie's voice dropped to near silence as she opened the door. It was here that she found Nicole, lying on the bed in a fetal position. Nicole was looking away from them, and out of her bedroom window. Natalie stepped gently, as if walking a tight rope. Both she and Elizabeth immediately feared the worst. Nicole was still. Too still. Still enough to be dead. Natalie and Elizabeth could hear one another taking labored, deep breaths in rapid succession. Neither wanted to take another step. Nicole was the strongest of the three of them. Neither could imagine what would have caused Nicole to commit suicide.

Nicole, sensing the girl's fear, responded to their entrance with a stillborn sniffle. She might have been terribly depressed, and shattered, but she was still in control here. There was no force on earth, even the crushing news of her parents ill fated relationship falling apart, that would cause her to lose complete and total control over the domain she ruled. While Natalie and Elizabeth were her best friends, they were also her greatest threats. They could usurp her at any time, and as such, Nicole had to rein them in as needed.

"Nicole? What's up girl?" Elizabeth questioned, walking three steps behind Natalie, as if she were the latter's Moslem wife. Natalie placed a hand on Nicole's thigh, taking more pleasure in it than she should have. She eyed the O'Leary from head to toe. Natalie came to rest her gaze on Nicole's tear streaked face. Nicole's wide eyes stared vacantly out of the window.

"That bastard got you pregnant, didn't he?" Natalie's voice carried venom more potent than that of the vicious African Black Mamba. "I always knew that he was an ass. I told you, too. Don't worry. I still have the number to the clinic where I went when I had that little accident. My dad still thinks I had lipo." Natalie laughed. She laughed off what she would find out in therapy years later was one of the most traumatic experiences of her life. It was ironic, in it's way, the

American girl who had been adopted having an abortion. She was a walking postcard for both sides of the always polarizing abortion debate.

"No." Nicole gave her head a sparse shake. "I'm not pregnant. I think Chad touches himself more than he ever touches me." Nicole referenced her longtime boyfriend.

"And Veronica." Elizabeth chimed in, broaching a very touchy subject.

"That's not true. Everyone said she was lying." Natalie turned to Elizabeth with a scowl. Bringing up Chad's alleged infidelity was not the best idea at the moment.

"Guys," Nicole sat up, frustrated even further by their arguing. "It's not Chad or that thing with Veronica, who we know isn't lying but we won't admit that publicly. It's my parents."

Nicole wiped tears from her cheeks. She would be damned if she'd cry for those who didn't care about her.

"What?" Natalie asked. She had her own sneaking suspicions. Her mother and father talked at night. Often times they even argued over whose fault it was and what would happen to the kids. Natalie had thought they were arguing about another of her aunts, until she heard her mother use their names. Harold and Elaine O'Leary. Instead of feeling sad, Natalie felt happy the moment she heard that.

"They're getting separated." Nicole's lip began to tremble. Her resolve not to cry from moments ago wasn't so strong when she forced herself to verbally admit the truth. She bit down. Natalie and Lizzie leapt to her with open arms, enveloping their hurting friend.

"Oh. You poor girl." Natalie rubbed Nicole's back. Secretly, Natalie was a bit relieved. Young girls may be best friends, but jealousy always runs underneath the surface. It's a calm trickle that slowly develops into a raging river of lies, backstabbing and gossip. Most would call it unhealthy. Americans call it a rite of passage. While young boys are taught fellowship and brotherhood (bro's before ho's and all that), young girls undergo a rigorous test of nerves and patience that no man will ever understand.

Natalie had always held her jealousy of Nicole in check. Nicole was the princess. All the guys asked Nicole out first. Nicole always came first because if Nicole wasn't okay, no one was okay. They weren't allowed to be. People rushed to Nicole's side and ignored Natalie and so the resentment always had a little fuel for the fire. However, they were best friends and this in turn kept her jealousy to a minimal level. Now though, Natalie had one area where she could one-up Nicole. At least her family was still together. Natalie smiled on the inside, while frowning and supporting outwardly.

Elizabeth thought Nicole was lucky to have the family that she did. She had no problem understanding how Nicole was feeling now. When she was 10 years old, Elizabeth's parent's had gotten divorced. Her mother had taken a liking to a steelworker. They lived together now in Massachusetts, the first state that allowed them to same-sex marry, as owner/operators of a lobster fishing boat. Lizzie lived with her father and sporadically spoke to her mother. The happy couple adopted a daughter three years after they eloped. Lizzie hadn't gotten a Christmas card or birthday phone call since.

"Oh, sweetie, when?" Natalie asked.

"I don't know." Nicole sniffled in frustration. "They didn't give me a date. I don't know how these things work." She snapped. Elizabeth and Natalie knew then that they were in unstable waters, and had better watch which way the conversation sailed.

"That's so sad." Elizabeth stroked Nicole's ruffled locks. "Tell me what I can do to help you."

"I know, pills and a drink." Natalie beamed. Getting Nicole drunk could make her even angrier, but that was rare. Natalie was betting that it would sedate her and calm her down a bit.

"Already tried that." Nicole sighed. "Besides my mom is passed out in her room downstairs and I'm trying NOT to be her today. God, of all things, I don't want to end up like her. Look what she did to me. Is that what I'm gonna do to my kids one day?"

"Then let's go somewhere," Natalie pushed herself away, holding Nicole by the shoulders. She looked directly at her best friend. "Let's go out and do something. We've got that pep rally tonight. We can't handle the crowd without our fearless leader."

"Okay," Nicole gave a weak agreement. "I guess I could use a bite to eat. Let me throw some stuff on."

"We'll be downstairs." Natalie turned to the door, motioning for Elizabeth to follow. Lizzie gave Nicole's arm one last squeeze, mouthed an apology with exaggerated pouting lips and left.

Nicole met them in her living room nearly an hour later. She wore her planned sweat outfit, to match her pep squad sisters, but was without any makeup. Oversized black glasses covered not only her eyes, but also her eyebrows and nearly all of her cheekbones. She pocketed the keys to her car and house as she entered the room. Natalie and Elizabeth turned at the noise. They had been immersed in the same daytime talk show that had been playing when they arrived.

"Hey, Nicky." Natalie smiled, glad to at least see her friend up and moving. Nicole returned a sickly form of the same facial expression.

"So where to?" Nicole asked.

"I think Jin is working at her parents restaurant today. She always has the hookup on some free sake." Elizabeth grinned. Jin was a former member of the pep squad who had graduated the previous year. Her parents owned and operated a Japanese Steak House/Sake bar. Jin was paying her way through college by working there.

"Not really in the mood for Jin." Nicole discarded the idea. Nicole liked Jin. She just didn't want to sit around drinking sake. Jin's mother let them hang out in the kitchen and drink, but had a tendency to talk the girl's ears off. Nicole wasn't in the mood for it. The last thing she wanted to hear was another story about just how sexually inept Jin's father was.

"Well then let's just hit the mall and see what we come up with." Natalie suggested in frustration. She had no idea what Nicole wanted and was already tired of trying. Nicole would have to meet her halfway if they were going to do anything at all. Surprisingly, Nicole agreed to this course of action.

"Fine. The mall. Let's get a drink for the road and go." Nicole's mind was all over the place. At the mention of sake, she wanted clarity. Now she wanted to numb her feelings again. She hadn't forgotten her earlier feelings about becoming her mother, but she couldn't think of a better way to cope than satisfying her addictions.

The girls nodded, too full of cowardice to question Nicole's actions. Nicole led them into the kitchen. Natalie moved to the cupboard to retrieve three shot glasses. Nicole rustled through the cabinet above the stove finally selecting her mother's half gallon of vodka. She eyed the glasses at the table level as she poured three even shots.

"To you, Nicky," Natalie toasted. "We know you'll get through this."

Elizabeth nodded.

"Thanks." Nicole's smile was gaining strength. They simultaneously knocked back their drinks like sailors. They dedicated another to having a good day. They dedicated another to putting on a good rally. And then they left.

Chapter Three: Adventures in Babysitting

Nicole neglected to drive. The pills had her on a body high. The alcohol from the entire morning had her stumbling drunk. Elizabeth, while being able to hold her own on most occasions, was comparatively a lightweight. She hadn't eaten breakfast and was terribly dehydrated to begin with. The three shots were already causing her head to spin somewhat. Being the least intoxicated, Natalie put the top down on her VW Beetle and accepted her designated driver role. Elizabeth sat in the passenger seat with Nicole on her lap. They sang along with the local pop radio station, ignoring the drivers they cut off, the pedestrians they nearly killed and the red lights they ran.

It didn't matter what song the station played, the girl's knew them all. Modern radio had changed vastly from it's early years. Now, you were lucky to hear music instead of advertisements at any given hour of the day. And each station played the same 15-20 songs by the same 15-20 artists incessantly, over and over and over and over... So the girls knew every song on the station on any given time by heart. When a new, studio polished, cookie-cutter produced hit came into the rotation, they had only to wait an hour or two to hear it played several times and memorize it. If the girls had wanted, they could hop on the internet and download 1 or 2 remixes that didn't add any musical quality, but just exchanged a verse or two with a guest star who never had anything pertinent to say. This was the state of American music. Video killed the radio star. The internet killed the entire industry.

"So who are you going to live with." Elizabeth asked during one of the absurdly long commercial breaks.

"What?" Nicole wasn't thinking straight. The transition from mindless modern music to actual cognitive thought took more time for her in this state.

"Your parents," Elizabeth coached her into the subject. "Yours will be different than mine. I'm sure you'll get to choose which one you want to live with when they divorce."

"Lizzie!" Natalie admonished. "They're just separated. And even if they do divorce, Nicole will be off at college by then. You don't just get divorced overnight. It takes months, if not years for some people. And they may get back together. Let's not even talk about this."

"No... she's right." Nicole sighed behind her glasses. "I was planning on going here, to DePaul University. I was going to stay at home just because I could. I suppose now I would have to live with my mom. Or whichever parent Jackson doesn't live with."

"Is he ever going to move out?" Natalie rolled her eyes, even though Nicole herself had just admitted to planning to stay at home after graduating high school. Hypocrisy is unknown to the young mind, when it applies to oneself.

"Jackson will move out when he finally settles down into a prison cell." Nicole laughed. "Seriously, I guess I would live on campus and make my parents pay. They ruined my plans. They can shell out a little for it. Besides, who wants to live at home with mom and pop, or either one, right? I mean, that's me starting a new phase of my life, might as well start it completely fresh, without the baggage of either one hanging over me."

"You guys remember Becka Griffith?" Elizabeth became very excited. "From sophomore year? She was the heavyset one who tried out when we were on the cheer squad."

"Yeah." Natalie flinched at the mention of the cheer squad. She wanted to slap Elizabeth. How many times would she have to tell her not to mention anything to do with Veronica? The cheer squad used to be Nicole's territory, until the yin to her yang managed to gain control of the team.

"You know where she is now?" Elizabeth referred to the aforementioned Becka Griffith. "Florida. Key West."

"What's that have to do with anything?" Natalie was a bit exhausted with the topic already. She made a hard right pulling items from a newsstand in her wake.

"Her parents got divorced," Elizabeth confided. "Her dad really wanted Becka to go with him. She told him she wanted a car and a beach adjacent house or she was staying here with her mom. So he moved to Key West and bought her the jeep she wanted."

"Ooh. Nicky, think of it." Natalie beamed jokingly. "As much as your parents make and with how much they love you, you could probably get your own house."

They all laughed together. The idea pained Nicole inside. A house was merely a modified shed without a family to inhabit it. The family is what made it a home. What good was a place to put your stuff if the people who mattered most to you weren't there to share it.

"Yeah," Nicole played along, hiding her true feelings. "I should do that. But I promise no matter what, I won't leave you two. Even if it means living in the same state as Jackson."

The local shopping mall was like any other yuppie, money-swallowing pit. It's five corners were anchored by top tier department stores, 1 movie theater with 12 screens & stadium seating, and one sports store. The parking lot remained full during business hours. No matter the time, if the doors were open, the capitalistic consumer zombies shuffled through the interior with handfuls of cheap plastic and ornately decorated cloth paper.

The mall also doubled as the perfect daycare as well. Parents of this era had an alternative to the television: dropping the kids off at the mall. It served as a communal meeting place and dating center. Parents could send their children in with obscene amounts of money and allow society to raise their offspring. Posters teach them their morals. Store displays help them set their goals. The food court offers the fried and baked passage to obesity that every American child requires. Not only did it erode the blood vessels but the food court also served as a multicultural center. You had your Italian pizza shop, usually most tolerable of all the eats available. There was the BBQ joint, whose employees were as greasy as the food. Somewhere there was Asian fast food that served as a source for all things Chinese/Japanese/Korean.

The shopping mall. Only man would have the diabolical inspiration to design the vicious trap that led to his own downfall. If ever there was a moral fiber or shred of common sense in America, it was stripped down, reprocessed, repackaged and sold at Aberzombie & Itch during a midnight madness blowout. Of course all of the labor in said process had been outsourced to some other country willing to do the dirty work, because us Americans, we like to keep our hands clean.

Nicole and her gang of two made their way to the food court first. Your average person would have passed out long ago from all that Nicole had ingested, but Nicole lived this drunken, drugged out life more or less every day. She admitted her tolerance, but denied her dependency. She was an addict. This title fit only because she was well off. Had she been poor she'd just be called a junkie. She had learned early on that maintaining herself with these intoxicants coursing through her meant she must eat at regular intervals. The girl who drank on an empty stomach often ended up washing worse than vomit out of her hair. Nicole wasn't one to make a fool of herself.

The mall was busy as usual. More than a fair amount of young adults their age were mingling about. It was an excessive amount if you considered that it was the middle of the day on a school day. The blissful, self-destructive ignorance of youth led them here instead of concentrating on their studies. Today was no abnormality. Teens often ditched class to "hang out", here. It wasn't a secret. Parents and truant officers knew about it; they just refused to do anything about it. Even though society was expected to raise these children, they weren't allowed to criticize or discipline them. Woe unto the man or woman who told another how to raise his children, even if that job was left up to the village. The mall was a safe haven for kids and they congregated here. This was the royal court of the teenage wasteland Nicole lorded over.

Most all of them present knew better than to ignore Nicole's entrance. She was after all, who they wanted to be or be with. She, Natalie and Elizabeth were akin to a Holy trinity. Their security at the top of the noble class was understood. Everyone within eyesight waved, nodded, or stared with a smile, dulling the fangs they would bare in the private sector. They didn't all like Nicole & Co., but they damn sure honored them. Nicole's wrath wasn't something anyone tended to invite. She was cunning, cruel, and vastly more intelligent than any of her peers. These qualities are what had allowed her to ascend to her status in the first place.

The trio ignored them all, for the most part. Some were able to get a slightly visible nod from Elizabeth, who couldn't perfect her icy bitch role the way Nicole and Natalie had long ago. These people were beneath insects to Nicole. If there were anyone here she cared about, she would have known they were here before she arrived. These people here were what she would never be, no matter how hard her life was. They were entrails, waiting to become chum for the sharks like Nicole to tear apart. Nicole basked in the glow of jealousy that beamed from the audience's eyes. She knew exactly what they thought of her. She knew how intense their desire to be her burned. It was tragic that they would never realize that their adoration was what made her this pubescent princess. That was her advantage. Nicole knew that the little people were necessary for her to step on in order to reach her throne.

"So where to?" Elizabeth asked. She was tired of standing still in the middle of the room. At times, she hated being around Nicole because the attention was always there. She longed just to relax, and be herself for once, with no one watching. That was never the case, though. Being one of the queen's court meant that she was under public eyes at all times. She wasn't allowed to make a misstep. If she did, Nicole had to clean up the mess, and in the process, Elizabeth would be the lucky recipient of some form of punishment from the queen.

"I don't know. I'm on the Atkins diet, so I can't really have any carbs." Natalie glanced at the nearest restaurants, refusing to meet any of the eyes staring back at her.

"Ugh." Elizabeth sighed loudly with exaggerated disgust. She placed her hands on her hips, which were a full size smaller than Natalie's. Natalie flinched. It was a jab that didn't go unnoticed, but went unmentioned. Elizabeth knew she'd never replace Natalie as Nicole's 'BFF', though she was close. She did however, have to show just how much she was worth to Nicole's status, and what she could offer the image of the group that Natalie couldn't. "You should try the South Beach diet instead. You get some carbs, but it's mostly proteins."

"So it's the Atkins, but you get to cheat." Nicole laughed.

"No." Elizabeth recoiled. "I lost 3 pounds on the Atkins, and then 10 on the South Beach."

"Oh my god. Ten pounds? How fast?" Natalie was hooked. The earlier jab would be forgiven, if the secret to the amazing loss in weight would be revealed. "I've only lost a pound and a half in two months on the Atkins."

"One month and maybe a half for me." Elizabeth smiled, sticking her hips forward just slightly.

"Bitch." Natalie smiled.

"Guys." Nicole hooked her arms through Natalie's on the right and Lizzie's on the left. She did this to grab their attention, but also to steady herself. She was drunk and high on pills and would eventually lose her footing. She needed some support, and would not make a fool of herself in front of all these people. "How many times do I have to tell you there's one diet. Eat smart and exercise. And calm down. We're seniors in high school, not aged models trying to hang on to our fading careers. You didn't need to lose 10 pounds, Lizzie. I can see your entire hipbone, for Christ's sake. And you Natalie, you're perfect. We're eating at Hot Dog on a Stick today, both of you."

"Whatever, Miss-I-never-gain-weight." Natalie sighed. She and Elizabeth didn't put up a fight though. They stood in line and ordered as they were told. Nicole waited for each of them and picked up the tab on her father's credit card. Nicole's diet had not been a lie. She worked her body many hours to maintain her figure. She had never been bulimic, anorexic or had any other eating disorder. She had never taken a diet pill, nor had she subscribed to any diet other than one that made sense when you looked at it. She watched what she ate, and exercised regularly. Nature took care of the rest.

"So, how's things with that Jeremy kid?" Natalie asked as they sat down, secluded from everyone else. Nicole clamped a hand over her cousin's mouth and looked around. No one of importance was within earshot, Nicole guessed. She knew that everyone there was wearing out the corners of their eyes watching them.

"Don't say his name out loud." Nicole hissed. Natalie peeled the fingers from her face one at a time.

"Oh, right," Natalie kept her voice low. "So, how is he?"

"He's nice." Nicole blew her off.

"He must be if you did him in a Wal-Mart bathroom." Elizabeth laughed. Nicole shushed her.

"Stop it," Nicole pleaded with a smile. "He's different. Not just 'cause of the bathroom, but we talk, you know. When I can find time to see him. He's not like everyone else."

"So you're saying he's better than us?" Natalie baited Nicole.

"No," Nicole rolled her eyes. "He's just different. He's not like us."

"He's not one of us. He's a bottom feeder." Natalie clarified.

"Be nice," Elizabeth chided her. "We love our Nicole, even if she's screwing common folk on the side."

Elizabeth and Natalie laughed. Nicole slumped slightly in her seat.

"Oh my god. You guys are so mean." Nicole knew she was could be more cruel than both of them at times. She was forced to hold back a smile. "He's nice, and very sweet."

"Look, I don't care who he is. He's better than the prick you're with now. You didn't answer me either." Natalie kept at her. "How are things with him?"

"With who?" Nicole felt two large hands come to rest on her shoulders. Her eyes grew large as she looked across the table at Natalie. She knew this new voice.

"With you." Nicole grabbed her boyfriend's hand and looked up at him. He stood with his usual five or six cronies. They were all beta males who pretended to be alphas. Without a pack, they wouldn't know how to breathe, let a lone run.

Chad was indeed what would be typically referred to as a fine male specimen. He stood over six feet tall. His dedication to swimming kept his body chiseled and firm. He wasn't muscle-bound; he was an even 200 pounds. That might have seemed heavy but with a minimal amount of body fat, he was an Adonis. His blond hair seemed to change with the seasons. With the coming winter, it had lost some of its golden luster and gained sandy strands here and there, activating a natural form of highlights. He kept it cropped shorter on the sides and moussed to perfection on the top. The blue of earth as viewed from the moon would be the best way to describe his eyes. They were firm and unyielding. He radiated with a confidence that none but Nicole and Natalie ever saw through. Due to the pep rally later that evening, he and his team wore their Letterman jackets, as swim team regulations forced them to do.

"Oh, so how are things with me?" Chad thought he was extremely funny. He wasn't.

"Great, Chad. Things are great," Nicole was a bit snide. Knowing that Chad hadn't overheard allowed her to relax into her usual mood. Despite what Chad liked people to think, they all knew the truth: Nicole ran the relationship. Nicole was the dominant one, and she didn't bend to anyone's will, even Chad's. "What are you guys doing here? Are you going to the assembly this afternoon?"

"Sure thing, we'll be there when we go back to school." Chad squeezed Nicole's shoulder. Nicole winced. "We got out of class by saying we were going to a funeral."

"Classy." Natalie commented. Chad ignored her.

"Eric Macguire got shipped home today." Chad elaborated without being asked to. Eric Macguire was the senior everyone wanted to be when Nicole and her class were freshman. Nicole had even gone on a date with him. Once. It didn't work out. After high school, Eric enlisted in the Marines. He had served in the infantry and died when a car bomb exploded next to him in the armed forces latest area of operation.

"That's sad." Nicole lamented. It was hard for her to recall his face at first. She felt ashamed, her mind's eye looking into what she finally remembered of his features.

"What, I'm not man enough for you?" Chad was hurt.

"No, Chad. It's sad that someone we know died. That's all." Nicole gave him the tone that let him know the discussion was over.

"We still on for tonight?" Chad abruptly changed subjects, looking to redeem his manhood. He figured a question like this showed his posse who was in charge.

"Huh?" Nicole had forgotten that they had plans for the evening.

"You, me and the guys were going out, remember?" Chad was insulted that she had forgotten. He moved from standing behind her to standing beside her.

"Uh, yeah. I forgot, sorry. I had some issues this morning with my parents, so it just slipped my mind. Sorry." She apologized profusely. She also gave Chad a route to redeem his self-infatuated ways. She opened the door for him to ask about her problems. He didn't.

"Lame." Natalie whispered.

"What?!" Chad's attention snapped to her. Chad and Natalie didn't get along any better than a conservative Baptist minister and the prize girl at a bunny ranch. "What was that, bitch?"

"You heard me, obviously." Natalie rolled her eyes. "You, Nicole, and your butt-pirate brigade out for a night on the town? That's a lame date. It's beneath the goddess that's decided to bless you with her presence."

"We ain't no faggots." One of Chad's teammates piped in with zeal. His name was Eric Betha, younger brother of mentally retarded newsboy Walter (Wally) Betha. Eric B., that was his nickname. He was Chad's best friend and a complete asshole. He specialized in masochistic chauvinism. He hadn't had a regular girlfriend or girl friend since grade school. Being Chad's friend was the only reason Eric B. was popular at all.

Chad had him as a friend because Eric did whatever Chad told him to. He was the little attack Chihuahua that circled the pit bull, yapping until your ears would bleed.

Nicole, Natalie and Elizabeth hated Eric B. for reasons all their own.

"Damn right." Chad agreed, slapping hands with Eric. He turned to Natalie again. "Sounds like you're the one in love with Nicole, dike bitch."

"And she's your cousin, inbreeder." Eric B. spewed gasoline onto the fire.

"Guys," Nicole put her hand up in the air. "Can you all get along for five minutes, please." It wasn't a question. It was an order. Either the feuding parties would reach a treatise or Nicole herself would enter the fray.

"She started it, but we were out of here anyways. Later." Chad gave Natalie the finger and walked off.

"What an ass." Elizabeth sighed.

"Sorry," Nicole looked to her friends. Elizabeth's face was red with rage… and shame. Nicole could hear the huffing breath of Natalie signaling her anger. "I don't know why you two have to hate each other." She told her cousin.

"He's a jerk, Nicole. You could do so much better." Natalie flipped off Chad's back as he and his group left the building.

"Natalie…" Nicole tried to calmly end the argument, but knew that there was no way to have her boyfriend and best friend co-exist peacefully.

"I'm sorry." Natalie spoke. She knew her hatred of Chad tore Nicole up inside. She also knew that Nicole was with Chad partly because she had issues about being alone, and mostly because it was what society expected of the popular girl. As much as Nicole thought she was pulling the public's strings, she didn't realize the detailed way they pulled hers. Natalie didn't fully realize this yet, either, but she did see how Nicole's various obligations and responsibilities were slowly eating her alive, no matter how well Nicole exercised and watched her diet.

"So, how was he? Jeremy, I mean." Natalie asked, ignoring Nicole's earlier order that she cease and desist saying the name aloud.

"Back to this again?" Nicole smiled. "Do you truly have to know? I haven't talked to him today, okay? Imagine if anyone finds out about Wal-Mart though. They'll think I'm a bigger slut than Veronica." Nicole didn't want to go into the subject any further. She allowed the conversation to continue as reconciliation for the events with Chad moments earlier. She herself was surprised at her current affair, and didn't completely understand it yet. With her life in the condition it was after this morning, she couldn't see how the two were related, or just how tightly intertwined they would become.

"Nobody would believe it. I still don't know if you're lying." Elizabeth smiled through her lemonade.

"It happened." Natalie assured her. "Look at her face. She glows when she talks about it. Look at how excited she is."

"I am not." Nicole blushed.

"Well, I call bullshit on that one." Natalie waved her hand above her head as if volunteering.

"He works here, you know." Elizabeth revealed.

"How did you know that?" Nicole asked, a restless passion stirring visibly beneath her features. There was a slight touch of jealousy to her voice, as if that information was only meant for her. It was obvious to the other two that Nicole had known that Jeremy worked in this mall all along. Natalie thought it entirely possible that Nicole suggested they come here for that very reason.

"Oh my god." Natalie slapped Nicole's shoulder. "Look at you! What's happened to my ice princess? You are in love."

"Shut up." Nicole tried to sound serious, but failed. " I just... I don't know. I don't know why I did it. I just did. And it felt good. It made me feel good. Not just like 'I had an orgasm good,' but really good, you know? It felt like I was with someone who didn't care about the most popular girl in school. He didn't care that I was me, or that you were my friends or any of that. He just, he dug *me*, not what I am." Nicole was almost in a daze, and then abruptly, she woke up. "So how did you know that he worked here, Lizzie?"

"Sweetie," Natalie fluttered her eyes, placing a hand over Nicole's. "School's still in. Jeremy's in class, where we're supposed to be."

"No," Elizabeth interrupted. "He's here. He takes the school-to-work classes with me. He doesn't have class for half a day, three days a week. He works here, late, I think." Now that was something Nicole didn't know.

"Oh... We have got to talk to him." Natalie grinned.

"No way. Chad might be back." Nicole shook her head routinely, but her heart nodded vigorously.

"So what?" Natalie slammed her drink on the table. "Look at you. Look at how just talking about him makes you feel compared to how Chad makes you feel."

"Chad's not the reason I was down today, remember?" Nicole shifted the conversation. She had made a peace offering to Natalie earlier, but not this time. This time she would take the conversation where she wanted it to go. At the moment, she wanted it away from Jeremy.

"Yeah, of course I do." Natalie's eyes fell to the floor, properly admonished.

"God, I need another shot." Nicole wiped her tearing eyes. "I cannot go to that assembly like this. I have to make that speech to everyone, and imagine me, crying like a baby in front of everyone. This thing with my parents is going to wreck my life." My carefully crafted, delicately balanced life.

"I think you've had enough to drink so far today." Natalie cautioned with a smile. No matter the fragile intricacies of their relationship, Natalie would always look out for Nicole. Natalie would literally die for her.

Elizabeth decided to join Natalie's argument for a trip to see the young man who made Nicole glow. "C'mon. Let's go talk to Jeremy. It'll cheer you up, Nicole." As much as Nicole wanted to control the day's talks, she was outnumbered. Her friends wanted to get her mind off of her parent's announcement. They knew that if she were preoccupied with something that made her so happy, she wouldn't feel so bad. Elizabeth could identify with Nicole, but needed help consoling her.

"Fine," Nicole gave in. "Let's go." Nicole let Natalie assist her to her feet. She pretended to resist a little. In reality, her heart was racing. She was excited to the point where she had to stop herself from trembling. She wanted to see Jeremy again. There was something about him...

"He makes me smile." Nicole uttered as her friends stared at her.

"What?" Natalie asked.

Nicole realized she had been thinking aloud. Her body felt light and warm. Some from the alcohol and drugs, some from her feelings.

"Nothing." Nicole smiled. "Just thinking out loud. We're going to The GAP, right, Lizzie?"

"Yeah, just up here around the corner." Elizabeth confirmed, pointing vaguely to the east. As the moved to walk, Nicole stumbled and clutched onto Natalie's shoulder. The drugs were at their peak. She had lost control of her motor function. Natalie and Lizzie helped her to steady herself. They had all practiced assisting one another at one point or another. They knew how to escort one of their own so that none but the most attentive would notice the inebriation. Nicole had a very limited amount of musculoskeletal regulation. They walked as a group, snubbing anyone who looked familiar and ignoring anyone who didn't. They parked in front of the GAP and stared in. The store was freshman cool at best, to Nicole and crew. They would never shop at the GAP, for themselves or anyone else. It was all trashy khakis and trendy shirts with awful craftsmanship, which were never in fashion, despite what their butchered pop melody commercials would have you think.

"Do you see him?" Natalie asked. They each searched the establishment with the keen eyes of young women with determination.

"No. He wears those black-rimmed glasses, right?" Elizabeth asked with a sour taste.

"Yeah." Nicole quipped, her tone more than enough to indicate that she liked the glasses Jeremy wore, and that no one better say another word about them. "He works in the back a lot, I think. He said he was a stock boy of some sort."

"Then we're out of luck." Natalie suffered the premature defeat.

"No." Nicole caught Natalie's arm, steadying herself. She was energized now. Adrenaline had begun to counter some of the intoxication. She had come this far and would be damned if she would turn back without at least a try. They had hassled her about talking to Jeremy, and now they would help her do it. "I have an idea."

"Natalie, distract that guy at the register." Nicole walked into the store, pulling her friends along. Natalie walked to the register, tucking her shirt in the back, so that it pulled tighter on her breasts, and twirling her hair like an idiot. Men always fell for the stupid girl twirling her hair. Nicole pulled out her cell phone and dialed information. She found the number to the store, and had them patch her through. The woman standing next to Natalie's target answered the phone. These were the only two employees visible.

"Welcome to the GAP, Stacy speaking." She was eerily cheery.

"Hello, I'm looking for a Jeremy?" Nicole asked, sneaking toward a door at the back of the store. Natalie had the male's attention at the center kiosk. He wouldn't be a problem, ever. However, GAP-Stacy would be. Nicole vaguely recollected her face and connected it with the name. She had graduated the year before them, but that didn't mean she wasn't known to them. Nicole had been on top of her teenage world for a few years now. GAP-Stacy was one of the people Nicole considered average. The kind who took out student loans to go to community college and couldn't afford to pay them back. They majored in liberal arts or some other crap and wondered why they couldn't find a job in that area with a degree earned through credits almost entirely derived from throwaway classes. Nicole couldn't remember much about Stacy besides her name, which meant GAP-Stacy was just about a nobody. What Nicole didn't realize is that GAP-Stacy may have been going to community college, but she was majoring in business administration, and had a five year plan that would see her taking accelerated courses and earning a Master's degree either in marketing or advertising. GAP-Stacy, the nobody, would be telling Nicole what was the hottest new fashion and Nicole would listen and pay good money earned from her father's work to follow said advice.

"Jeremy...?" GAP-Stacy was confused. "I'm at the counter with David. Jeremy must work in back."

"I think so." Nicole imitated GAP-Stacy's "very stupid, but well endowed" tone of voice. She was trying to stay quiet so that the girl wouldn't notice through background noise that she was right there in the store.

"Hold on." GAP-Stacy told Nicole. She put Nicole on hold and paged Jeremy over the in-store intercom. Having handed off that responsibility, she took notice of Nicole and Elizabeth, who were just standing near the back door doing nothing. Nicole smiled, and waved GAP-Stacy over.

"Hello?" Jeremy suddenly answered the phone.

"Hey, it's me." Nicole announced, expecting to be recognized. She rarely introduced herself, not to people who had damn well better know her. Jeremy was a bit more than surprised at the phone call. He dropped the phone and something else. Nicole heard the crash over her phone and behind the door.

"Can I help you?" GAP-Stacy stood before Nicole and Elizabeth. Nicole glanced over her shoulder to make sure Natalie still had the male attendant's attention.

"Yeah. Stacy, right? Didn't you go to our school?" Nicole flattered the girl by remembering her name.

"Yeah. Nicole O'Leary and Elizabeth, right? I think I remember seeing you two around." Both girls knew it was an insult. GAP-Stacy remembered Nicole just fine. That's why she had slighted her in that manner, to get back at her. GAP-Stacy had hoped that college would allow for a new start, but a funny thing happened: she couldn't stop being herself. College, even community college wasn't some magic portal that suddenly changed who you were and what made you. If anything it seemed to help you refine those characteristics, while maybe picking up a few accents on that basic design. GAP-Stacy wasn't the prettiest girl in any of her classes. She wasn't the smartest. She wasn't the most popular. She was still plain old Stacy. A five-year plan that had been successful up until this point didn't make her stop hating her years in high school. It damn sure didn't stop her from taking a little get-back from Nicole right then and there by pretending to barely remember her.

Nicole pushed Lizzie toward GAP-Stacy. "She needs the perfect pants and boxers for a boyfriend of two months. It's his birthday and Homecoming is going to be here before we know it."

"I know what you mean." GAP-Stacy smiled. Elizabeth looked at Nicole in a sort of shock. Nicole grinned.

"What size is he?" GAP-Stacy asked.

Elizabeth looked from GAP-Stacy to Nicole.

"24," Nicole answered. "He's a 24."

The woman gave Nicole a sideways glance.

"Oh, he's my cousin." She identified the reason she knew the waist size of Elizabeth's boyfriend. It suddenly struck Nicole that a 24 was a bit small. "And he's been on chemo for the past few months."

"What?" Jeremy said over the phone.

GAP-Stacy smiled and led Elizabeth away.

"I wasn't talking to you. About that." Nicole told Jeremy. "Are you right behind the back door at your job?"

"Yeah, why?" He couldn't hide his excitement.

"Come out to the front desk and see me." Nicole knew just how to tease with her voice and get results.

"You're here. Whoa. Hold on a second."

He placed Nicole on hold. She stared at the door handle inches away from her. When the door swung inward, she pounced. Flying like a rocket she smacked into him, knocking them both to the ground. The door handle clicked into place behind them.

"Hey there." Nicole smiled, leaning in closer to him. She was lying on his chest and he flat on his back. His hair was mussed, and his glasses skewed across his face. The right lens lay across his nose, fogging with each breath he took.

The back room was empty, save for the two of them. Very few of the fluorescent lights that hung overhead were working. The ones that did were blinking on and off intermittently, begging for new ballasts. The décor here was nowhere near the avant-garde design that shoppers saw. The walls here were unfinished cement and drywall. Pipes protruded through from the floor to the ceiling, many leaking imperceptibly from poorly maintained joints creating patches of mildew stink and water stains.

Jeremy was taken aback by Nicole's sudden advance. She pushed her face closer. Strands of peach fuzz on the tips of their noses jitterbugged across one another. Jeremy's heart raced. Nicole could feel it beating within him so hard she could almost hear it. He could smell the sweet strawberry-vanilla of her perfume. Her breath was all at once warm and cool, laced with the afterthought of the lemonade she had washed down her hot dog with earlier. His face, even in the sterile fluorescence, was flushed red and hot. Her's was covered very finely in a sheen of sweat, produced from a mix of excitement and her body detoxifying the numerous chemicals in it.

"Ni-Nicole?" Jeremy stuttered. The smart thing to do was lay there. The professional thing to do would be getting to his feet.

"Heya, kiddo. How ya doin?" Nicole flipped her cell phone shut and pocketed it.

"O-Okay. What are you doing here?" Jeremy had no idea what to say. He wasn't one with enough courage to make the first move. Not just with Nicole, but with any girl. Nicole debated telling him the truth. In the end she decided it might be best to get to know him a bit better before revealing the damaging truth of her insecurity and frailty.

"I was just in the area with some friends and I thought I might stop by to say hello." She remembered to keep her voice calm, coy and collected. "Good thing you were up for it, huh?"

The double entendre was cheesy and not lost on Jeremy. He felt the throbbing in his loins. He knew there was no possible way he could hide it from her. His nervous system kicked into overdrive.

"Yeah, lucky me." He grinned uncomfortably.

"Yeah." Nicole awkwardly agreed. She brushed her lips down across his, touching more with breath than with skin. "Lucky you."

She kissed him, closing her eyes. It was short, more of a massage for the lips. Jeremy relaxed, closing his own eyes just as she retreated. Nicole laughed softly, and sat up. She minimally ground her hips into his before abruptly standing. As she stood, she grasped Jeremy's hand and pulled him to his feet with her. He straightened his glasses while trying to create something manageable of is curly brown hair. Determined to change for no one, it stayed a mess.

"So," Nicole smiled, teasing the corner of her mouth with her tongue.

"So," Jeremy blushed. He attempted to place his hands over the unsightly and blatantly obvious bulge in his pants. "How did you get back here?" he questioned. He pretended to scan the room, as if someone might be coming. He hoped Nicole's gaze would follow his so that he might sneak a hand into his pants and manually position his penis into a less obvious position. (Yes ladies, we do that if we have to).

"Same as you." Nicole answered. "I walked in the door. I thought you saw me as I came flying in to you."

"Yeah. That was a dumb question." He admitted.

"Yeah. It was." Nicole slightly tilted her head, intensifying her stare. She was openly studying his reactions to her. It was all part of the game that kept her in control and him in the hot seat. "So what time are you off tonight?"

"Probably around nine, when we close, like usual. Why? Does Chad know you're here?" His mind began to fly about through the possible scenarios that all ended with him being pummeled.

"Let me worry about, Chad, okay?" Nicole tried to ease his fears. "I was wondering when you were off because I thought you might try to come by the pep rally."

"There's an assembly this afternoon? Isn't the game tomorrow?" Jeremy was confused. He wasn't into school spirit, pep rallies or assemblies. He went, when they were mandatory. When they weren't, he skipped out on that. He usually had to work right after school, and if he didn't he had chores to get done.

"Yeah, it's terrible scheduling, but I really couldn't care less," Nicole conceded. "I guess you're working later in any case, huh…"

"I can try to get my boss to let me off early." Jeremy tried to adjust to her wishes. "She's usually pretty cool about that."

"GAP-Stacy seems a little uptight to me." Nicole laughed. "Don't worry about it. Just give me a call later tonight. At my house, not my cellphone, okay? I'd really like to talk to you."

Jeremy noticed the serious tone creeping along the edges of the conversation.

"Are you alright?" He asked, placing a hand on her arm. The passion of his mini-Jeremy suddenly emptied.

"Yeah," Nicole lied, backing away a step. "For now. I just took a few drinks and a couple of my mom's pills. But I could use someone to talk to later. Okay?"

"Nicole, you shouldn't drink and take pills. You shouldn't be doing either, at all." Jeremy's swell upbringing led him to be a bit motherly. Nicole was not amused. The last thing she was in the mood for was a lecture of any sort.

"Not now, Jeremy. Please. Just be the one person who doesn't try to coddle me and who I can talk to without consequence. Please." She asked.

"Okay." Jeremy nodded eagerly, fearing his transgression might have cost him his chance with Nicole.

"So, tonight. Call me." Nicole didn't ask. She instructed with assertive statements.

"Yeah. Sure." Jeremy tried to sound cool. Nicole didn't see it that way. She saw someone whose word she could trust and that was a rare thing in her world. It gave her a sense of hope, yet another feeling she wasn't sure still existed until this moment.

"Don't keep me waiting." She stepped forward. Her confidence intimidated Jeremy. He almost backed away from her. She let out an impish giggle. He let a puny smile escape. She kissed his cheek and scooted out of the door.

"Excuse me?" GAP-Stacy was right outside the door as Nicole exited. She was surprised and rather curt.

"Sorry," Nicole made like an idiot. "I thought there might be a bathroom back there." She gave an innocent grin and scanned the area. Her friends stood outside the store laughing at her.

"Well there isn't." GAP-Stacy snapped. "This isn't a public restroom, those are out there." GAP-Stacy motioned to the interior of the mall.

"Oh, I know." Nicole kept her cool. She wanted to slap the hell out of this girl. "That guy working back there told me to get out. I am so sorry." Nicole didn't bother to see how GAP-Stacy would react. She brushed past her with a moderate shove of the shoulder. GAP-

Stacy let out a short gasp. By the time she recovered, Nicole was out of the store.

"You two suck." Nicole told the ladies waiting. She gave them each a soft punch in the shoulder.

"You looked so scared back there. What did you think, they were gonna call the cops or something?" Natalie laughed.

"Yeah. Ha. Ha. Ha." Nicole mocked.

"It was funny. And you owe me $63.77." Elizabeth held up a sack. "For my cancer stricken lover's clothes."

"Oh. You actually had to buy something, huh. I'll pay you back. Let's go." Nicole said with sincerity.

"So what'd he say? What did you say?" Natalie asked as they began to walk out of the mall.

"We just talked for a second or two." Nicole gave a rather obscure explanation. "He's gonna call me later." She elaborated.

"Won't you be out with Chad and the boys?" Natalie set the lure.

"For a little bit," Nicole admitted. "I'm going to start feeling sick around nine and be home by ten." Nicole plotted.

"You're so bad." Elizabeth believed that. She envied the audacity of Nicole. Lizzie wasn't nearly as outgoing. Like most girls her age, she had self-esteem issues. Her friends did as well, but they had mastered the art of hiding such flaws. Elizabeth tended to hold her insecurities on one sleeve and her heart on the opposite. It was well known that she was a sucker for cheap lines, and that any quip about the size of her thighs would produce tears. Her thighs in reality were perfectly healthy, and could be no better size. It was her self-regard that was twisted. Some of it was from the constant hammering the media gave young women about their bodies. Most of it was from her dysfunctional family. She had encountered so many potholes on the road of life that she expected defeat. She expected to lose. Were she ever able to discard these encumbrances, she could change the world. For now, she primarily lived vicariously through Natalie and Nicole. She was the Moon to Natalie's earth. Natalie was the Earth to Nicole's sun. Besides, the one time Elizabeth had let loose, it ended in disaster...

Chapter Four: Where's the beef?

Elaine O'Leary was a woman with a story. Sadly, her story was one that was repeated too often in modern society. She had sold out. She allowed her goals and standards to be lowered because it was a given expectation that a woman must do this to be a "good" mother. To understand this fully, we must go back several years. Gift me a moment of your time to give you, my dear reader, perspective.

Born Elaine Walker, she was an only child of a working class family in Chicago. Her father, Eldred Walker, worked in the Stockyards of Chicago, which are non-existent today. He worked on the kill floor, amidst the blood and guts. The entire Walker family would never forget the smell of Eldred when he came home every evening after backbreaking shifts slaughtering livestock. No matter how many years go by where you are exposed to it, the natural human instinct to be disgusted at the stench of rotting flesh and meat will stay intact. After awhile, no amount of showering or laundering will erase the putrid stink. It eats into your clothing and flesh and stays with you the rest of your life, if you expose yourself to it for too long. It's like a bad fart from a man with rotting guts that just won't go away. Most of the modern world had no idea what it was like, but Elaine O'Leary would never forget the smell, because it had been burnt into her DNA.

Eldred Walker had married in his twenties and in 1954, Elaine Walker was born. She came into the world kicking and screaming, a stark opposite to the silent and obedient woman she would play later in life.

Some would say this was due to the nurture vs. nature aspect of life. Perhaps that obedient woman ideal was cultivated in her far too long, and her true self needed to emerge. Maybe that's why she began kicking and screaming again later in life while asking for a separation from her husband. She had to go back. She had to return to who she was.

Although Eldred had hoped for a son, he never regretted having Elaine. She was a smart girl, always the top of her class. Eldred drilled the need for education into her, because he didn't want her to end up like him. He wanted Elaine to have more. Even though most of the world believed a woman's place was in the home, Eldred always hoped that his daughter would have the chance to do more. He never used the word "if" with Elaine, always the word "when". "When you graduate from college." "When you become famous." Eldred refused to foster the idea that Elaine would ever fail. She was his baby girl, and she would be successful if she worked hard. Eldred always believed that.

Elaine's mother was a comely woman who married Eldred straight out of high school. They had met at a local soda shop one day as Eldred decided to spoil himself after the Yards closed early due to a worker's death. The factory wasn't allowing the employees to grieve, they just happened to have the death as someone from the newspaper was in the building, which meant instead of grinding poor old Jeff Hamburg (ironic, no?) up with the meat like they normally did when someone fell into a grinder, they had to actually sanitize and clean their machines. Even though the early 1900's saw the publication of The Jungle, by Upton Sinclair, which in turn led to tougher regulation of the meat industry, the changes were lobbied for by the meat packing industry to prevent the government intrusion they were truly worried about. Thus, the corrupt industry remained so, and Jeff Hamburg was only spared being packaged with the rest of the beef because a lone reporter happened to witness his tragic demise. Not that the factory manager didn't try to slyly offer the reporter a bribe. The reporter himself happened to be fresh out of college, on his first assignment with the paper. He was still thinking that his written word would change the world, as all writers do when they first put pen to paper.

Jeff Hamburg's death led to a pivotal point in our story. It gave Eldred Walker the day off from work. Eldred went into the local soda shop and happened to open the door for a young woman. Her name was Rhoda Peerless. She was a pretty girl, popular and attractive enough to be fending off the local boys and college men. She had just graduated High School. Eldred was two years her senior but looked much older, due to his hard work at the factory. As Rhoda accepted his chivalrous opening of the door, Eldred commented on the weather. Rhoda agreed that it was indeed a nice day out. Eldred took a chance. He was never a man to know fear in his heart. He asked Rhoda right then and there to allow him the pleasure of her company for a walk in the park. Rhoda giggled along with her friends who she had come to meet that were standing nearby, and promptly refused. She couldn't just go walking in the park with any old strange man that smelled like steaks, now could she? Eldred offered again, refusing to give in that easy. Rhoda was charmed by his rugged looks and merciless pursuit of her. She offered Eldred a deal, if he would promise her the biggest house and the fanciest car, she would indeed allow him to take her for that walk. Rhoda thought that she had surely outsmarted the young factory worker, but she was wrong. Eldred may not have been a scholar, but he was educated. Eldred had learned the lessons of life the hard way, through hard work. His answer to Rhoda was this, "I can only offer you the love of my heart. It may be little bigger than my fist, but inside, it's boundless. I will love you forever, and give you all that you desire, if what you desire is an honest man to love you back. The house and the cars won't matter if we have each other." It was sappy and almost unbelievable by today's standards, but this was the first half of the century. People talked like that in their everyday vernacular. Rhoda noticed her friends weren't giggling anymore, and neither was she. She was crying. She accepted Eldred's soda, and his walk in the park. The rest as they say is history.

Elaine was just graduating high school when the stockyards collapsed, figuratively that is. The entire industry began to decentralize. Work at the factories had been slowing for years, moving to other parts of the country. Try as the unions might, no amount of political power and bribes can save a failing industry that the public won't support. Eldred was caught in this crash. In the 1920's the Stockyards employed over 40,000 people. Eldred moved from slaughterhouse to slaughterhouse as they all moved and closed. In 1971, the last of the Yards closed, driven to the end by advances in refrigeration and trucking, making the industry abandon the need for the refrigerated rail car driven Chicago Stockyards.

Eldred had nothing left to do in life. There was nowhere else to go. He retired and his baby girl who was now a woman went off to college. She kept to her father's ideals, and valued his beliefs in hard work and education. Elaine was blessed to grow up not in her mother's era when women went to college to abandon their learning for homemaking. Instead, Elaine entered college during the middle to the end of the sexual revolution. She was of the generation that had been blessed to witness the civil rights movement, and the progress of women's rights. Elaine's father supported her in her liberal thoughts. He had worked many years with many immigrants and knew that a man was only as good as his word, no matter his skin color. Eldred also wanted his daughter to have a chance to achieve her dreams, so he supported her when she joined the National Organization for Women (NOW) in 1967, however unpopular it was with the rest of the country.

Elaine's mother supported her was well, although for a much different reason: she lived vicariously through her daughter. Elaine would have the opportunity to be the independent woman her mother had always dreamt of being. Elaine didn't have to be tied to the house with the kids. She could have a real career, of her choosing, and she could experience life like her mother never was, nor would be able to.

After graduating high school, Elaine enrolled at Northwestern University. She had known Harold

O'Leary from her days in Chicago. They had attended the same high school, and ran into one another occasionally. Harold took her to see a movie. Once. Here on the Northwestern campus, Elaine came across Harold once again. He was majoring in Biology, hoping to transition over to the Master's program for Molecular Science and Biology at the Illinois Institute of Technology. Elaine was in the middle of her third undecided semester when she ran into Harold again.

Elaine had moved away from home to an apartment that she rented with 2 female roommates who also attended Northwestern. The three girls had gone out to a rather large gathering for a keg party. The party had been a bust for Elaine. She wasn't an idiot, and she didn't want a man who was one either. The tough guy jocks didn't impress her. The activists had all started turning into simple potheads or they were laced with so much LSD their breath would blow your mind. Elaine had man troubles of the worst sort; She couldn't find a decent one.

Elaine had left her roommates at the party (they were suckers for a little dirt weed), and had stopped at a 24-hour gas station to buy a Coke. There was no one in the store, save for Elaine and the store owner, or so she thought. Elaine was surprised to find a man in the back, looking rather indecisively at the sodas in the case, as if he were deciding the fate of the universe. And then she recognized him.

"Harold?" Elaine smiled, cigarette dancing in one hand, her hip bolstered with the other.

He turned to her with a startled look. He wasn't a small man, but he wasn't the tallest either. He kept himself in decent shape, and didn't go for the current trend sweeping the nation of looking like a homeless hooligan. Elaine could dig that.

"Oh, Elaine? Is that you?" Harold readjusted his thin frame and thin-lensed glasses. He knew it was her.

"Yeah, It's me. What are you doing here?" she asked.

"Oh, just trying to figure out which of these sodas has the largest sugar to caffeine ratio. I have a huge exam in the morning-" Harold was cut off by Elaine suddenly.

"You have an exam. Where are you going to school? Here in town?" Elaine realized that was a stupid question. Where else would he be in school if he had an exam in the morning?

"Yeah, I go here, to Northwestern." Harold motioned up the block with his left hand, toward the school.

"Really? I haven't seen you around. I go there, too. What's your major?" Elaine asked.

"Biology, for now. I'm transferring to Tech to get my Masters." Harold stuck out his chest slightly.

"Uh-huh. Well it was nice to see you. And it's Dr. Pepper, by the way. Dr. Pepper has the most caffeine." Elaine reached past him and took out a bottle of Coke.

"So, uh, I'll see you around, I guess." Harold said. Elaine heard the slight jitter in his voice, and knew that she had him hooked.

"Yeah." Elaine moved back past him, purposely brushing her breasts against his arm. She sauntered to the checkout counter, and suddenly turned back. Harold, ashamed at being caught staring at her backside, flushed and waved. Elaine was flattered, and intrigued. She walked back down the aisle, and made Harold's day.

"Listen, Harold, I don't usually, do this. But you're an old friend. Maybe an old boyfriend by some standards. Why not come to my place with me, and have a drink?" Elaine put herself out there, but it wasn't that daring a move. Any idiot knew that Harold could only say yes. Elaine didn't really have a chance to be rejected here.

"Sure, that sounds nice. Maybe I can buy you dinner." Harold offered.

"Harold, it's 1 in the morning. A lonely girl invited you back to her place to have a drink. We can figure out what to eat when the sun rises."

Two months after they met that night, they married. Elaine's friends didn't like Harold much and Elaine soon moved out of her apartment and into the house that Harold's father rented for him. Harold came from old, American-Irish money, much of it dirty. Six months after they married, Jackson was born, and Elaine made the hardest choice of her life. She dropped out of school. The girl with the 3.87 GPA just gave up on her future. Harold continued on, supporting them with his family's money. Once he became the one the family was depending on, Harold changed. He became more controlling, and unyielding. Elaine could look past it, because she had tried the other fish in the sea, and there wasn't one she could say had any flavor she enjoyed in the slightest. So, if Harold was just beginning to leave a tad bit of a bad taste in her mouth, well, that was better than what else was on the menu, right?

Elaine's parent's weren't happy with her decision to leave school, but they understood it. They weren't big fans of Harold either, but they both agreed she could have done much worse. And before the thought of the marriage had time to grate on them too much, Jackson was born. The Walker's were grandparents, and the new baby took all their attention away from the possible mistake their daughter had made, mostly. Eldred never forgot his dreams for his daughter, and always made sure to tell her that he thought she should renew her quest for a career, and not be satisfied with just being a homemaker, unless that was truly the route she wanted to take with her life. Being a respectful man, Eldred did keep this type of conversation to his private moments with Elaine, and didn't ever bring it up in front of Harold.

This was the story of the American woman. They struggled and sacrificed for freedoms that many would abandon in the name of their families. It's an honestly valiant decision, but one that leaves many women unfulfilled and unhappy.

Elaine's life began taking that turn around the time Nicole entered Junior High School. Some of her friends thought it was because she and her daughter began to grow apart at that time, but it was more than that. It was more than just growing apart from her daughter. It was losing her daughter that started the downward spiral for Elaine.

The morning that she and Harold broke the news to her daughter, Elaine's heart finally broke. She saw the defeat on her daughter's face. She felt the failure of her life. She knew that because she had not done the one thing a mother should always do, protect her child, Nicole had been damaged forever. The alcohol and pills had numbed her pretty well up until that point. She was depressed constantly, spending her waking hours inebriated and drunkenly crying herself back into sedation or sleep.

Today, after she rushed from the kitchen, away from Nicole's dumbfounded face, Elaine ran to her bathroom. She dug into the cupboard under the sink and found her stash: a half-gallon bottle of Vodka. She took a swig, ignoring the sting, and drank until she was forced to come up for air. She looked back at herself from the mirror as the burn crept up her throat, through her brain and settled behind her eyes. Tears burst through, trying to douse the flames, and seared the mascara and eye shadow from her face, dragging them in paths down her cheeks. She clenched her teeth, wanting to scream out in horror at the monstrosity she had become. Eventually, the grinding of her teeth let her know that she was going to break each and every tooth in her mouth into pieces. Elaine thrust her hand into her mouth, that meaty little webbing between your index finger and thumb, and she bit down. She bit hard, and slow, until the taste of blood that began as just a dribble eventually became a torrent. She screamed into her hand, muffling the sound into a loud hum.

When she was done, she rinsed her hand with vodka, knowing that human bites are one of the filthiest that one can acquire. Then she rinsed the vodka away with water. Once she was sure her hand was clean, she took some antibiotic ointment from the medicine cabinet and spread it on her still bleeding wound. Next to the vodka's proper place, in the bottom cupboard, was the first aid kit. In here, Elaine found gauze, bandages and tape, which she used to dress her injury. With her hand wrapped tight, she took another small sip of vodka, and put the alcohol away, along with the first aid kit.

Elaine slowly washed her face, and cleaned her inky, black tears off of the bathroom counter and sink. She took two Percocet for the pain, and her Prozac, which had helped her depression in exactly zero ways. With renewed vigor, Elaine bolted from the bathroom, and to her bedroom, where she retrieved her purse and car keys. She left the house in a hurry, realizing that her alcohol stash was getting low. Since she had delved into and then succumbed to the grasp of alcoholism, she always renewed her stock when she was nearing only two day's worth of liquor in her home. To her that was 3-4 gallons of vodka or any other heavy spirits.

Elaine had to drive far from home to fulfill this wish. She lived in the suburbs; there wasn't a liquor store within five miles of her that opened before 10 a.m. No, Elaine had to drive across town to someplace a bit more... neglected. Elaine weaved in and out of traffic with total disregard for the lives of those around her. She was upset, and on a pharmaceutical high. She didn't care who was in her way. Even though she had a supply of alcohol at home, her addiction was in control right now. Though the bottle was literally miles away, Elaine could still taste the spirits on her tongue. She desired that burn to drizzle down her throat and warm her insides.

She pulled up to a rundown brick building that had been painted white at one time, but now stood colored a dim gray where graffiti didn't cover the wall. Black, wrought iron bars covered the windows and door. Faded ads for cigarettes from at least a decade prior fought against a layer of dust to fulfill their destiny of advertising death. One man slept under a blanket so covered in dirt and grime that it was like a wave of filth. His clothes, beard, and contents of his shopping cart matched. The only thing near him that looked remotely clean was the bottle of whiskey at his side, and the brown bag it peered out of. He grunted at Elaine as she walked past; too tired and drunk to even beg clearly.

The small man behind the counter greeted Elaine by her last name, familiar with it from her many trips here with her credit card. Elaine gave him a short wave as she made her way to her section. She wasn't here to shop, just to restock and she knew right where she needed to go. In the vodka aisle, she grabbed three of the cheapest half gallon jugs. Making her way to the counter, her eye caught a bottle of wine on sale. It wasn't top shelf, but it wasn't Mad Dog 20/20, either. She snatched it as well, almost dropping her purse. She juggled her items to the counter and plunked them down. The store owner attempted to make small talk, but Elaine wasn't reciprocating. She merely handed over her credit card and remained silent.

As she left, Elaine threw her vodka in the car and took out the bottle of wine. It was a cheap bottle. The label gave it away. So did the twist off cap and plastic cork. Elaine removed both and sat next to the homeless man she had passed earlier.

"Harold and I told Nicole that we have decided to separate today." Elaine said out loud. The homeless man grunted, sitting up.

"I know you heard me, Butch." Elaine sighed, obviously acquainted with the man.

"Yeah, wha? Oh, yeah, Elaine. Hey. So, you told her, huh?" he asked, wiping drool from his cheek. Elaine took a swig form the wine and handed it to Butch. He set it next to him and began digging in his shopping cart. From what would appear to be a random, wadded up plastic bag, he acquired what he was looking for. Inside he found several alcohol pad hand-wipes that he had taken from a popular fast food restaurant that specialized in greasy fried chicken. He wiped his hands, and then the top of the bottle.

"How'd she take it?" Butch pulled a dirty plastic cup from his cart. He poured himself a glass of the wine and drank it all in seconds. Before Elaine could speak, he poured himself a second glass.

"Not well. Not well." Elaine took a drink from her bottle. "And me being the useless parent I am, I didn't help matters at all. I've failed, Butch."

"Hey, it ain't over yet. Look at me." Butch banged a hand on his shopping cart. "This is what you call failed, sweetheart. I got nowhere and nothin'. I don't know where my kids are, and can't even remember their names anymore half the time. My family's all dead, or want nothing to do with me. I eat trash and spend more days than I care to say passed out in my own vomit or piles of shit. You ain't failed yet, Elaine."

"You don't understand, Butch. This is different. Things happened. I should have been there for Nicole. I should have defended her. I should have looked out for her best interests, not my own, or my husbands. I didn't do that. That's my only real job, and I fucked it up, Butch. And she's paying for it. I just want to hold and hug her, and I don't even know how to talk to her." Elaine guzzled from her bottle loudly.

"So just do it. Do it however you can." Butch advised, drinking from his cup.

"It's not that simple, Butch. She knows what I did. And I don't think there's any way to say that I'm sorry."

"There's always a way to say you're sorry, and a way to forgive, if you love each other." Butch advised, tipping his cup toward her indicating he needed a refill.

"Then why are you here, Butch? You could do the same with your family: find them and apologize." Elaine suggested.

"Me?" Butch laughed out a mouthful of frothy spittle. "Shit, Elaine, I told you I was a failure. You know why? Because I don't care no more. You still do. I stopped caring a long time ago and just began walking this earth waiting to die because I was too chickenshit to take myself out. And here you are, pissing and moaning, sharing drinks with a homeless guy outside a liquor store. But you know what, when you're done, you'll get back in your car, drive back to your pretty little suburb, and cry yourself to sleep in your designer sheets. You know why you'll do that? Because you still care. Me? Done caring. I'm a piece of shit, and my family knows it and the thing that would be best for them is for me to just die so that they can say 'At least he's not suffering anymore,' the way people do to make themselves feel better about that hopeless family member that passed away from cancer, or in my case, stupidity. Go home, Elaine. I love ya to death, but you need to get out of here. Go home and figure out how to fix your life, before ya do end up like me."

Elaine took his words in and figured she might as well listen. She doubted he was as apathetic as he was playing it, but that didn't take any validity from the rest of his speech. She still did care; he was right about that. She should be at home. Even if it was her destiny to spend the rest of her life piss drunk, she should be doing it at home. Too many people were like Butch with no place to go, no warm bed to sleep in and had no idea where their next meal would come from. Elaine didn't have to worry about any of that. She had been well provided for in life. She had a home to go to. This made it even more unacceptable for her to pretend her life was in the dire straights that this homeless man spent his every waking minute in.

"You're right, Butch. I better go." Elaine hauled herself to her feet.

"Been nice knowing you, Elaine. But look here, I don't want to see your face again. You go get things right with your family, okay? At least try. At the very least, get things right with yourself. Shit, if you can do that, the rest will come naturally, I suppose." Butch licked his lips and closed his eyes. His breakfast of liquor was warming in his belly. It was time for a nap.

"Thanks, Butch." Elaine wiped a tear from her eye.

"Goodbye, Elaine." Butch said dully, shooing her on her way.

Elaine listened to part of what Butch had to say. She drove home. Once there she drank herself silly and passed out on the couch.

Chapter Five: War. What is it good for?
(Absolutely Nothing?)

The girls took their time making their way back to school. Nicole decided that with the support of her friends, she could face the rest of this day. Besides that, her reputation wouldn't let her stay home. She never intended for anyone besides her two best friends and Jeremy to know what was happening in her home life, but in case the news did get out, she could not look devastated. The crying girl might think she's getting sympathy from all the classmates who lend her a shoulder and a hug, but in reality they're all laughing inside; laughing at the trials and tribulations of others, no matter how terrible and life shattering.

Nicole, Natalie and Elizabeth hadn't wanted to return, but what was a pep rally without a pep squad? Natalie didn't bother taking the freeway. She cruised along the city streets at a fair pace. Nicole spent the moments rubbing her arm where Jeremy had touched her. It still felt warm. She was charmed by his sense of chivalry, as the stereotypical cobra in a wicker basket is by an Indian man with a flute sitting in a dusty alley in Bangladesh. Nicole had let Jeremy know she was in trouble, and he wanted to help. He wanted to make it right for her. Despite his inability to make this wrong right, she was enamored with him even more just because he attempted such an act. He was willing to fly blindly into the tempest that her life was becoming with no thought for himself. Nicole, being a cynical bitch, couldn't believe that such a being could really be alive, let alone in her life. Even now, her mind conjured up possible schemes that Jeremy must be running, because she couldn't wholly believe someone to be that honest and true. Jeremy must want to use her or her situation for something. Even as the devil sat on her shoulder whispering these cruel nothings in her ear, Nicole knew in her heart that they weren't true. Jeremy was a genuinely good person. That was part of what attracted her to him so.

"So what do you think of the war." Elizabeth prodded during the car ride, referring to current political world events. Such things fascinated her. While most teens sat around watching music videos, she often spent the night fixated on 24-hour news channels. The mention of the deceased former classmate had stuck in her mind. It wasn't every day someone you knew was going to be flying home in a casket covered by an American flag, and secreted away from the prying eyes of the press who might want to tell the story of how that young soldier died. At least it wasn't for the generation before them. Sadly, it was becoming a regularity for Nicole's generation.

"It sucks. War sucks," Natalie blurted. "But we have to do it."

Nicole kept silent. She didn't really want to weigh in on the issue... yet.

"It's kind of our duty, as Americans, right? I mean, who is going to stand up for these people if we don't? Truth Justice and the American way, right?" Elizabeth gave an unsteady agreement. She had noted that Nicole hadn't spoken up yet, and didn't want to cross her unintentionally.

"Well, the rest of the world doesn't understand evil the way we do." Natalie elaborated. "We've been blessed with a leader who'll stand up for the liberty of all people in every nation. Evil dictators have to be overthrown. If we hadn't stopped him when we did, he could have been the next Hitler." Hitler, the end-all be-all of despicable human beings. After Hitler's massacre and genocide he suddenly entered the popular vernacular as the absolute lowest example of human filth in any conversation, the one exception being campfire stories at White Supremacist summer camps. While he had hoped to leave a legacy as the first leader to dominate the modern world and ethnically cleanse it at the same time, he merely made himself into the closest to a human caricature of Satan that the world had ever known. So much so, that some say when a comparison of one human being to another devolves into comparisons with Hitler, the debate/conversation has at that point lost all value and meaning. That's how low Hitler had become on the scumbag list. And deservedly so. He was so low that being compared to him could suddenly make a conversation meaningless; The reason being that no one could think of a worse example to compare anyone to. Christ found a way to forgive Judas, but Hitler? Nah. He's a-burnin' in the big fire downstairs, no matter how many times he says he's sorry. So it came to pass after World War II that any world leader needing to be seen in the public's eye as a really bad guy was compared to Hitler, because if you could draw even a shoestring strong tie to Hitler in your argument for one being evil, your opponent couldn't find a greater evil to throw into the mix, except big old Lucifer himself, and in that case you'd have to be interacting with someone who believed in the devil to begin with. Wasn't it every good man's duty to stand up against Hitler? This is Hitler's lasting legacy: Just bringing up his name ruins any and all conversation not directly related to World War II.

"So what about all these protestors?" Elizabeth played a half-hearted devil's advocate, smartly not falling entirely for the Hitler escape that Natalie had tried. She was still playing the fence until Nicole weighed in.

"Ignorance," Natalie explained. "They just don't know any better. The pastor at our church says socialist special interest groups fund them. I think they're just out to cause trouble. Anarchists, you know?"

"Yeah," Elizabeth sighed in agreement. "I mean, why fight against your own country? That's no way to support our troops. They go over there and stand up for what we believe in and then these people protest them. No one wants to die for people that hate them."

"I don't think soldiers want to die at all." Nicole piped up. Her plainly obvious statement stunned her friends. The other two girls hadn't pondered this idea. Too often, people talked of the valor and bravery of dead troops. Too little did they speak of the fact that no soldier wants to die. "But I don't think it's any disrespect for someone to protest anything in this country. That includes war and the troops fighting them. Think about it. These troops believe enough in American ideas of freedom to go and die for them. A citizen exercising these rights for any reason is a celebration of our fighting forces in itself. We tell them it's their right as Americans to speak freely, but then call them traitors when they do. That's trivializing the death's of our soldiers right there. The protestors are actively using the rights that those soldiers stood for. That's doing a hell of a lot more with a dead military man's career than any 'patriot' trying to shut the protestors up or degrade them. Why have live babies grow up to be dead soldiers, for our rights, if we refuse to use them and denounce those who do as traitors?"

Why indeed?

The car remained silent for the rest of the ride to school. Nicole had put the girls in an uncomfortable position. They actually had to think about something outside their trivial high school lives. Looking at the big picture can be scary and it scared all three of them into contemplative silence.

They arrived just two hours before classes were released for the day. The girls didn't bother going to any class at all. Their last hours had already been cleared to prepare for the rally. The pep club was basically in charge of building student spirit and running assemblies. Nicole, Natalie, and Elizabeth had been in other clubs, up until last year. Now in their senior year, they delegated all of their tasks to the lower-classmen in the pep squad. This only worked because the other members knew that they could be considered "in" if everything went well. There would be hell to pay if anything went wrong. Nothing ever went wrong.

The girls headed straight for the gymnasium where today's event would be held. The large room was decorated from the rafters to the walls to the floor.

Streamers in the school's colors were littered from the rafters and down the windows. Hand painted signs that the girls had made weeks in advance were hung about. Blown up pictures of the star player's freshman yearbook photos had been mounted on the walls. The large bleachers were the old wooden style that would fold up into the walls. Many a young girl had lost her virginity under those bleachers while the home team was playing. There was also the inevitable urban legend of that one kid who was crushed under the bleachers at some point in the school's history, even though no one had ever died there.

Currently, the large hall was nearly empty, save for fifteen or so people. The pep squad members who were already present were standing next to the freshmen cheerleader squad going over a few of the event's details that involved both groups. Here, the stage was set for an outstanding confrontation. Nicole didn't know of anyone that she couldn't get along with, if she tried. She did, however, acknowledge that she had an archenemy.

Interlude: The Man in Black
(every hero needs a good villain)

Veronica Barbossa was a Venezuelan immigrant/American citizen, depending on her mood. Her father came from a long line of Venezuelan oilmen. Her mother was a relief worker from America. They met when Mrs. Barbossa traveled to his home country with the Red Cross. Veronica's mother died after being attacked in a guerrilla raid when Veronica was only two years old. Stricken with immense grief and a wanting to have his daughter know her culture, her father moved to America. He remarried a Sears catalog model named Anna Schwartz a year later. She was the only mother Veronica had ever known. The New Mrs. Barbossa was drunken and unfit. Veronica loved her, emulating all her worst behaviors. Her new stepmother encouraged the daughter she didn't give birth to in all the despicable activities that no respectable woman would put herself through. Of course, Anna was only doing her best, and teaching behaviors that she thought were best. Anna felt that she had a grasp on the world, and knew just how to get ahead. She did end up marrying into a whole lot of money after all. She could guide Veronica toward the same end. Anna overlooked the fact that she was hollow and dead inside spending every waking hour vomiting up her last meal or guzzling bottles of wine.

Due to their obvious similarities that neither would ever admit, Veronica and Nicole were friends until Veronica made a pivotal mistake in the third grade. She kissed Ben Reilly behind the handball courts. Ben and Nicole, who had been his girlfriend at the time of the incident, broke up. Veronica and Ben stayed together off and on until the tenth grade. That was the year Ben overdosed on cocaine. It had been his first try, Veronica's 1036th. She used the drug and her left index finger (scarred terribly on one side due to overexposure to stomach acids) for weight control. She was an addict in denial, but her addiction was controlled by her incessant need to be perfect. Two days after Ben died, there were rumors of her calling Chad and them hooking up. Nicole didn't believe it that first time. She did, however, act in public as if she did. There was no other option, because even if it were untrue, enough people believed it to be true that Nicole had to treat it that way to save face. Her sway over others minds wasn't powerful enough at that point to convince them otherwise. She couldn't allow the situation to make a fool of her. Not like with Ben Reilly. With unrelenting cruelty, she forced Chad to tell her the truth in the privacy of her room. Then Nicole forced Chad in public to condemn Veronica and her story. Nicole watched as Chad recited from memory every word that she had written for him. The entire school watched Veronica running away in tears. The plan worked, that time. Veronica was humiliated and Nicole shone brighter than ever. That was not to be the end of this twisted love triangle, though.

Veronica was now the captain of the cheerleading squad. She had been merely a co-Captain when Nicole and her crew were on the cheer team. Nicole had quit over a year ago. This too stemmed from an event between Veronica and Chad. Natalie's birthday party had been down on the lake that year. Nicole brought Chad with her. Lizzie drank too much and felt the gastric repercussions. Nicole drove her home, forcing Lizzie to hang her head out of the window the entire ride. Meanwhile, Chad and Veronica took advantage of the alone time. They were caught in the middle of a sexual act involving Veronica's mouth and thumb. Some of those watching were scarred for life. No one would forget that day. It only helped the rumors of Chad's possible homosexuality grow. Nicole quit the cheer team, claiming that she couldn't be so close to a girl who could be that filthy. She made Veronica out to be the worst whore in the history of man, and claimed to be "handing over" the cheer team to Veronica because it was beneath Nicole now. It was a weak excuse, but Veronica took it. It was a rare win over Nicole and everyone knew about it. Many of them waited each and every day even now, over a year later, expecting some sort of horrid vengeance to be leveled from Nicole's camp toward Veronica.

When Nicole took over the pep squad, she knew that dealing with Veronica would be unavoidable. Both groups were often required to work together for school events. She merely kept her distance. If she had any hand in planning the event, she made sure to let the cheer team know their time was going to be cut short only minutes before they were to perform a routine. Veronica would complain to administrators, but Nicole always had her tail covered with a perfectly acceptable excuse. It was usually that Nicole took a little too long with her speeches that generally started off the assemblies. This rally wouldn't be different. It may have been a pep rally, but everyone there would be expecting a cheerleader performance.

Nicole marched over to her old cheer squad. Most of the girls were still her friends. A few had switched to Veronica's side, in exchange for better floor positions during routines. Natalie tried to stop Nicole by grabbing a shoulder but Nicole shook her off and shot a look back at her that let Natalie know that she had better not try it again. Even Elizabeth cringed. Though Nicole had relinquished control of the team, she hadn't conceded the territory. She wanted to appear here to make sure that Veronica felt her presence. Nicole had to make it clear that anytime she wanted, she could be back in that uniform and in control of the team as co-captain again.

Nicole put on her biggest smile. She greeted all of the girls, except Veronica. The girls stopped practicing the cheer they were working on, and moved to meet Nicole. Veronica felt her control over the girls slipping, just what Nicole had intended. Veronica wasn't one to be slighted. She pushed her way past them all, and stood face to face with Nicole. All talk within the gym ceased. Veronica smiled. Nicole returned a vampiric grin. Those still within the four walls around them settled in to watch the confrontation. No one spoke, and quite a few of the students actually held their breath. It was an old west showdown. All they needed was for a ball of sagebrush to come blowing past them as they each fondled a six-shooter attached to their hips.

"Nicky!" Veronica continued the charade of glee. "How are you?"

"Good. Excited about the assembly?" Nicole tilted her head. It was all a façade that fooled no one. Everyone present knew that there was a lake of bad, bad blood between these two.

"The assembly is the last thing on my mind. I heard Natalie rushed to see you earlier. I hope everything is alright at home." Everyone heard what she said, and heard her giggle at the end of the statement. It was as if a challenge to a duel to the death had been issued. People heard Veronica moving in for the kill and no one wanted to miss the carnage. Nicole's mind ran through a number of controlled responses. The drugs and alcohol were easing her inhibitions aside as she stood there.

"You know, Veronica, your mother's a slut and your father got rich supporting the terrorists who killed your real mom. I don't see anything funny." Nicole finally blurted out through her smiling teeth. She took a step back, as if releasing that gem of venom had taken a toll on her. It was really too much to have to deal with Veronica right now. Besides that, what Veronica had said struck a little too close to home. Did Veronica somehow know about what was happening? No. *That's impossible*, Nicole told herself. It was a weak shot, that just so happened to resonate with Nicole, but there was no way that Veronica could know what was happening in the O'Leary household.

"What?!" Veronica was shocked. She took a hand to her chest and looked about the gym. Nicole sighed. Then she let loose a haymaker as Veronica turned to face her again. The blow snapped Veronica's head back. She tried to adjust and recover, but the momentum was too much for her to overcome. As she fell backward, the cheer team who had been standing behind her separated. Veronica crashed onto the floor, banging the back of her head on the hard wood. The blood from her split upper lip landed on the floor in front of her feet just as her noggin smashed into the glossy pine. She began flopping on the ground, playing for attention. Through tears, she threatened lawsuits and the wrath of the local District Attorney. Nicole laughed.

"Go clean yourself up, Veronica. You're uniform's a mess." Nicole shook her head.

"You'll go to jail for this." Veronica pinched her nostrils to stop the blood flowing from there and kept her head tilted back to look at the ceiling. Blood gushed down the back of her throat causing her to swallow continuously. Her cheer team helped her to her feet, careful not to sully their own uniforms.

"Calm down," Natalie tried to diffuse the situation she had initially wanted to prevent. She realized now that Nicole shouldn't have come in to school at all. She knew they hated each other, but had never expected them to come to physical blows. Veronica had just gotten in that one shot about Nicole's family on the wrong day, at the wrong time. Because of that, the young Mrs. Barbossa ate a five sided fistagon sandwich.

"Really," Nicole echoed. "Why would you blame me for your cheerleading accident anyway?"

"What are you talking about?" Veronica was truly confused now. She didn't know what Nicole was playing at, but she knew something shady was about to happen. It was that moment when the fall guy in the bank heist suddenly realizes that the rest of the gang has set him up to *be* the fall guy, and there's nothing he can do about it except squeeze his butt cheeks tighter than a vise for the 10-15 year prison sentence he'll be looking at.

Nicole stepped forward, leaning in close to Veronica's ear. The victim tried to back away, but Nicole insisted. She placed a hand on each of Veronica's cheeks. Her lips came so close to Veronica's ear that it almost appeared that she was kissing her.

"We wouldn't want anyone to find out about you and Mr. Wade, would we?" Nicole whispered ever so softly. It was perhaps the quietest deathblow in history. Veronica immediately stopped fidgeting. She hadn't expected Nicole to bring this information to light, ever.

It was over a year prior, just after Natalie's birthday party where Veronica and Chad had fooled around. Veronica had been having a relationship of sorts with Mr. Wade, head of the school's history department. Nicole happened upon them in a supply closet by accident. She had been searching for old trophies to add to the new display case in the main lobby. Nicole had found them in an old, unlabeled closet in the basement, near the old swimming pool that that they used to use before Antonio Valdez, Olympic medal winner, raised all that money to build the new athletic center.

Rarely did anyone come down to the old pool after the new one was built. It wasn't filled anymore. At least not with water. Old gym supplies, desks, chairs and other junk sat within the pool now. After it's closure, it also earned the obligatory ghost story. Supposedly a young girl somehow found her way down here and managed to die. The sheer creepiness of the huge, abandoned room helped support the story. It also helped to keep most people out, except for the hardcore marijuana smokers who needed a good place to hide. The room's vacancy made it ideal; Not only for pot smoking, but also for an illicit, illegal teacher-student relationship.

When Nicole stumbled upon Veronica and Mr. Wade, she promised not to tell, but she did snap a video on her cellphone of the two stumbling around, trying to put on their clothes. Nicole promised silence not because she wanted to help, but because Mr. Wade agreed to give Nicole, Natalie and Elizabeth an A for the year. This was why Veronica figured that Nicole would never reveal anything about the incident to anyone. She had continued the relationship with Mr. Wade because she didn't see any reason why Nicole should tell and risk her own future as well. Now, though, Nicole had brought the encounter to the forefront of this war.

"Fine." Veronica agreed immediately, in just as quiet a tone, through a gulp of bloody mucus and saliva. She mustered an arm up and shoved Nicole away. "So what if I fell? It's still my squad and we still have practice girls." Veronica turned to her team. With the skill of a slave driver, Veronica coerced the girls into practicing. She then made her own way to the school nurse. Natalie moved to Nicole's side as they watched the beaten enemy retreat. Those in the gym moved back to their previous duties, but the level of chatter had been turned up a notch or two. Several people were already on cell phones, texting classmates about the incident.

"Did you just blow that Mr. Wade ace card you had?" Natalie asked. Elizabeth's eyes begged for an answer as well.

"Maybe, maybe not." Nicole kept the truth to herself. "What I did do was remind her that no matter how tight you shut the door, someone's always able to drag at least one skeleton out of your closet."

"You're a sneaky bitch." Natalie pinched Nicole's arm.

"That's the only reason it worked. She never saw it coming." Nicole turned to the rest of the Pep squad, the girls who had been waiting for the trio to arrive. "Now, let's make sure our posters are hung right, and get that T-shirt slingshot ready." The general was back in her saddle, rallying the troops.

The assembly came without any further incident. Veronica even reappeared, albeit with a fat lip and gauze taped over her nose which wasn't broken as it turned out. She had to refrain from participating, and sat with the freshmen cheerleaders in the front row. Nicole ran the microphone to coordinate the event. They started with words from the principle, Mr. Anderson.

Mr. Anderson had planned on changing lives when he graduated from college. He had planned on shaping the minds of future world leaders. He had known from the day that he left high school and entered college that he would do his part to change the world. That had been over thirty years ago. He had long since lost his passion. Nowadays, he merely showed up for the paycheck. Most days that meant showing up late and hung over. His staff noticed. They all took on a rather lax and uncaring attitude. As long as they were paid, they would keep showing up. Mr. Anderson waited impatiently for each day to end, pretending to be teleconferencing in his office. Most of the time, he was masturbating to free internet porn of an illegal, prepubescent nature. The idea of public education entices some of the brightest people, who hope that they too can make a difference in the lives of young people. Then these new teachers find out just how poor public funding is for schools. They find out how they are judged based on standardized tests. No longer can you teach them for the future, you just teach them in preparation for that standardized test, because guess what, those standardized test results will decide the future funding for your school and even your district. Gone are the days of teaching what you should to future generations for their success in life. Nowadays, public school teachers are forced to take low paying jobs with piss poor supplies just to train kids which bubble to fill in on some standardized paper test that will tell the world that the kids aren't all right, no matter what their score is.

Mr. Anderson now sat with his arms crossed in the front row, with his sidekick, Vice Principal Draven, at his side. Nicole then introduced each member of the team. There was a bachelor auction using fake money that was thrown into the crowd by Nicole's girls. The coach gave a few words, boring everyone. Nicole took the microphone near the end one last time. She had been scheduled to give a speech of her own before the cheerleaders took over. As the pep squad quieted the crowd, Nicole went over the words in her head. She had prepared and memorized it nearly a week ago. As she stood alone, in the center of that room with everyone staring at her, she decided to ad lib a little bit.

"How's everybody doing?" She asked with more zest than usual, receiving a thunderous roar back. "Well-" She tried to continue, but they were cheering still. It was because of the punch. Word had gotten around the school that Veronica didn't fall of her own volition. The entire student body was cheering Nicole for manhandling Veronica. Nicole took control of the situation by repeating herself with a bit more force. One of her pep squad members stood, and motioned for the crowd to shut up.

"Well," Nicole continued as the crowd quieted. "You all know why we're here. I don't really need to give you an explanation. What I do want to do is ask if we should be here right now." She felt the glares of the school staff. "I mean, we all have other things to do, right? I know more than a few of you that should be home studying."

This brought some laughs from those gathered. Nicole discreetly glanced about the room. In the corner of her eye, she caught a figure standing in the shadows of one of the side entrances that was supposed to be closed. One cautious look was all it took for Nicole to recognize Jeremy. She quickly looked back to the crowd, scanning to see if any of them had seen the mysterious observer. No one was looking, as far as she could see. Chad hadn't noticed her eyes diverting that way. That's all that really mattered.

"Let's get one thing straight," Nicole continued, grabbing their attention. "I know we'd all rather be off drinking in the canyon right now." Nicole referenced Tahrongy Canyon, a popular hangout thirteen miles outside of town. "And maybe we should. I mean, there's really no point in being here, is there? We're supposed to be here to gather school spirit, but we all hate this place. This is just an elitist gathering to build testosterone and self-esteem for the sad few of you who believe minor athletic achievements can make up for that hollow feeling you have inside. It's stupid, really. C'mon, ladies, do these mindless apes really need another reason to act like idiots?"

The females in the audience cheered, screamed and yelled, shattering eardrums. The vice-principal stood to his feet, sensing that this speech wasn't going to turn itself around. Mr. Anderson slowed his cohort, just to be sure that they weren't acting hastily. Inside, he knew this situation could only end poorly, and he wanted to see the carnage. He felt that the school system had failed him, and he wanted oh-so-bad to let this assembly degrade into a shame on the face of that system. Nicole moved a few steps further from them both. Her hand tightened around the wireless microphone. The crowd began to quiet as she spoke more.

"Can you believe the school actually pays for this? Our parents pay taxes for this crap! We could use new books, computers, teachers... We could use this money to give some of them a raise and make the daily grind worth their time. Maybe then we could get rid of this antiquated ritual, and cut to the getting wasted portion of the night we're all looking forward to!"

Nicole dropped the microphone as the vice-principal and Mr. Anderson rushed towards her. Chad stood and urged everyone to run to the canyon. That's the only part of her speech he had understood. The crowd listened, rushing for the main exits. Well, most of them. The band members stayed seated, along with the student's who saw no acceptable GPA below 5.0. These select ten or twenty students kept to their seats, fearing the possible wrath of the school's administration. Even if they had wanted to leave, none of them had the slightest clue where to go in Tahrongy Canyon. They had never been invited, and wouldn't be. Years later they would be the social elite while most of the jocks and cheerleaders were working as average insurance salesmen or realtors in the same areas they grew up in. Chad smacked one of the band kids in the back of the head as he ran by. Nicole was so caught up in her own anarchy, she didn't notice the principal had gotten close enough to grab her. She was reveling in the chaos as the few teachers present tried to stop the fleeing students who had bottlenecked at the doors. The head administrator began to yell at her as his partner took to the mic in a futile attempt to restore order.

Nicole ignored them all. She wrestled herself free, and fled to the exit Jeremy was at, far away from anyone else. The principal debated chasing after her, but calming the masses was his priority. He quickly decided to try and control the exiting student body. He knew Nicole. The entire faculty did. Finding her later to mete out punishment wouldn't be difficult.

He began to demand obedience from the fleeing crowd. He resorted to begging as the large auditorium emptied. Every student had left eventually, except for Veronica who wasted no time in voicing her outrage.

Nicole slid out of the exit she had been aiming for, slamming the door behind her. It locked automatically. No one had followed her though. The entire student body had run to the parking lot. They were headed to the canyon to get drunk, as she had suggested. There, in that darkened hallway, Nicole smirked at Jeremy hiding from eyes that could no longer see him.

"Wow, Nicole. That was-"

She grabbed him by the collar and pulled him to her. He was amazed at her clandestine strength. She pressed her lips to his with more force than he was expecting. Jeremy fell back into the assorted lockers behind him, and Nicole with him. A padlock tunneled its way into his shoulder blade. As soon as he found some stability, he pushed her away, ignoring how good it felt to have her with him.

"Nicole! Someone could see us here. Chad would kill me," he hurriedly looked around. No one was in sight within the building. The student body had gone outside to the parking lot. They were moving to congregate together at Tahrongy Canyon, as Nicole had instructed them. She laughed off Jeremy's admonition.

"No one's here, Jeremy," she reassured him. "It's just me and you. I'm so glad you came. It meant a lot to me." Nicole smiled through her lasting haze of alcohol and prescription drugs.

"Yeah." He gave an out of place reply. "I'm guessing that speech wasn't rehearsed." Jeremy tried using light humor to mask his body movements as he stepped back.

"Nope," Nicole confirmed. " I just made it up on the spot. It was my weak attempt at improvisation."

"I'd say you did pretty good. But you're going to be in serious trouble." The tone of Jeremy's voice let Nicole see that he genuinely cared for her. He was falling for her.

"You let me worry about the trouble, okay. I can see that you're worried enough about us being together." With her reminder, he glanced about again. Being with her brought about the feeling of joy, and visions of the Chad's teammates thrashing him.

"I thought you had to work..." Nicole's statement demanded an answer.

"I did. I mean, I do." He stammered. "I just took a long lunch, and had someone cover for me. I have to get back soon, though."

"And what are you doing later?" She inquired, toying with the strings of her sweat pants.

"Nothing. Studying, I guess." He honestly answered, trying not to notice the physical signals she was sending. "I've got a chemistry exam coming up."

"Of course you do." Nicole paused as her cell phone rang. She debated not answering until she saw the i.d. of the caller.

"Hello." She flipped it open and pressed the phone to her ear. "What's up, Chad." Nicole grinned, looking right into Jeremy's eyes.

Jeremy took a step away. Nicole took three steps toward him. She was toying with him. His fear at being caught was evident. He hadn't deduced, as Nicole had, that Chad followed the herd at her command.

"Yeah." Nicole spoke into the phone. "I'll be at the canyon."

She put her free arm around Jeremy's neck.

"What?" She asked Chad. "Yeah, I can get you something to drink. I always do, don't I?"

She lightly pressed her cheek to Jeremy's. He could hear her boyfriend on the other end of the line, and it petrified him.

"I didn't ask if she's coming or not, Chad, but she's my best friend so it's a distinct possibility, don't you think? Yeah. Okay."

Nicole listened to Chad while silently kissing Jeremy's neck.

"Love you." She whispered as her lips brushed the bottom of Jeremy's ear. It was unclear to Jeremy which of them she was referring to. She snapped the phone shut, and placed it in her pocket.

"That was Chad." She told him what he already knew. "He's on the highway right now, headed to the canyon with the rest of the sheep. I've been tasked with bringing him some beer. You want to stop by there later, maybe?" Nicole didn't get her hopes up. Her tone let Jeremy know that she didn't expect him to say yes.

"I don't think that would be the best idea." Jeremy tossed the notion aside.

"I didn't think so." They laughed together. Nicole stepped back. "So. I better get going then. I'll call you later, okay?"

"Sure." Jeremy agreed.

"I promise." Nicole swore. "It might be really late, but I'll call, okay?"

"Okay." It was Jeremy's turn to not get his hopes up. She was the most popular girl in school and for that matter any school that was within 20 miles. She was going to a huge party in a canyon full of drunk jocks and beautiful people. He figured she'd forget that promise after the third drink or so. Nicole squeezed his hand and walked away. Jeremy watched her go, and then followed her path to the parking lot. He exited the building and made his way back to work.

Nicole found her two best friends waiting at Natalie's car in the parking lot. Natalie and Elizabeth were sharing a cigarette and yelling reassurances to passersby that the trio would indeed be making an appearance at the canyon tonight.

"What the hell was that about?" Natalie laughed as Nicole neared.

"I don't know." Nicole averted her cousin's eyes. "I just got tired of it all. Pep rallies, assemblies, it's all bullshit. Mindless, brainwashing, elitist bullshit. And it really was only a dress rehearsal for the canyon tonight. Whether I told them to or not, there would have been a party in Tahrongy tonight. Even the teachers and administrators knew it. There is after every pep rally or whatever. I just told them in there to confirm it, but I bet not one police officer shows up out there tonight.

Plus, I think I might have taken a pill or a shot too many earlier."

They all giggled.

"You know you're gonna get it when you get back to class." Natalie said. "You'll probably get kicked off of the team, leaving me and Lizzie to take over." Natalie stamped her cigarette out.

"We'll see." Nicole said cryptically. She moved to open the car door.

"We are going to the canyon?" Elizabeth asked.

"Of course we are." Natalie sighed. "I bet we have to buy Chad some beer on the way, like usual." She rolled her eyes and opened the driver's door.

"Oh, quit complaining." Nicole opened the passenger door. "Jackson gives it to us for damn near free anyhow. And you don't have to come, Natalie. I can drive Lizzie and myself out there."

Natalie rolled her eyes and stepped into the car. They drove to the liquor store where Jackson worked. Nicole hated her brother, but the fringe benefits of his job were nice at times. Before he had become an employee of Ridgeway Liquors, the girls had to use more desperate options for their liquor supply. First, they could steal their parent's provisions. This had to be done carefully and only in small amounts. The other option was to employ the services of one of the city's many homeless people. Once Jackson had landed this job, he allowed the girls to buy whenever they felt the urge to do so.

Natalie parked at the curb in front of the store. Nicole left the car almost before it had stopped moving.

She stormed off without a word, proceeding into the store alone.

"Are you guys going to fight like this all night?" Elizabeth turned to Natalie.

"Does it matter?" Natalie barked, looking away.

"Well, yeah, it does. It is her life, Natalie. You always freak out as if everything she does, you are doing, like it affects you. It's like you're in love with her or something." Elizabeth stared intensely as Natalie continued looking away.

"Oh my god!" Elizabeth took notice of what had been before her for years. She was physically rocked by this revelation. "You. Are. So. In. Love- With her."

Elizabeth paused pointing in the store at Nicole's back.

"That's kinda gross. You are cousins. Maybe not blood related, but still." Lizzie grimaced.

"Shut up." Natalie sighed stifling a sniffle and wiping a lone tear from the corner of her right eye. Natalie got out of the car, and Elizabeth followed suit.

"You better not say a word." Natalie threatened as they walked into the store. Lizzie had much more to ask, but couldn't. She filed her questions away in the back of her mind, and promised herself she'd make Natalie explain in further detail as soon as possible.

While the girls had been talking in the car, Nicole had been in selecting the party supplies. There was the always present homeless man truly trying to get more bang for his buck. He only had one dollar and twenty-three cents. This state of financial shortcoming left him with few options. If he could gather just one dollar more, he could buy two forty-ounce bottles of malt liquor. Nicole brushed past him, and moved toward the freezer that contained premium beer. She selected a case of Budweiser and moved to the counter. Jackson sat behind the register. His throne was a folding chair. He rested here, focused on reruns of *The Simpsons* on a small black & white television. He hardly glanced toward Nicole.

"That all for you?" He mumbled his uniform customer greeting.

"No, idiot, I need my usual bottle of rum." Nicole demanded some service. Jackson sat up at the sound of a feminine voice. Realizing who it was, he sighed audibly.

"Oh. Nicky. Where's your friends?" his mind didn't want to leave the track her voice had put it on. He turned behind him, grabbing a fifth of spiced rum.

"Don't worry about it, perv." Nicole threw a $20 bill on the counter. Natalie and Elizabeth entered the building.

"Ahh, ladies, right on time." Jackson glanced through slits at the girls. His relaxed eyelids hid devilishly bloodshot eyes.

"Jackson." Elizabeth grinned at Nicole's brother. She had entertained a crush on Jackson from the day she had met him. Natalie wasn't as big of a fan. She knew what Nicole knew. Natalie looked away, keeping her eyes on the TV behind the counter.

"So, this all for you girls?" Jackson didn't look away from Lizzie.

"Jackson, we get the same thing almost every week." Nicole's tone was extremely firm. "What do you think? Is this all we need girls? Just ring it up you idiot before I have to come back there."

"Maybe I should check you girls for ID." He didn't look at her when he threatened her.

"Shut up and get my change." Nicole slid her money closer to him.

"Hey, we can all be friends here, right Elizabeth?" Jackson snatched the money up and began operating the register. Nicole grabbed the box of beer and shoved it to her gawking friend.

"Take that to the car, Elizabeth." Nicole gave a direct order. "Put it in the trunk."

Nicole refused to stop staring daggers through her brother. He handed her $5.76 in change.

"Thanks prick." She snatched her bottle. Natalie followed a step behind.

"You know, one of these days, you're gonna regret treating me so bad!" Jackson warned her. Nicole was surprised to hear such a threat from him. She couldn't believe that he would ever take on a victim role. She didn't want him to know that he'd gotten to her though.

"Up yours." She scowled, disappearing in a huff of frustration and anger. She shoved the change she had gotten in the homeless man's hand as she barged past him. The door was closing shut behind Natalie and Nicole before he could offer his thanks.

Nicole arrived at the car in a much calmer state. "Wow. How bad do you want to nail my seedy brother, Lizzie?" Nicole asked as Natalie opened the trunk. Lizzie tossed the box of beer in the trunk.

"You'd be surprised how much some people desire others." Elizabeth hazarded a sideways glance at Natalie. It was a message that Natalie had better do something if this continued, to save Elizabeth, or the secret would be out. She could see Natalie gritting her teeth.

Nicole was in her own world, and didn't notice the subtleties of the exchange. She plopped into the passenger seat, scrunching in with Elizabeth. With the zest of an addict, Nicole opened the bottle of rum and took a long swig. Imitating the best pirate, she wiped her face from lips to chin on her forearm and passed the bottle to Lizzie. Natalie started the car.

"He's probably got warts or herpes or something." Nicole was still concerned by her friend's infatuation with Jackson.

"It's not like I wouldn't use a condom, Nicole, God!" Elizabeth mounted a poor defense.

"Lizzie! He's just gross, period. I'm not saying that in the 8-year old sense that he's my brother so he has cooties or something. He's filthy and he gets around." Nicole was blunt. "Trust me. He's not what you expect."

"How would you know?" Lizzie questioned her cryptic statement.

"Lizzie's just caught on the bad boy image." Natalie laughed, trying to mellow the tone of the conversation and dull the daggers she felt Elizabeth's eyes throwing at her.

"At least I go for the attainable." Elizabeth bit into Natalie with a grin. Natalie's laughter stopped. She turned up the stereo and pop princesses serenaded them the rest of the way.

The girls could see the canyon party long before they could actively participate in it. A bonfire was visible at the base of the main canyon road from the very top edge of Tahrongy. The canyon itself was hundreds of feet deep. A small creek ran along the edge of it, mirroring the highway. The canyon spanned a mile and a half in length, and at it's widest measured out at a mile even. The canyon was a crescent shape and eventually emptied out with the creek into a lake: Lake Tahrongy. The highway had a separate exit for the winding road that plowed down the canyon edge at a steep angle. Trees clustered about the stream, some daring to spread further away than others. There was a large clearing at the widest point of the canyon. This is where the main bonfire had been lit. Two smaller fires had been lit along opposite edges of the clearing. One near each of the kegs that had magically appeared in the back of pick-up trucks when the party had been announced. Cars were parked all around the clearing where the fires blazed. Some were occupied with fogged up windows, most were not.

Most of the students were clustered within their separate cliques. They were close to one another, but not too close. Every few feet, one small pod of people would come within inches of another, but there was adequate space for one to move about comfortably. Nicole spotted her significant other rather easily. He and his usual suspects had gathered with the affluent jocks. Nicole knew the conversation in this area would be focused on two things for the night: sports, and false reports of encounters with female anatomy.

Natalie, Nicole and Elizabeth were greeted by several people before they finished stepping out of the car by the "OhSoCloses", as Nicole called them. These were the kids who were "Oh So Close", to being considered popular. They would do anything to rub elbows with the social elite. The commoners didn't realize how much better off they were outside the castle. Their place at the bonfire was out at the edges. The popularity of one dictated how close he/she could stand to the fire. In essence, if you weren't cool, you weren't able to keep warm. You stayed chilly. And everyone knows chilly's never been cool.

Nicole brushed past the OhSoCloses briskly, but not enough so that their dignity was no longer intact. These people were the power. She knew that. Under her arms rested Chad's case of beer. Natalie passed her the half full bottle of rum after taking a drink. Nicole hadn't been completely sober since she woke up that morning. Her problems lingered on the edge of her consciousness, content to bide their time. Nicole had never needed to deal with the obstacles that independent adulthood presented. Her culture had raised her to see problems as targets for cash. Her mother and father threw money at every obstacle in their path, and Nicole's. Nicole knew that the bombshell that had rocked her world today couldn't be bought off. She wanted it all to end, but didn't have the heart for suicide. She would attempt to drink and drug the abomination away. Slowly she sauntered toward Chad.

"About time you showed up." Chad made jokes at Nicole's expense to impress his friends. They giggled, as their role dictated.

"Shut up and take your beer." Natalie had somehow gotten a hold of the bottle of rum and was taking another drink.

"You had to bring her, didn't you?" Chad snatched the box of beer from Nicole's arms and handed it to one of his stooges.

"We really have to go through this every time we all get together, don't we?" Nicole sighed.

"Hey, I didn't start with her." Chad held his hand up to feign innocence.

"Nope, I started it," Natalie confirmed. "But don't worry, Chad, I've got people to talk to, so I won't be standing around here for awhile." Natalie tilted her head awaiting a response. Nicole grabbed Chad's attention by slipping an arm around his waist. He turned his attention to assisting Nicole with a public display of affection. It was drunk, sloppy, and very immature, as teenage kisses tend to be. Natalie rolled her eyes. She led Elizabeth away by the arm.

"We'll be back, Nicky." Natalie called over her shoulder. "We've got to circulate and get away from all the gay over here. I think I saw David Ocean earlier. I've got to get him to call me."

Nicole broke her lip lock long enough to wave her friends away.

"So I heard about what you did to Veronica." Chad opened a beer, and handed it to Nicole.

"I bet you did. I'm sure she told you herself." Nicole hinted at his infidelity, and turned away. Some of his friends snickered. Chad didn't see any humor in the remark. He felt he had paid the price long ago for his misdeeds. It didn't matter to him that he was still abusing Nicole's trust at every opportunity. He believed that if he didn't get caught red-handed, he wasn't guilty.

"C'mon Nicole," He pleaded. "You know it's only you, for me." His tone held a bit of a warning as well.

"It was only a joke," Nicole shrugged his comments off. "So, did you see her at the assembly?"

"Everyone saw her." Chad was excited to move on. It always exhilarated him to discuss the misfortune of others, even if it was his mistress. "It looked like a brick hit her."

"Yeah, it was pretty sweet." Eric B. jumped into the conversation. The remora always stuck close to the shark. Eric had a bit too obvious of a crush on Nicole, and it showed more when he drank. Nicole often disregarded him because she didn't have time for little fish. Although, there were times that she desperately needed favors. At these moments, she didn't hesitate to abuse his infatuation.

"Good." Nicole felt proud. "I'm sure I'll have to answer for it when I see her again."

"Ha!" Chad laughed like a boar snorting. "Forget about her. You're gonna be in for it at school for that assembly stunt."

"Yeah." Nicole said flatly. "I don't really care." She drank from her beer as Chad opened his. Her mind began to slow as her eyes took on a glossy covering. She knew she would have to watch her drinking now. Even with her habitual abuse, she couldn't fight off the effects of intoxication forever.

"Holy shit, was old man Anderson mad. He looked like he was gonna kill you." Eric B. tried to grab her attention.

"Yeah. That's gonna go down in history as the best assembly ever." Chad held Nicole a bit tighter.

"I'll get out of it somehow. On Monday." Nicole sighed, and looked at Chad.

The small talk and drinking continued for a few hours. In that time, Natalie managed to find and give her phone number to David Ocean. She spent some time behind a tree letting him feel her up before she found Elizabeth again. Elizabeth, unlike her peers, had an open heart and over-active caring complex. As such, she spent her time hitting on the few freshmen that had dared to show up. Her boyfriend was a no-show, which would undoubtedly help Natalie formulate extensive theories on his homosexuality.

As Natalie made her way to the gaggle of youngin's gathered around Elizabeth, she adjusted her bra. In doing so, her gaze brought her to an unexpected acquaintance. Jeremy had arrived at the party. He was looking around, unsure of himself. Jeremy had never attended a social gathering of this magnitude. His circle of friends never did anything this wild. He almost never drank and didn't dare stay out later than he was allowed.

Jeremy wasn't sure why he had come here. He knew he was infatuated with Nicole, but coming here was suicide. She had indeed captured him with her antics. Jeremy held no notions of Nicole suddenly leaving Chad to be with him. Jeremy understood his role; he just wanted to see her. He had to see her. She occupied every moment of his day. He dreamt of her at night. He just had to see her again. So, Jeremy skipped his trip home, and left work early. He didn't bother to eat, and his stomach was voicing it's anger at the situation.

"Jeremy?" Natalie walked up and tapped him on the shoulder.

"Yeah?" He was startled. Jeremy didn't expect anyone in attendance to recognize him.

"Hey-ey". Natalie's last note lost some of it's pseudo-cheeriness as she realized how poorly things would go if Jeremy had come to profess his love to Nicole or perform some other fool's errand.

"So, what are you doing here?" Natalie asked, gently taking Jeremy by the arm. As he began to talk, she ushered him slowly toward a dark empty field where they wouldn't be seen together. And more importantly, where he wouldn't be seen at all.

"Well, I mean, I just came to see-" He was cut off by her hand clamping over his mouth. She looked around. They hadn't yet reached their destination, and anyone could hear them right here. She was sure many people were even watching her. That was fine, as long as they were given no idea about his feelings for Nicole.

"Do not say that," Natalie warned. "Not out loud. And definitely not here." She moved him faster. They had to get to the cover of night, where it would be safe to talk freely. They walked in silence until the jarring noise of the party was a low hum behind them. Natalie stopped, turning to face him in the moonlight. He noticed the cold glow of the glitter in her makeup as she smiled at him.

"Sorry to seem so rude, but we still don't know who else might be out here. So do not say her name, understood?" Natalie coached him.

"O-okay." He stammered

"You shouldn't even be here. What are you doing?" Natalie was hard on him, but she was acting that way in his best interests. Chad and his apes would beat the tar out of the baby if Jeremy even publicly hinted at liking Nicole.

"I know, I know. I just had to see her. She seemed... different today. I just wanted to make sure that she was alright." Jeremy looked to her face for some sign of agreement about Nicole's current mental state.

Natalie listened to him, and couldn't help but pity him. She had no idea what Nicole was doing with this kid. She was sure that her best friend had no idea Jeremy's feelings had grown into such a strong force. It was silly and romantic. Natalie had ideas all her own, though.

"Oh, Jeremy." Natalie brought a soft hand to his shoulder, and then hugged him. "If you are in love with her, Jeremy, you'll never talk to her again, for both your sakes."

"There's no, 'if.'" He tried to move back. Natalie stopped him, and let herself initiate the separation at a much gentler pace. "I really do care about her." Jeremy was firm.

"Then go to her. If you really care about her that much, go to her and Chad and tell her." Natalie dared him, waving an arm flippantly toward the party.

"That's not what I meant, by coming here." Jeremy explained. "I just wanted to see her. That's all. I didn't even want her to see me. I just wanted to see her, and make sure she was alright."

"Jeremy," the distant light of the fires danced through the trees and across half of Natalie's face. The other half was glistening in pale blue moonlight. She grinned slightly, and took Jeremy's hand. "You do deserve better than this. You're going to end up heartbroken, or worse, broken. It doesn't have to be that way..."

Natalie let her voice drift off and moved in closer to him. She gently whispered in his ear and guided his hand to the waistline of her pants.

"I can give you everything she can, and more." Natalie promised. She felt Jeremy's body respond positively against her leg. Jeremy's blood pressure rose as his heart began to beat hard enough to vibrate his entire body. Natalie slowly coached his fingers into unfastening the drawstring on her sweatpants.

"You wouldn't have to hide like this." Natalie very carefully let his hand go. She waited for any sign of his hesitance, in case she had to coax him more. He didn't know what to do when his hand found her crotch, but he left it there. Next, she took his other hand and snuck it up her shirt, under her bra.

"You could be out there, with me, in public, having everything you want..." Natalie gave a low coo, and Jeremy responded with a hardly audible guttural moan of his own.

"Nicole never said we couldn't fool around, did she? I mean, you aren't her boyfriend or anything, are you?" Natalie gyrated against his hand.

"No... I guess I'm not" Jeremy agreed.

"And if you were with me, you could be around her every day, couldn't you. You could see her anytime you wanted. You could pretend to be stopping by to see me, and, well, I could leave the two of you alone... some of the time." Natalie bent her head into his neck, gently biting her lip.

"Yeah." Jeremy agreed, eyes rolling up to the sky. He had never experienced anything like this before, except for his Wal-Mart run in with Nicole. He had fooled around with a few girls before, but nothing like the debauchery he had faced with Nicole, and now Natalie. He was not prepared.

"Maybe Nicole's keeping you a secret because she knows how popular you'd be if she dated you openly. You're a smart, good-looking guy. Maybe she's keeping you all to herself when she should be sharing you. You could have me. You could have us both. Maybe even at the same time. You'd like that, wouldn't you?" Natalie coiled a leg around his calf, preparing for her own climax.

"Ye-" Jeremy pulled away before finishing his sentence. His re-entry into reality was so fast and vicious, he almost threw her to the ground. "No. No. What's going on here? You're supposed to be her friend. Her best friend." He snatched his appendages from within her clothing. Natalie grinned trying to calm him down, hiding her frustration at not being able to reach a happy ending.

"Just testing you kiddo. Can't let just anyone play with my best friend's heart, now can I?" Natalie stepped away from him and tied her pants. The moonlight once again seemed to overtake her, beating out the warmth of the fire, and she was drenched in it's cool blue glow. "You're right, she is my best friend, that's why I had to make sure you were serious before letting you go any further with her."

"Oh. Okay..." Jeremy bought the story, only because he hadn't had to deal with conniving plots before this. He had no idea about the layers of deception that coated high school females.

"Well," Natalie adjusted her bra once again. "Come with me. I'll show you Nicole. It's something you should see, in any case." She slipped an arm around his shoulder, and walked him back toward the party.

About the time Natalie was giving her phone number to David Ocean, Nicole was walking to Chad's SUV with him. She was drunk, and on the edge of blacking out. Nicole was cognitive of the fact that she was following Chad to his Ford Explorer. It was what they did about this time through any party they attended. Chad's truck wasn't always the destination. Often it was a bedroom or motel room or even one of their homes. But in the canyon, the destination was the truck. Once or twice they had wandered off into the woods, but Nicole hated having to wonder what was crawling on her out there. Then there was the foliage she had to brush off of her clothing so she didn't look like some random tramp.

Nicole accepted Chad's help as she climbed into the back seat. After all the years they had been together, she had a pretty good idea of how the interaction would proceed. It wasn't as if Chad broke from his routine too often. When he did, it was usually to try some disgusting act he had seen in a porno that Nicole had no interest in trying. At least not more than once.

While maintaining consciousness, Nicole wished she were somewhere else. She wasn't in the truck against her will, she just wasn't truly in the mood. However, she understood this to be her role in the relationship. Sex with Chad was merely one of her duties. It was one of the things the "OhSoClose" girls and some guys wished they could have. Performing this duty helped cement her position in the social elite. Working to remain the most popular girl around often meant working with Chad, on her back.

Being with Chad wasn't particularly gratifying, either. Nor did it take that much time. Sexual encounters between Nicole and Chad were often over before her body had any natural reactions to the process. Translation: it was a rare day that he got her juices flowing.

She watched him fumble with his zipper, cursing under his breath. With his current state of inebriation, he would never get it done. Nicole had let him blunder about on his own a few times before when he was this drunk. It was a trial that Nicole didn't want to repeat tonight. She just wanted to get it over with, and move on. Soon enough they could leave, and she still planned on fulfilling her promise to Jeremy about calling him. She unsnapped her bra to guarantee that it wouldn't take him all night, and then helped him unzip and remove his own pants before his genitals ended up on the wrong end of a wardrobe malfunction.

Less than three minutes after they began, Chad finished. It was at this time, that Natalie was standing alone with Jeremy in the shadows on the very edge of all the parked vehicles. They had taken a wide route to avoid the party-goers who weren't drunk and on their way home. A few times, Natalie had shoved Jeremy into the bushes when someone who mattered enough walked by. After the third time this happened, Jeremy began throwing himself into the brush whenever anyone drove or walked past them. They made good time, even after taking the extended route. Natalie stood with an arm on around his shoulder. The other arm was extended before them. She was pointing out to Jeremy exactly which SUV Nicole was in.

"There. Your beloved Nicole is in there right now. You happy?" She tried to hurt him for his snubbing of her earlier. Her voice was mocking and vicious. It surprised her when she felt his body jerk in pain at her words. She regretted her actions immediately. Jeremy was as naive as Nicole had said he was. He was not ready for the world he was getting into and it was going to destroy him. All in the name of puppy love..

"She's in there with Chad?" Jeremy stood still, looking on at the white SUV rocking back and forth gently. His voice was flat. Natalie had expected it to be cracking in pain by now. She figured he would cry, but he didn't. Natalie checked the area to make sure no one was watching them. She and Jeremy were a safe distance from the action, but she couldn't help being paranoid.

"Look, Jeremy, I don't know what's going on between you two. I do know I hate who she's with now, and you seem like a nice guy but... Look, just don't get your hopes up too high, alright." Natalie said with a sincerity she didn't even know was in her. Jeremy might have been naive, but he recognized pity when he heard it. Natalie continued, "I'd hate to see you get hurt. Emotionally or physically."

"I get it. I'm a geek to you. Or some kind of a nerd, or whatever. But I can take care of myself. At least I like to think so. I'll be alright." He looked at Natalie as the words bit back at her. At that moment, both he and Nicole smiled like they meant it and thought of each other.

Jeremy left Natalie and made a silent exit from the scene. Natalie was tempted to follow him. She really had started to feel bad for the kid. She didn't follow him though, because she cared for Nicole more than anything. Nicole would need her help and watchful eye tonight.

Nicole herself exited the SUV wearing Chad's lettered jacket as Jeremy was driving out of the canyon. She walked with Chad back to their original posts. Natalie wiped a tear from her face and made her way toward them as well.

"Hey, who's next?" Eric B. gave a jackal's grin looking from Nicole to Chad and then back again.

"You fuckin' wish." Nicole huddled closer to Chad.

"Where's pretty, little, Elizabeth? She was giving everyone take a turn at last year's homecoming." Eric replied. The others laughed, including Chad.

"That was rape, you asshole," Natalie appeared, cheeks suddenly flushed, fists balled at her side. "She was passed out."

"Wait, wait, wait." Eric tossed his beer aside and puffed his chest. "I didn't hear her sayin' no?" he turned to his friends. "Any of you hear her saying no? Me either." He turned his attention back to Natalie. "In fact, by the way she moaned, I think she liked it."

The guys all broke out laughing. Natalie raised one of her fists and stepped forward. Nicole, mildly placed a hand on Natalie's arm.

"Elizabeth said it never happened, Natalie." Nicole's voice was firm. Her eyes bit into Eric. She let him know with a lethal glance that he was straying awfully close to a line he did not want to cross. He was adventuring into the wilds of the world, where being Chad's friend could no longer protect him and he would be at her mercy. "She said they made it up. I don't know about you, but I believe my best friend over these R-tards."

That was an outright lie. Nicole didn't believe Elizabeth. Lizzie had gotten the abortion two months after the incident in question. Nicole knew that Lizzie only admitted to sleeping by choice with Eric, not the rest of them. Elizabeth didn't want to be known as the girl who had a train run on her in a puddle of her own vomit. Just as Natalie wouldn't allow Nicole to be hurt, Nicole did the same for Elizabeth. If the lie is what Elizabeth wanted to live, Nicole would support that and do her best to kill any inkling of the truth any time it crawled from the grave she had dug for it and reared it's contemptible head. If Nicole publicly supported Lizzie's story, others believed it. This was the power of her influence.

"Shut your friends up." Nicole elbowed Chad in the gut with meaning. "Or I'll tell everyone how much your swim team practices, 'Veronica's specialty' on one another."

"That's the line right there!" Eric jumped forward. "We ain't no fucking faggots!" He slapped one of his friends in the back with no homoerotic thoughts whatsoever. That time.

"That *is* a lie, Nicole. Don't tease them like that." Chad tried to exert some sort of control while retaining his dignity. Eric and the gang smiled.

"Chad, I said shut them up, not me. If there's any lies being told here and now, it's that filth about Elizabeth." Nicole forced them all to acknowledge that the lioness is the one who truly runs the pride.

"Maybe," Eric conceded. He knew that Nicole was going to allow him no more attacks on Elizabeth's reputation that night. "But we still ain't no queers."

"Damn right." Chad agreed. "In fact we ought to head to Delmar Park right now and teach some fags a few lessons." Chad pumped up the hate levels. Nicole shook her head. Natalie grabbed her arm and the two began to walk away. They had to find Elizabeth; it was time to go.

"I'll see you later, Chad." Nicole's voice was thick with disgust.

"Yeah." Chad and his gang made their way to his truck.

"I wish they'd quit talking about Elizabeth like that." Nicole brushed her hand through her hair. She smiled at Lindsay Worol, on of the school's star volleyball players who waved at her.

"I wish they'd just admit they're going to troll for a little man meat themselves. Then you could dump him and we could be rid of them all. As for Elizabeth, I wish she'd go to the police." Natalie said simply. Nicole stopped and they looked at one another. Nicole was not happy. Her displeasure swam across her features like an oil-slick taints ocean water. She whispered delicately in Natalie's ear.

"I meant what I said back there, Natalie. Lizzie said it didn't happen, okay? It means everything to her that everyone understands that. Don't even joke that it ever happened. Even between us. If we show in any way that it did happen, that we think it happened, people will begin to believe it did. Okay?" Nicole looked at Natalie. She was gritting her teeth so hard as she closed her mouth, that there was an audible squeal escaping her cheeks.

"You're hurting my arm." Natalie conceded Nicole's point and looked at her wrist. Nicole looked down as well. She didn't remember grabbing Natalie by the arm, but apparently she had. Nicole apologized and released her grip. Blood came rushing back into pale white flesh that had been left with deep impressions by Nicole's hand. It would bruise, they both realized immediately. Natalie would be wearing long sleeve shirts for a few days.

"I won't say anything about it again. Promise." Natalie assured Nicole. "But just so you know, I hate Chad and his friends. I'm really getting fed up with them, Nicole." Natalie stepped back, waiting for Nicole's usual rebuttal, but it didn't come. Normally, this would start an argument that the two would continue through the rest of the night, eventually ending in one of them storming off and not speaking to the other for a day or two.

"I know. Me too." Nicole agreed, strangely. No one was overtly listening in on their conversation, but they were watching. Nicole could feel them staring at her. She could see their sideways glances and overheard her name in their conversations. She readjusted her royal crown (Chad's jacket), and made sure to keep a smile on her face. They continued walking.

"You too?!" Natalie was aghast. This had never happened before. Natalie had begun to think it might not even be possible. Nicole coveted her social status so much, Natalie figured she may end up marrying Chad, or some other college jock just like him. "You never agree with me on this? Wait, this has something to do with a certain khaki selling someone, doesn't it?"

"I don't know. Maybe." Nicole acquiesced with a shrug. She stopped to shake her head once at a hideous sweater that a freshman she had never seen before was wearing. The girl instantly understood the message and shuffled out of view. Nicole actually liked the sweater. She just didn't want the freshman to be seen with it by too many people so that Nicole herself could wear it later and appear to be one of the first to do so.

"He was here. Tonight." Natalie took a chance. Jeremy could very well replace Chad, with a bit of help. She had no worries about him telling Nicole about Natalie's attempt to lure him into bed with her. Jeremy wasn't that forward, as far as Natalie believed. Even if he was, she was sure that her story of just wanting to test him would pan out just fine. Nicole might be a little angry, but the important thing is that she would believe Natalie. That meant if Nicole did get mad, she'd eventually forgive Natalie.

"What?" Nicole turned to her best friend.

"He came here. I think he was actually going to try and hang out with you." Natalie teased her with a wink and a smile. They both thought of what would have happened if Jeremy had tried to approach her.

"Chad would have killed him." Nicole was horrified at the thought.

"I know. I steered him home. You had better be careful with that boy's heart. He's in love with you." Natalie put her observation out in the open.

"Or I'm falling for him." Nicole kept her voice low and looked away. Natalie begged for more information as they walked on, looking for Elizabeth. Nicole bit her lip and remained silent on the subject. Her grin and out of character actions told Natalie all she needed to know though.

Once the girls had rounded up Elizabeth, they decided it was time to head home. The party was being flooded with freshmen and that meant that it was no longer cool. Natalie, who had drank the least, drove the girls. She stopped at Nicole's house first. As Nicole exited the car, they exchanged good-bye's.

"You going to school tomorrow?" Natalie asked.

"What time is it? Midnight? One?" Nicole tossed a hand in the air, not expecting an answer. "I'll probably stay home. I don't want to have to deal with what happened at the assembly today until next week at the earliest." Nicole let out a sigh. The car ride and walk to look for Elizabeth had allowed her to sober up. A little.

"You going to call him tonight?" Elizabeth began to pry.

"Jeremy? Yeah, I think so. Probably." Nicole gave a sinful grin.

"You're so bad." Natalie said with an even mix of encouragement and admiration.

"I know." Nicole agreed with a nod. "I'll see you guys tomorrow night or something, alright?"

Natalie and Lizzie nodded. Nicole shut the car door and took the long walk up to her front door. She stopped on the way in to fix the lawn gnome that had once again been knocked down. She noticed the curtains pulled back in an upstairs window at her neighbor's house. Mr. Kirkland was peering down at her with a smug look on his face. Nicole waved with an obnoxious smile, and then flipped him off. Jack Kirkland stormed away from the window shaking his head. She could hear his voice as he complained about her behavior to his wife. This was a rather regular occurrence. Mr. Kirkland kept a close eye on his neighbors. Nicole wondered why he didn't complain like that when she was drunk enough to flash him her breasts.

She didn't bother checking to see if the front door to her house was locked. It never was. This was safe neighborhood. They lived far from the crime, or at least that's what the statistics and newspapers told them. People weren't openly dealing or using drugs on street corners. The police answered promptly to any call made, thus scaring away many would be corruptors of the innocent in these parts. It may have been crawling with people lying to themselves and deceiving everyone else, but it was a safe neighborhood.

Upon entering the house, the sound of the television was immediately audible. It's lifeless glow doused the living room, a breathing ray of stupidity. A fitness guru of some sort was selling the "newest", and "best" exercise equipment at a price you just wouldn't believe and it could all be yours for three simple monthly payments. Nicole didn't bother with sneaking about. She had never had a curfew, and came and went as she pleased. It wasn't up to her to respect others in her home, it was up to them to respect her. After all they had put her through, they owed her that. With great grades and no sort of criminal record, her parents didn't believe she needed any control placed over her. They also didn't want to endure the shouting match if they ever tried to discipline Nicole.

In the living room, her mother was asleep on the couch. A glass of vodka and water sat on the table next to the liquor bottle it's primary ingredient originated from. The water had been ice cubes hours before. Nicole took a blanket that lay across the back of the love seat next to the sofa, and placed it over her mother. She gently removed her mother's glasses and set them on the table. Her mother let escape a small breath, but Mrs. O'Leary's eyes remained shut. Nicole discreetly scooped up the glass and bottle mentally admonishing her mother for being such a sloppy drunk. Nicole could teach her a thing or two about at least looking respectable when you pass out.

"We got a phone call tonight." Her mother's eyes never opened. The voice cutting past the television noise startled Nicole. Nicole regained her composure and focused her gaze upon her mother's rosy cheeks. It creeped her out to hear that dry, cracked voice coming from her mother's solemn face. She felt as if the corpse at a funeral had just spoken to her. A shiver went up her back and down her arms, where the finest of hairs that were just beginning to grow back from her last shaving stood on end.

"Yeah. I kind of... had a breakdown of sorts." Nicole found the softest, warmest tone she could manage without slurring her words. "It won't happen again, I promise."

"I know this is hard on you." Her mother's hand pointed at her from under the blanket while her eyes remained closed. "We never wanted to hurt you, you know. I explained this all to the principal. I think things will be okay. I'm sorry we're such poor parents, Nicky."

Nicole immediately bent and kissed her mother's forehead. She felt the clammy sweat on her lips. The stench of the alcohol her mother's body was desperately trying to detoxify assaulted her nostrils. Nicole suddenly wondered if her mother had ever seen her passed out in her room and had this exact experience. She recoiled, faster than she wanted to. Her mother might have been drunk and passing out, but Nicole knew her mother could probably still sense her daughter's movement. She didn't want her to think Nicole was disgusted with her.

"You're not a bad parent, mom." Nicole whispered, backing away as quietly as possible. She moved quickly to the kitchen. Standing there in one place had been a terrible trial for one as drunk as she. Her balance was off and would be that way for the rest of the night and part of the morning. She avoided falling down, but teetered slightly to the right as she entered the kitchen's open doorway.

Again she was surprised, as she saw a figure sitting at the kitchen table. Nicole didn't bother with the lights. The crisp moonlight shooting through the kitchen window, coupled with the glow of the television behind her let her know all she needed to. Nicole stopped, and then continued, pretending not to notice Harold sitting alone at the table. She moved to the cupboard to put her mother's therapy supplies away.

"I thought I heard you come in." Her father's voice was calmer than she expected.

"Daddy." Nicole greeted him curtly. "We were all out at the canyon."

"So I heard. Your mother and I dealt with the school."

"Yeah, she just told me that." Nicole informed him, coldly.

"Did she now? I'm surprised she's even awake. What else did she have to say?" He quipped.

"Nothing." Nicole lied, unsure of whether he had overheard them talking.

"Figures. Nicole, how do I put this, we never meant for it to end up like this. You have to understand that. I never- I mean-" He suddenly stopped. He thrust his hands before him on the table and flexed them into fists out of discontent.

"What do you want from me, daddy?" Nicole let her frustrations take control. "You want me to be your confessional? Do you want me to wash your sins away? Do you want me to tell you to donate money to the collection plate and say your prayers? I'm your daughter, not your savior. You should have started caring this much months ago, instead of letting her slip away like this. But all you have ever cared about is work. You've never cared about us; me and mom. You just cared about you. You and your research, your awards, your accolades, your company."

"Nicole, you don't understand-" He tried.

"No, daddy, that's the problem: I do understand. All of it." Nicole stormed up to her room.

"I did all that for you!" Her father put his head down on the table and began to cry.

Nicole sat on her bed and debated having a good cry herself. Instead, she picked up her phone, and called Jeremy. He answered before the first ring finished.

"Hello?" His voice was barely a rustle. Unlike her, he had rules that he dared not break. He had no intention of waking his parents at this hour.

"Jeremy? It's me. Were you up?" Nicole heard muffled yelling behind his voice. Jeremy assured his mother that it was just a wrong number before he spoke to Nicole again.

"Hey, Nicole. Yeah, I was up. I mean, I was studying," He regretted that as soon as he said it, and attempted to fix it. "or whatever." It was a Band-Aid over a bullet hole that had no chance of being successful. Nicole smiled. He was cute when he tried to lie.

"So, you free tonight?" Nicole let her emotions crack her normally solid voice.

"You okay, Nicole?" He didn't bother to hide his concern as others would. Nicole could swear she heard him jump to his feet.

"Yes. No. I don't know. I feel like... I'm tired, you know?" She began to cry freely.

"Tired of what?" Jeremy asked. He could tell that she didn't mean that she was just physically worn out.

"Breathing." She stated candidly.

"Nicole, don't do anything stupid." It was a corny clichéd phrase, but it was the first thing that came to his heart, and mind.

"Or what?" she teased, caught off guard by his sincerity and passion. With that one sentence, he had brought her minutely out of her depression.

"I'll be mad at you." He said with a smile that traveled miles over a telephone line and landed squarely on her heart. His ploy worked. She laughed for a few moments and then calmed herself. They both waited for the other to speak.

"Will you come over, Jeremy?" She asked after the prolonged silence.

"Now? Tonight? Nicole, we have school tomorrow. My mom-" Jeremy knew she was serious, but this was something he had never even attempted to do. It would be direct disobedience of his parents and their rules. 'No', was not an acceptable answer to Nicole. She knew how to turn the cogs of a man's mind.

"Please." She begged, that coy, playful tone beckoning him.

"And what about your parents?" he tried.

"I need you." She admitted, not directly answering him to let him know that her parents wouldn't be a problem.

The phone was again silent. Jeremy thought it over. He weighed the risk of being caught sneaking out by his parents vs. the reward of seeing Nicole now, tonight, drunk and probably willing. Like any man in the prime years of his raging hormones, Jeremy's desire for the female touch seemed to win the argument.

"Okay." He agreed to her request. Then he tried to figure out how he was going to explain this to his parents. He couldn't imagine how much trouble he'd get in, but he was willing to put himself in harm's way, for her. "I'll be there in a few minutes, okay?"

"I'll be waiting." Nicole felt such a surge of joy that she stopped crying immediately. "Jeremy?"

"Yeah?"

"Thanks." Nicole smiled. It was a word she didn't say often, and rarely meant when she did.

"No problem." Jeremy smiled back. He moved to hang up the phone so fast he missed the cradle, and the receiver crashed to the floor. He hurriedly snatched up the receiver and set it lightly back where it belonged.

Jeremy had never snuck out of his house before. Coming home after curfew was a rule he'd broken on occasion, but by no more than half an hour, and never on purpose. His parents would ground him for this, for sure. In fact, he wouldn't be surprised if they took his car away for good. That punishment didn't outweigh the fact that Nicole needed him. She had actually said that: *She needed him.*

Chapter Six: 'Secret lovers, yeah, that's what we are...'

Jeremy thanked god that he lived in a single story house. It had taken him a few minutes to try and decide just how he was going to sneak out, and he was made acutely aware how much easier this task would be, having to only get out of a one story house.

He turned off his bedroom light and listened. He hoped his parents had fallen back asleep by now. The phone call had woken up his mother, whose yelling had woken up his father. Jeremy walked to his door and opened it to look down the hall. His parent's room was down a ways, but even from here, he could see under the door that there was no light on in there.

The window in his room was his only way out, he figured. The front door was old, creaky and loud. Just walking down the hall from his room would irritate the old hardwood hallway floor and had woken his mother in the past. Nothing terrified Jeremy more than getting up to pee in the middle of the night, only to find his mother in the hallway checking on him as soon as he finished. She was a bit overprotective at times. What Jeremy didn't know is that she was this way because he was her first and only child. She had two miscarriages before he was conceived, and his difficult birth had ended with her complete hysterectomy. This is why she watched over him so closely. To Jeremy, it was just his annoying and overbearing mother who checked up on him when he was peeing in the dead of night.

The window was the only way for him to sneak out of the house. It looked menacing in the moonlight.

The panes mocked him and his fear. Jeremy swallowed and unlatched the makeshift exit. With a gentle tug he opened it just a crack. The sudden change in air pressure caused his slightly open bedroom door to slam snug into it's frame. Jeremy cursed, listening for his mother's excited voice. He expected her to come running down the hall, hands grasping for him, at any second. She didn't. He sluggishly opened the window, attempting not to cause any more sudden noises. It obediently slid on it's track in silence; though it still grinned at him with lion's teeth, awaiting his next false move so that it could capitalize.

Once Jeremy had gotten the window all the way open, he let the cool Illinois night breeze blow over him. He took a deep breath, and prepared to cross the threshold. With a few, tugs, he jerked free his window screen, and let it fall to the ground outside. He slipped on his shoes, and hefted one leg over the edge. He could feel the ground just inches under his leg and decided to hop over the rest of the way. As he did, his pants were snagged on the window frame. The jeans ripped freely down the seam as Jeremy fell to the ground with a thud. The neighbors Labrador fell into a fit of barking. Jeremy cussed the dog and the window in whispers. He rose to his feet. There was no sound within his own home. Jeremy decided to use the barking dog as cover. He slid the window shut faster than he had opened it. As he was nearly finished, the window gave a shrill cry, shattering the serenity he had been trying to protect. It was as if the window had decided to laugh at him. Jeremy's eyes darted about to see where this metal on metal scream came from. The corner of the window that had caught his pants had been bent. It was on the interior of the window frame, and his weight had bent it to the point where it was now eviscerating the window's aluminum housing. A glint just past the window caught Jeremy's eye. His car keys were still sitting conveniently on his nightstand. Jeremy stomped the ground cursing through frothing spittle. After all that he'd been through, he had to start over again. There was only one spare set of keys to his car: the set on his dad's key ring. Walking to Nicole's wasn't an option, she lived too far, and honestly, Jeremy was scared to walk that far, this late, alone. He had no choice but to go back in his room and get his keys.

Thankfully, as he crept the window open, it made little noise. The damage in that area had already been done. Jeremy boosted himself onto the window sill and tried to hop into his room. Unfortunately, he caught his pants on the same troublesome corner. His one whole pant leg was now torn wide open. He fell to the floor of his room and was sure that the entire house shook with him. Still, there was no reaction from his parents. Jeremy felt lucky, and then neglected. While it was nice that no one had come in to check on him, it was also a bit sad. Someone should notice all this noise in their child's room at this hour. He remembered the numerous times his mother had come to check on him for the slightest noise in the house. Now, she was nowhere to be found. Either he was overestimating the degree of noise he was making, or she had fallen deep asleep.

Jeremy took it as a sign that he was supposed to go to Nicole's house and hopped to his feet. He snatched his keys. No longer caring about the noise he caused, he didn't try to silence their jangling. He shoved the keys into his pocket, which proved pointless. His pocket had been ripped wide open. His keys fell flat to the floor. Jeremy didn't listen to see if anyone was awake. He scooped up the keys, and dropped them in his back pocket, which still had all of it's integrity.

The window still smiled at him. The jagged edge had been bent back to it's original position by his last fall. Jeremy leapt over the sill without a problem this go round. His anger at his mother seeming to have forgotten about him disappeared when it came time to shut the window. His bravado was itself, false. Now that he was back outside the home, and technically breaking the rules, he wasn't willing to take a chance on his parents catching him. Once again, he shut the window in baby steps, just to be sure. It closed in silence this time, satisfied in the damage it had already caused.

The wind picked up outside, causing the blonde, near invisible hair on his arms to rise. As the breeze wafted through his ripped pants, he suddenly wished he had taken the time to change them inside. With a sigh, he slid past his home and into the driveway. Jeremy's twelve year-old, beat up Toyota was parked on the street.

He decided not to start the car in front of the house. He had lost his muffler a few semesters back, and his compact sounded like a semi. Instead, he put the car in neutral, and pushed it an entire block away. Once at this safe range, he started it up, and sped away, confident that he had successfully pulled off this minor teenage caper.

Jeremy lived in a less affluent neighborhood than Nicole. He wasn't poor, but he was lower-middle class. His house was a good 10-15 minute drive from Nicole's. He wasn't sure what to do once he got there. He had been to her house once, though not inside. He and his friends had thought about attending a party at her house, but chickened out, knowing they weren't invited. It would have only been a spectacle of ridicule and possibly an ass kicking.

Throwing pebbles at the window was the best idea he could come up with to let Nicole know he had arrived, though with his luck, it'd probably shatter the pane. As he neared her house, he turned off his headlights. Two houses away from hers, he turned off the stereo, only to realize that her parents couldn't hear inside his car. He stopped two houses past hers, and parked. The neighborhood was dead quiet. Jeremy slid his door shut by leaning on it, so as not to make any more noise. The air was still chilly, and he shivered. Huddling his arms to his body, he walked towards her house. He grabbed a pebble from next to one of the lawn gnomes, and stood there. He had no idea which window was Nicole's. He leaned against the large tree in the front yard, and pondered his next move. There weren't many options he could come up with as he juggled the rock in his hand.

"It's on the second story, to the far right." An angel spoke above him. Jeremy fell away from the tree and to the ground in shock. His ripped pants left little to the imagination as he looked to the heavens. Nicole was sitting in the tree above him, smoking a cigarette, wearing only a T-shirt and boxer shorts.

"Yep, that window, that's my room." She smiled. "Now get up here."

"Up the tree?" Jeremy clarified her simple order.

"Yeah, and then follow me across this branch to the front patio roof. Then we climb onto the main roof and then into my room. But hurry. It's cold out here. I just took a shower and my hair's wet." She instructed.

Jeremy scrambled to follow her, snagging his pants on the tree a few times. Once he came to the branch she was on, she nearly killed him. She clamped him in a hug and sapped nearly all of his balance. Jeremy teetered and fell back onto the tree trunk for support. The rough bark dug into his back, but he didn't notice. The scent of her freshly shampooed hair dug into his nose. The warmth of her body serenaded him. He was entranced.

"Thank you for coming." She whispered.

"I'd do anything for you, Nicole." He whispered back.

Anything?, she thought. Her hand, with fingers like silken tendrils clasped onto his. She carefully led him onto the patio roof and into her room. With years of experience she maneuvered across the tree branch like some sort of wood elf. He could hear voices coming from her room. The nearer they drew, it became clear that he was hearing the radio, not parents.

"So, you go this route often?" He asked her.

"Nope. Not since I was 14 or so." Nicole shook her head. "But I know you've never done anything like it, and I thought it would be fun."

"So how do you sneak out now?" he asked, curious if anyone had as hard a time as he had.

"I don't." Nicole discarded the idea with a laugh. "I just come and go when I want. You think my parents are gonna kick me out or something?"

"Mine would." Jeremy muttered.

Nicole stepped through her large double-door window. She turned to face him with a smile.

"Mine wouldn't."

Jeremy shook his head at her audacity. He had never had the nerve to dream about the transgressions she described. That is, until he'd met her. She gave Jeremy a sense of independence and daring. He gave her genuine care and friendship.

As Jeremy entered Nicole's room, she slammed the windows shut with complete disregard to anyone else's sleeping habits in the house. Her room was the forbidden zone to Jeremy. He'd been in the private quarters of 2 females who weren't family. And those were lab partners from school. Nicole's room was a den of magnificence. Every guy in school would give everything to be where he was right now. Her parents spoiled her and it showed. Her laptop computer cost more than his car. Her small, but plasma flat-screen television sent shivers down his spine. The walls themselves housed a collection of hundreds of immaculate porcelain masks which had caught Jeremy's attention.

"There's over 200 of them in here." Nicole nodded to her walls. "Natalie thinks they're creepy."

"I guess they could be." Jeremy conceded.

"What do you think?" Nicole sat on her king-sized mattress.

"I think it's cool." He smiled at her. She smiled back with a short laugh.

"I've been collecting them since I was 4. Every time I see one I like, I buy it. No matter where I am." Nicole patted the bed next to her oblivious to the analogy that no matter where she went, all eyes were on her, and she was never alone. "Come, sit."

As Jeremy sat she curled her knees under the long T-shirt she was wearing.

"So, that thing I told you on the phone..." she started.

"About being tired?"

She stared at the floor. He stared at her.

"Yeah, about that, it's all true, you know. I hate my life."

"Nicole-"

"Wait, let me finish. I know it's stupid. I know how blessed I have been in life. I know how much I have been given that others haven't. I know all that. I also know that money really isn't shit. It's a quick fix. You can always find another little this or that to buy that makes you feel good for a little while; but nothing you can buy makes you feel good forever."

"Nothing makes you feel good forever." Jeremy interjected.

"Not even heaven?" She knew he'd have to lose this battle.

"Well, heaven, I mean, sure, I guess. But I'm not sure that you get into heaven, if you, you know, do something to yourself."

"Why not?" Nicole tested him.

"Because the Bible says that, I'm pretty sure." He answered, very unsure.

"So. Maybe the Bible's wrong. If God's all knowing, all-seeing, all-everything, maybe he could forgive me just that one sin. Just that one." Nicole explained.

"But you'd have to pray for forgiveness, right, and you'd be dead."

"Who says the dead can't pray?"

"I don't know. Sounds like a question for Ben Reilly." Jeremy referenced the ex-schoolmate who had overdosed some time ago.

"Ben's been dead a couple years now."

"Exactly." Jeremy smiled and Nicole caught on to the dark humor.

"Ben did kill himself." Nicole continued in a sober tone. "Maybe it is a good question for him."

"So you should wait and ask him when you see him. When it's really time. Don't rush things." Jeremy was quite pleased with having diffused the situation.

"See those." Nicole nodded toward her desk where her laptop sat with a screen saver featuring the latest MTV sensation. Jeremy's eyes searched. It took him a few sweeping glances to focus on a pile of round red pills.

"They're my mother's. She has them for depression. I was going to take them all tonight before I called you." Nicole explained. Jeremy silently rose to his feet. He shoveled the pile into his hand. She watched him walk into the bathroom. The pills made several small plops as they hit the water. Then the toilet flushed. Jeremy felt the leftover heat and humidity from her shower. The room smelled of lilacs and bubble gum. He emerged with confidence.

"Now you don't have to worry about that." he smiled.

Nicole giggled.

"My mom has, like, 12 bottles you doofus."

Jeremy made for her bedroom door. Nicole leapt to her feet and grabbed him.

"Stay. Stay with me." Nicole looked into his eyes. "Not sleep with me, but lay here with me tonight."

Jeremy nodded. Nicole brushed her hands across the light switch. She guided Jeremy to her bed. She helped him undress and noticed his pants again.

"What happened here?" she said, slipping them over his boxers.

"Long story. I'll tell you in the morning."

She took him under her blanket and curled into his waiting arms. Here, she slept. Her body worked it's way out of the chemical dungeon she had sentenced it to. Jeremy slept well, but often woke to make sure his reality wasn't a dream.

In the morning, Nicole woke first. Being the best at everything meant hard work after partying. She had conditioned herself to wake sometime between 5 and 6 a.m. each morning. Today, the clock readout said 5:23 when she first opened her eyes. She worked on her studies an hour and a half. Every few minutes, she'd steal a glance at Jeremy who slept snugly in her mound of pillows. Once her studies were caught up, and she felt comfortable with her knowledge on the subjects, she showered. The sound of running water ignited Jeremy's nocturnal senses. He slowly awoke to a nagging call from his urinary system. Shock greeted him. He had forgotten where he was. His memory quickly reset itself, and it all came back. He rose from the bed and stretched. He had never slept in a bed so comfortable. Nicole had closed the bathroom door, but Jeremy couldn't have gone in there to pee with her in the shower anyhow. He clamped his bladder muscles, hoping she would be out soon. While trying to ignore the growing distention in his lower midsection, Jeremy decided satisfying his curiosity might help. As any average man or woman would, he began snooping through her room.

His quest started innocently enough. He flipped through a few papers on her desk, and was impressed by her advanced trigonometry papers with no sign of eraser marks on them. Her nightstand contained a few interesting items. There were several photographs of Nicole's family, dating back to her adolescence. Most of them were photos of her with her mother. Few were of Nicole alone. The other majority featured Nicole and her friends. Jeremy saw no signs of her father or brother in any of them.

Nicole's dresser was next. It was a large antique made of red mahogany wood. Intricate designs featuring elves, fairies, sprites, and flowers trailed up the legs and around the edges of the drawers. Brass knobs with the initial O engraved on them sat at the ends of each drawer. The dresser had been hand crafted by her great grandfather on her father's side. It had been handed down through the generations, and was actually a wedding present to Nicole's parents. In her dresser drawers he found three cartons of cigarettes, various bottles of liquor, and more. In the back of one drawer, he came across a stunning find. First was a device he had no idea about. It had a few cords and wires, and a small control device. The words, "The Rabbit," were printed on both sides. Behind this device he found several pornographic DVD's. He was holding one (Cuties with Booties IV) and "The Rabbit" device as Nicole emerged from the bathroom.

"Get a little bored?" Nicole stood, hands on her hips. A large towel wrapped around her tightly, covering her body. It hung from her breasts to her mid-thigh. Steam rushed from the bathroom and nestled about her feet. She appeared as an angel perched upon a cloud.

"Oh, I was, I mean-"

"It's okay." Nicole stepped to him. She gently pried "The Rabbit", and DVD from his clutches.

"I didn't mean to violate your privacy." Jeremy's head bowed in shame. Nicole laughed and put her toys back where they belonged.

"Sometimes," she turned to him as she shut the drawer. "Sometimes, girls get lonely, too."

"Understandable." Jeremy muttered. He was becoming increasingly uncomfortable.

"Did you know the pornographic movie industry makes billions of dollars each year?" She asked him quizzically.

"Really?" Jeremy gave a generic answer.

"Yep." Nicole looked puzzled for a moment. "And yet, conservatives with views like my father are constantly railing against porn. It has to be one of the most profitable private industries that's entirely legal. Yet, those supposedly in support of private industry hate it."

"Well," Jeremy countered. "I can see how it may not sit well with other beliefs. You have to give religious views a consideration."

"Why? This is America. Shouldn't church and state be separate?" Nicole argued.

"Not necessarily. 'All things in time. All things in moderation.'" Jeremy quoted an unknown source.

"Who said that?" Nicole asked.

"Not sure," Jeremy admitted. "Probably an Asian philosopher."

"Huh," Nicole put a finger to her lip. "I like that. Maybe you are right. But I still don't see any reason to ban porn."

"I never said we should ban it." Jeremy did not want to offend her.

"I know." Nicole smiled. She turned and began going through her drawers, pulling out undergarments for the day.

"So, I guess I better go get ready for school." Jeremy tried to keep the conversation going.

"We," Nicole stressed the word. "are going to get you some new pants. Then lunch, I guess. How's Olive Garden sound?"

"Wait," Jeremy was unsure. "It's Friday. We have class."

"Nah." Nicole waved the idea away. "Lizzie, you know my friend, Elizabeth, right?"

Jeremy nodded.

"She's a teacher's aide in the attendance office. She'll mark us present on all our roll sheets." Nicole explained.

"Can't she get in trouble for that?" Jeremy was somewhat naive on the subject of skipping class.

"Maybe," Nicole said, as if she hadn't ever taken the time to contemplate the idea. "If she does get caught. But she won't. We'll be fine."

"I'm not sure. My parents are going to be pretty worried as it is. They're probably out looking for me as we speak." Jeremy presented another roadblock to her plans.

"Why?" Nicole dropped her towel and began to dress. Jeremy turned his head away.

"Do I have something you haven't seen before?" Nicole gave him a quizzical grin.

"No, it's just impolite, I guess." Jeremy was honest, and a bit blunt on accident. Honesty hurts.

"Yeah, I guess," Nicole secured her bra in place. "Want to know a secret? We kinda like it when you look at us, sometimes. It makes a girl feel wanted, and sexy." She slipped a leg into her panties.

"I thought it just made guys look creepy." Jeremy yielded.

Nicole laughed, as she did a lot when Jeremy's innocence was on display for her.

"Ogling is creepy. Admiration and desire is sexy. You can turn around now, I'm dressed." She told him. Jeremy hesitated. His hormones forced his muscles to work. He turned his head to face her again. His anticipation was working on his nerves, but he didn't want to appear anxious. By the time he was able to view her, Nicole was buttoning her jeans.

"So, back to your parents, do they both work?" Nicole asked.

"Yeah." Jeremy struggled to watch her face and not her bra. It was hard for his eyes not to wander because she wasn't looking at him.

"Does your whole family eat breakfast together or something?" Nicole asked.

"No. Both my parents are usually leaving by the time I get up. And getting home late at night. They work long hours in the city."

"Good. They probably didn't even notice you were gone." Nicole slipped into a tight fitting baby T-shirt. The word, "PornStar" was branded on the front.

"My mom wakes me up every morning before she leaves." Jeremy elaborated, trying to hide his shame.

"Well that's a different story then." Nicole ran a hand through her short hair. "Call her. Tell her I needed a ride, so you left early."

"What?" Jeremy couldn't believe her.

"Yeah, explain to her that you didn't tell her because you figured she was tired from work and you didn't want to wake her."

"That won't work." Jeremy didn't want to even attempt the scheme.

"Why not? You haven't even tried. Plus, you have me, a 4.0 WunderGurl, to back you up. Go on. Call her." Nicole ordered. She nudged him with her hip towards the phone on her nightstand. Jeremy reluctantly picked up the receiver. He convinced himself that he had nothing to lose. Nicole's encouraging smile was a wrought iron reinforcement to his confidence. Jeremy dialed his home number, hoping to catch his mother before she left.

"Hello, mom? It's Jeremy."

Nicole could hear yelling on the other end of the phone.

"Yeah, I know. Wait, listen." Jeremy tried to calm his mother. "This girl, Nicole, at school, she needed a ride and I didn't want to wake you 'cause I knew you'd be tired and she lives a ways away and..." Jeremy stopped suddenly.

"What?" He asked. Nicole noticed the yelling had stopped. "Yes, a girl." Jeremy said with disgust. Nicole guessed his mother was surprised at his actual association with a member of the opposite sex.

"What? She's nice." Jeremy smiled at Nicole.

"No, mom," Jeremy rolled his eyes. "Yes, she gets good grades. "

Nicole gave Jeremy a "thumbs up" signal.

"Meet her? Mom- Yeah, okay. See you tonight. Thanks mom. Love you too. Bye." Jeremy hung up the phone, and stared into space.

"So? It worked, didn't it?" Nicole waited for him to answer the smug smirk on her face.

"Yeah," Jeremy looked at her. "I can't believe that worked. I lied to my mom, and it worked."

"Well, duh," Nicole rustled his hair. "I've been lying to my parents for years now. How could it not work? Seriously, you have to start trusting me, Jeremy."

Nicole called the school and set things up with Elizabeth. Lizzie agreed to assist her as long as Nicole told her all about what happened or would happen later that night. Nicole swiped a pair of her father's slacks, and threw Jeremy in them. Luckily he had his own belt, so they fit in a slipshod manner. They would suffice to get him to the mall. She retrieved a bowl of cereal from the kitchen, and let Jeremy eat in her room. As he spoon-fed the breakfast of champions into his mouth, she applied the socially acceptable minimum of make-up. When she took his dishes downstairs, she arrived just in time to see her mother passing out on the couch again. Nicole walked back upstairs, snatched her oversized black sunglasses off of her nightstand and led Jeremy to her car outside.

It was Friday and there was still the danger of someone from school seeing them together. To avoid this, Nicole drove to the other side of town. There was a chance for them to be spotted on this side of town, but it was much smaller. Thunder Ridge Crossing was the mall everyone who mattered went to. It was an outlet mall that sat in a prosperous corner of town. Thunder Ridge was the mall Jeremy drove miles to work at.

Crossroads Mall was in a poorer suburb named Romero. Romero was an area populated primarily by Blacks, Latinos, and Asians. Jeremy was scared of Romero and Crossroads Mall. Of course, his fear was primarily from rumors, not actual experience. Nicole wasn't scared at all. She shopped at Crossroads often to avoid the normal zombies at Thunder Ridge, but would never admit it.

"Are you sure we'll be alright?" Jeremy asked as Nicole parked.

"Jeremy," Nicole rolled her eyes. "If I thought for one second that we could possibly be in trouble, I wouldn't bring you here. In fact, protecting you is the primary reason for coming here. Now, show some backbone. Cowardice is unbecoming. Of anyone."

Jeremy nodded thoughtfully. Nicole led him into the mall. Jeremy was surprised that the mall wasn't in as bad a state as he had imagined from all the stories he had heard about it. There weren't drug dealers and homeless people littered about. The floors were clean and without bloodstains. The sound system pumped out the same elevator muzak that he heard at work constantly. The water fountain had clean water, not rusty brown sludge. Yes, the younger patrons seemed to be of a minority nature, but they could not have cared less about him being present. Nicole drew some glances, but that's what Nicole did. Jeremy felt okay. There was no threat. He was beginning to realize just how much he didn't know about the world.

Nicole led Jeremy through several stores. She didn't ask him any questions other than his sizes. Once she had these, she marched him and the sales associates through the various aisles. She told Jeremy what he would be wearing and why. All in all, she purchased him three shirts and two pairs of pants. One of these was a pair of jeans that he wore immediately. Nicole decided he needed new sneakers as well. This is where the trouble began. Had she merely been satisfied with the clothes, her life may well have taken a different course.

Nicole walked Jeremy over to the Foot Locker store. They (she) found a pair of sneakers she liked on him. As the saleswoman left to retrieve the correct size, Nicole and Jeremy sat waiting on a small bench.

"Well, well. Surprise, surprise. Look who was too timid to face authority today." A female voice said. Jeremy didn't know it, and didn't pay attention to it. Nicole knew it before she turned around. It was Veronica. Nicole wanted to hang her head in disgust, but she was in public and had a reputation to keep. Jeremy saw Nicole's body language change. She suddenly became tense and her arms turned a hot shade of red. She was angry and about to explode. The tension was suddenly spreading through the room and clogging them down. He turned to see who was talking to them.

"How's the paper-mache princess today?" Nicole asked. Jeremy looked at their guest, and the ramifications of her spotting them marched through his mind.

"Wow, Chad, you've sure gotten skinny and lame." Veronica poked a finger into Jeremy's chest. Before Nicole knew what she was doing, she slapped Veronica. Veronica's head cracked to her side. The bruises from the assault she suffered the day prior were visible on her cheek as she rubbed it. The sting of a second assault brought tears to the corners of her eyes. Within her nose, a small trickle began. Veronica wasn't sure if it was snot or blood, but wanted neither to be shown, so she sniffled quietly.

"Just can't keep your hands off me, huh?" Veronica took a step back. She anticipated being hit again, but Nicole had composed herself and refused to move.

"Veronica, this is getting old. Go, run to Chad and tell him whatever you want. I'm so tired of you. I don't know how we were ever friends. All you do is use people and tear them down. Maybe it's fate for us to remain separate, yet forever entwined, like the yin and yang." Nicole sighed. Veronica was not impressed.

"Oh please, sister. Don't get so high up on your soapbox that you forget how often you yourself chew up and spit out the little people. Who are you? Mother Theresa and this is your little Calcutta boy?" Veronica nodded toward Jeremy.

"Leave him out of this." Nicole knew she should play down her feelings for Jeremy, but she couldn't sit back and let Veronica attack him.

"Why? You don't want him to know about the real you?" Veronica turned to Jeremy. "She and I may not be friends, sweetheart, but trust me, I know her. Ask her to tell you about Cal Schnell. That was her nobody/charity case last year. Chad laid a thumping on that boy that made the news. Remember, Cal said it was a bunch of gangbangers, but it wasn't. It was Chad. Wasn't it, Nicole?"

Nicole remained silent. She looked away in recognition of the truth in Veronica's words.

"That's right, cabana boy." Veronica's fangs glistened. She slithered around Jeremy as she spoke. "Oh, you didn't think you were Nicole's first little excursion to normalville, did you? Cal made that same mistake. Then Chad found out. Chad and the rest of them found Cal, and beat him until they couldn't hear his whimpering anymore. I'm sure you saw the newspaper pictures. Chad tied Cal to a fence on Highway 281 and left him there. You know what Nicole did? Nothing. She left Cal out to dry; put the dog to pasture as some would say. Cal is still in physical therapy, by the way. He's trying to learn how to walk again."

"Shut up, Veronica. Just shut up." Nicole finally spoke. It was a tone Jeremy hadn't heard often from her. It was quiet, yet shaky.

"Can't stand the truth?" Veronica flipped open her cell phone, snapped a picture of Nicole and Jeremy, and then turned her back. She sensed the weakness in Nicole, and didn't fear any retaliation at the moment. She was wrong. Nicole lunged forward, only to find Jeremy catching her arm. He reined Nicole in, as Veronica remained oblivious to his heroism. Veronica had already begun chattering about her find into her phone.

"It's not worth it." Jeremy told Nicole. He let go of her arm, hoping she would calm down. Veronica, meanwhile had started to walk off, satisfied that she once again had the upper hand in her war with Nicole.

"Is what she said true?" Jeremy asked Nicole.

Nicole looked away, holding her arm.

"I was different then, Jeremy. I was..." It was hard for Nicole to think of Cal. She had put him out of her mind for some time. "I was like her. I'm not that person anymore. I don't know how to prove it to you. Cal and me, that was just sex, honestly. It was a game for me. I was a different person then. I promise you."

Jeremy used a finger to cautiously pull her chin. He looked at her and wondered if he was making the biggest mistake of his life.

"If you tell me, I'll believe you. People change." He sincerely told her.

Nicole looked into his eyes. She could see his fear, and it made him human. It made her love him. She had no way to reassure him. The danger of their affair would now reap whatever fruits it had come to bear, and they couldn't stop it. No matter how mighty King Arthur was, Lancelot still found a way to bed Guinevere. Only this time they had been caught red handed. The danger Jeremy was ready to put himself in for her forced open the blast doors of Nicole's heart. She had to let him in. All the way in. There was no turning back from this moment on. Nicole's phone began to ring. She looked at it and immediately tapped the touchscreen to end the call. She turned it off, and took Jeremy's hand.

"Let's go. I have something special that I want to show you."

Nicole drove Jeremy miles out of town into the hills he didn't know had been infiltrated by society. They entered a gated cabin community. Hidden within rows of trees and small, man-made ponds were small lots where cabins of varying sizes had been built. Nicole drove to a large cabin that overlooked 80% of the area, including the lakes.

"Wow. What is this place?" Jeremy followed Nicole out of the car. He took in a deep breath of pine and dirt. Too often in the city we breathe in what we call dirt. It isn't. That smell and grit in the city isn't dirt.

Jeremy knew that now. You only know that once you have tasted true, natural dirt in the air. That thing he could smell and breathe in the city, that wasn't dirt. It was filth. Dirt was natural and in its own way pure. This was the dust that went with the phrase "dust to dust". It was ancient and natural.

"This is my family's retreat." Nicole held her arms out wide. "My parents used to have a fifth wheel camper here." Nicole walked to the front door, searching her key ring. "They put up this cabin a while back."

Just in time for our family to go to down the tubes, she thought.

"We don't really come up here anymore." She said, opening the door. A dark, musty smell crawled out to greet them. Sunlight beamed through the cabin windows, illuminating the leftover webs of arachnid generations past. Nicole looked about as she stepped in. Memories of times from her earlier years came to life. There would be no going forward without regaining some composure. She took a deep breath and a step back.

"You okay?" Jeremy put a hand on her shoulder.

"Yeah. Sorry." Nicole turned to him, smiled, and then stepped over the threshold.

"Sorry it smells so stale in here." Nicole turned on a light switch in the kitchen as Jeremy entered the building. He gazed about as she opened the refrigerator.

"It smells, like I would expect a cabin to smell." Jeremy confessed. He looked at how Nicole's family had decorated the building. The two couches were a soft, tan suede, hardly ever used. Pelts, heads, and antlers of her father's various conquests were strung about the walls with care. Pictures of the family at differing ages and various stages had been hung up on the wall under the staircase leading upstairs or left on small tables at the ends of the couches. The two couches faced a brick fireplace.

Jeremy came to a picture of Nicole in her junior high years, and paused. In the photograph, she and Chad were hugging in front of the fireplace Jeremy now stood inches away from. In the background, Nicole's father was present with a smile on his face. Jeremy wondered if he'd ever be in such a position, or if what Veronica had said was true.

"Looks like Jackson, my brother, was here recently. Or at least in the last few months. There's some old Budweiser in here. It won't be the best, but it's palatable." Nicole called from the kitchen. She arrived at his side and shoved an open bottle in his face.

"That was ninth grade." She informed him about the picture while swallowing a sip from her own drink. "My parents love Chad. They're not so in touch with reality."

"Do you think they'd like me?" Jeremy asked.

"Of course," Nicole said directly. "I like you, therefore they will like you."

"And I can actually meet them someday?" He queried.

"Jeremy. A beautiful girl has sequestered you to a fortress of solitude, far away from the eyes of anyone and is now trying to get you drunk. If you really want to go meet my parents instead, I suppose we could do that."

Jeremy waited a second. Her argument finally won out, and he looked to her.

"Okay. Sorry. So what did you want to show me up here? Or was it just this place?" He asked. She grinned.

"Follow me." She led him up to the second floor of the cabin. They passed two doors, and a loft that had been converted to a bedroom. She opened two sliding doors and revealed a large bedroom. It was the size of his living room at home. By the decoration and hanging masks, it was obvious this was Nicole's room. She led him and through two glass sliding doors onto an outdoor patio. His eyes caught the decorative rifle hanging over the door.

Outside, Nicole introduced him to the grand view. Jeremy could see over the treetops and hillside. He could see down to the small ponds and one large lake. Boats and Jet skis left white trails behind them. Small dots that he assumed to be people bobbled about near the beaches.

"Beautiful, huh?" Nicole slid her arm through his.

"Yeah." He said candidly. "I can't believe you don't come up here more often." He admired the oranges and yellows of fall in the midday sun.

"It's just things with my family, you know." Nicole explained. "And I guess things with me." She looked past the horizon in the distance.

"What do you mean, 'things with you'?" he kept his voice low and neutral.

"I just, I feel like I'm losing sight of who I am. Or I could be finally finding out who I really am. I've let the bureaucracies of life dictate my actions and decisions for too long." She confided.

"Now you feel like you don't or aren't?" Jeremy was curious as to what she meant. He tried not to sound offensive.

"No. Not so much, I don't. It feels like I've finally awoke from a dream that lasted too many nights. I feel like I get to be who I always wanted to be." She sounded afraid.

"How is this a bad thing?" Jeremy was having trouble deciphering her mood, and her face remained blank. Nicole was still. As the cool breeze picked up, she whispered lightly, to no one in particular.

"I don't know,".

Jeremy started to question her on this, but her demeanor suddenly shifted. She clanked her bottle against his.

"Drink up, Jeremy. We've got a long day ahead of us."

They finished their beers on the patio as the noon hour passed. Nicole spent most of the time debating whether or not to turn her cell phone back on. While doing so, she told Jeremy several of the more sensational tales about their classmates. Being able to expose the dark hilarity behind the secrets of their school's elite caste was a privilege Nicole enjoyed dearly. Jeremy sat aghast at the lurid narratives of debauchery, betrayal and hatred. He had no idea that people who had numerous suicide attempts, STD's, a fascination with sexual depravity and vile acts walked the halls with him. Nicole was amused and encouraged to continue by his ignorance.

An hour or so later, she initiated sexual relations with Jeremy on the bear skin rug downstairs. They finished outside on the patio she had led him to earlier. Nicole smoked, standing naked, looking into the sky.

"You make me feel good, Jeremy." She ran a hand across her shirtless chest.

"That's a good thing, isn't it?" Jeremy did not understand why she would suddenly say something like that. He had no experience with depression.

"Yeah, duh." Nicole laughed, expelling clouds of methane and other such poisons. "I haven't had a reason to feel good in a long time."

Nicole looked at him.

"Whatever I can do to help." Jeremy smiled. Nicole's eyes grew very wide. Jeremy was afraid he'd upset her. Her gaze shifted as she looked over her shoulder at the tops of the trees surrounding them.

"Look," she whispered. Jeremy turned to his side in a flash. He didn't see what she was looking at.

"There." Nicole's hand snaked over his shoulder. As her motion stopped, her fingertip came to rest in his field of vision. He immediately targeted the family of squirrels she had been trying to call his attention to.

"Oh. Cool." He tried to sound impressed, but it was hard to hide the flat tone in his voice.

"Wait here." Nicole hopped away, and into her room.

"They still there?" she called out. Jeremy had kept the critters locked in his sights.

"Uh, yeah." He was hesitant, not understanding why in the hell she was so fascinated with rodents. He could hear a lot of commotion coming from her room. Suddenly, she appeared over his shoulder again. He turned to look at her as she chambered a bullet in a small, .22-caliber rifle.

"Ever handle one of these?" Nicole asked with a smile. Jeremy returned a feeble form of the gesture. He had never touched a gun before. "No matter, it's only a .22, which is little more than a BB-gun." Nicole informed him.

"You're gonna shoot one of those squirrels?" Jeremy was cautious.

"They're vermin, Jeremy. God will make more. He always does." Nicole sighed. Jeremy was shocked at the statement. He had no time to react, though. Nicole had finished loading the gun. She reached down, and jerked him by his arm to the patio railing. With no regard for safety, she shoved the rifle butt into his shoulder. He didn't resist. His comments had already made him seem like a creampuff. There was no need to disappoint her further. If killing squirrels made Nicole happy, Jeremy supposed he could do that.

She unwrapped his clenched fist, and placed it on the handle of the rifle. As his finger reached for the trigger, she slapped his hand.

"Never put your finger on the trigger until you are sure you will fire." Nicole sternly advised him. Jeremy nodded. Nicole turned him to face the squirrels. She stood behind him, and helped him bring the rifle into firing position. While she supported the elbow of his arm that wasn't pulling the trigger, she clasped that same hand on the barrel of the weapon.

"Look down the barrel, through that sight on the end, see?" Nicole gave him a crash course in aiming. Jeremy rested his head on the rifle, and Nicole readjusted it a bit. Jeremy turned the rifle to see the squirrels. Nicole kicked his ankles, forcing him to spread his legs wider.

"Keep your feet shoulder width apart, and face your target." She whispered in his ear. "When you see one in your sights, aim for the chest. When you're there, put your finger on the trigger. Keep your sights straight; holding your breath helps with that. Then pull the trigger. Don't jerk the trigger. Just pull it gently. If you jerk, your aim will be off, and then you'll be more likely to scare the thing away than kill it. Okay?"

"And that's a bad thing?" Jeremy posed a similar question to one he had given her moments earlier. He wasn't a fan of killing anything.

"Jeremy. It's a rodent. There's millions of squirrels in the world. If it will make you feel better, I'll skin it and make you a hat, okay? Just shoot. Try it. For me." Her voice had dropped to a whisper at the end. That was all it took to convince Jeremy. He had given his heart away, and now she was leading him by it. Somewhere in his fascination with Nicole, he was losing his common sense and free will.

Jeremy pulled the trigger with a firm jerk, despite her warnings. The rifle popped loud in his ear, but barely moved. He swore he heard a squeal. They watched the squirrel fall from the tree. Instead of lying deadly still, it began to twitch and squirm.

"Crap, you only winged it." Nicole snatched the rifle away, her face twisted in a disapproving scowl that she immediately regretted. She looked down the barrel herself. "And I can't see clearly to finish him. Shit."

"Now what do we do?" Jeremy felt ashamed for sacrificing his beliefs, but his fear that she would leave him outweighed that shame.

"Let's go see how bad it is."

Nicole walked back into the house, tossing the rifle on her bed. Jeremy followed obediently. She snatched a shirt from the closet, and put it on as they trotted down the stairs.

The squirrels wheezing and crying became distinctly audible as they left the house. No matter how hard he tried, Jeremy couldn't help but feel bad for it. Nicole was rather disgusted that she had to waste her time with the situation at all. Her body language alone made Jeremy question whether they did indeed have a future together. He was sure Chad never missed when he shot helpless animals with her. Chad probably fired a perfect shot every time.

The squirrel itself lay bleeding to death from a leg wound. The bullet had clipped the lower portion of the leg clean off. It couldn't move, but was desperately trying to escape. Like Nicole.

The squirrel's dark eyes darted around, trying to find the mighty beast that had wounded it. Sadly, the blood loss it had suffered had already caused blindness. The squirrel would never get to look Jeremy in the eyes.

"We can't leave him like this." Jeremy looked at Nicole.

"We could, but you're right on a level. Nothing should have to die like this. Not even a squirrel. I told you not to jerk." Nicole smiled as proper as possible for a succubus. Jeremy stared at the squirrel as she walked off back toward the cabin. She returned in seconds, with a large wood axe over her shoulder.

"Nicole?" Jeremy didn't want to imagine what was to come next.

"Close your eyes, if you must." She gave him allowance to be a coward. Nicole never took her eyes off of the animal. Jeremy tried to watch, but had to look away as she raised the axe. He tried to send his mind elsewhere, but found himself watching her through the corner of his eyes. Nicole swung the axe and relieved the squirrel's shoulders of their weight bearing responsibility with the precision of a surgeon. The animal didn't make a sound as the dry thunk of the axe ended its artificially shortened life. The body trembled for a moment, as the little blood left drained out. The eyes blinked, and then it was gone.

"Let's go back to town." Nicole walked back toward the cabin, dragging the bloody axe behind her. "I'll call Natalie and see what kind of trouble Veronica has caused. Then we'll figure out what party will be best to go to tonight."

"Party?" Jeremy was looking at the dead squirrel.

"Yeah." Nicole confirmed, her voice becoming quieter as she neared the cabin. "It's Friday, silly. The weekend's starting. There will be parties. There always are." She kept her voice light so as not to truly offend him as she insulted him. She had a snake's tongue that was sweeter than chocolate covered cherries atop a lake of molasses.

The dynamic duo dressed and headed back to town. As soon as she was able to get a clear signal on her cell phone, Nicole was informed by the onscreen display that she had 112 new text messages and enough voice mail messages to fill up her inbox.

"It looks like Veronica has been a Busy Beaver." Nicole commented, showing Jeremy the phone.

"Chad's going to kill me." Jeremy felt himself begin to sweat. It took all of his energy and effort to force his body to stop trembling.

"No, he's not. You leave them to me. I'm not that girl that Veronica told you about. Not anymore." Nicole attempted to reassure him.

"Yeah." Jeremy's belief in his statements was weak. He heard himself saying things that he couldn't stand behind, which was somewhat new to him.

"You don't sound so sure." Nicole laughed, picking up on his insecurities. She gave a façade of indifference, when in reality she was taking the situation very seriously. When Jeremy refused to elaborate any further on his own feelings, Nicole decided to call Natalie.

"Hello? Nicky?!" Where are you?! Oh my god, do you know what Veronica said?" Natalie could hide her animation no more than a Saturday morning cartoon.

"Yeah, I know. I wouldn't have taken Jeremy out like that, but so what? You know? Chad's too high-maintenance anyhow. Isn't that what you always said?" Nicole saved herself the time of having Natalie tell her what she already knew.

"No, I said he was an a-hole," Natalie corrected "But same difference now, I guess. This is a bit ballsy, though. How are you going to stop Chad from destroying Jeremy?"

"I'm not sure yet. We'll see when the time comes. What's the news on plans for tonight? Where's the party at?" Nicole began toying with ideas on how to salvage the entire situation she now found herself mired in. Nicole, unlike Jeremy, was able to fully simulate any confidence she lacked.

"Well, there's a few, but if you're really looking to handle this whole thing head on, Veronica herself is supposed to be having a party of some sort. Chad's face has been attached to hers all day, so I'm sure they're going to announce their engagement or something equally lame."

Nicole and Natalie shared a laugh.

"I guess that would be best." Nicole referred to attending Veronica's party. "Okay, meet me at my house around seven or so."

"Okay," Natalie dared not question the order. "Love ya."

"Love you, too." Nicole replied, running her finger across the touchscreen to lock the phone again. She and Jeremy traveled in silence for half an hour.

"So what happened?" Jeremy finally asked. He could hold his curiosity no longer. Never before had he willingly put his future in someone's hands without knowing that they planned to do with it. He felt that his end was coming at Chad's hand and wanted to know a little about how it may transpire.

"Veronica's throwing us a party." Nicole gave him the wicked grin of an enchantress.

"Yeah, right." Jeremy mistook her irony for playfulness.

"She is throwing us a party and we're going to be there." Nicole lit a cigarette as they passed a sign announcing that the city was only 10 miles away.

"This feels like courting disaster, Nicole. I'm scared." Jeremy timidly admitted.

"That's understandable." Nicole conceded while swerving around a family of five in a motor home. "Chad wants to kill you right now, I'm sure. To exacerbate that, I'm taking you to a party where he and his whole gang of misfit toys will be drunk and riled up. They've been talking about beating you up ever since Chad got the news. You have every right to be scared."

"So that's it." Jeremy was shocked by her admission that he was in the right to feel as he did. "I guess trembling in fear is all I have left to do."

"Jeremy, calm down. Enjoy the moment, and live on the edge a little bit. I told you it'd be okay, didn't I? And hasn't it so far? Okay then, trust me." Nicole attempted to console him.

"Live on the edge." Jeremy wanted to spit it out with contempt, but he was afraid of Nicole, so it came out more as a simple statement. "I'm the one who is going to get pulverized here."

"Jeremy," Nicole pulled the car to the shoulder of the road in a cloud of dust. Jeremy braced himself on the dashboard, to avoid smashing his face into it. "No, I haven't thought it all the way through, yet. No, I am not absolutely, completely, totally positive that Chad won't obliterate you tonight. Yes, I am pretty sure I can keep you safe. You're scared and you have no idea what to expect. I understand. But enjoy it. Life was meant to be lived. I will die before I let anything happen to you. I feel alive with you. And I think you feel the same way with me. In order for it to stay this way, Chad has to be dealt with. It had to happen sooner or later. I want to feel alive. I never want this to stop. And, I guess, before we go any further, I need to know that you feel the same way." Nicole played with her cigarette. Jeremy looked into her eyes, as dust settled about them. Her pupils were shaking behind a small wall of tears that had yet to break the levees.

"I'm sorry." I'm just worried, you know. I do want to keep what we have. I do want to be with you." Jeremy put a hand on her leg to massage the tears away.

"Then trust me. And enjoy the thrills while they last." Nicole smiled as her foot mashed the gas pedal nearly through the floor. The purring motor leapt into action. She cut off the same family she had whizzed past a few minutes earlier in the RV.

Life is Hell and Suburbia is a Lie

Chapter Seven: The bang and the whimper

Nicole pulled into her driveway around 5 p.m. that afternoon. Her mother's car sat in front of her. Jackson and a few of his friends stood on the front porch smoking cigarettes and passing a pint of brandy about.

"Great." Nicole muttered, mashing her cigarette into the ashtray.

"Who's that?" Jeremy asked. Jackson and his friends were pointing at Jeremy and Nicole and laughing.

"My older brother, and his rugged band of derelicts." Nicole opened her door. "Just ignore them."

"You want me to come with you inside?" Jeremy still was not acclimated to the environment that always surrounded Nicole. The excess and disregard for social standards were unfamiliar to him. He had become accustomed to hiding his relationship with Nicole in public.

"I thought you wanted to meet my parents. Well, my mom anyhow. My dad isn't home yet, but you aren't missing much there to begin with." Nicole closed her door as Jeremy opened his. She marched up to the walkway, and Jeremy followed.

As tough as Jackson attempted to act, Nicole still intimidated him. She threw her brother and his colleagues an unforgiving stare of disgust. Them avoiding her was like trying to catch a jumbo jet with one hand; There was no way to avoid it you simply tried to minimize the damage.

"If it isn't Nicky, the super-bitch." Jackson flicked ashes from his cigarette her way as she neared.

"Jackson, don't you and your degenerate congregation have anything better to do than bring down our property value by loitering in the front yard?" Nicole snatched the cigarette from his lips and stamped it out on the ground.

"Oooh. She's always got the 5 million dollar comeback." Marilyn, Jackson's girlfriend handed him another cigarette.

"Shut up, Marilyn." Nicole could feel Jeremy's nervousness radiating behind her. "Aren't your other johns going to get lonely with you hanging around here?"

"I'll kick your ass, whether Jackson likes it or not." Marilyn started to take a step forward.

"Please." Nicole waved her off. Jackson held out a hand to stay his beau.

"Chad came by earlier. Seemed mighty angry. That have anything to do with the square peg following you around?" Jackson motioned at Jeremy.

"You are such an ass." Nicole pushed him out of the way, and walked into the house. Jeremy followed.

"He had a fine-looking girl with him, too." Jackson called out.

"Looks like Chad traded up." Marilyn added.

Nicole stopped in the doorway, but ushered Jeremy past her. She turned back to her brother's girlfriend.

"Marilyn, don't make me escort you off of my porch and leave you on the curb with the rest of the trash. You better be gone by the time I come back."

Nicole slammed the door shut before she could hear any response. Jeremy stood waiting. Nicole took a moment to breathe and collect herself. Marilyn hadn't upset her. Her brother's best friend John McKenzie had been eyeing Nicole's chest with an untamed lust that she remembered.

"You okay?" Jeremy put a hand on her shoulder.

"Yeah, fine." Nicole left her insecurities in the past. Jeremy was already terrified enough. He didn't need her appearing weak or confused at the moment.

"You sure?" Jeremy made his availability for support known.

"Yeah. I just hate my brother. But what sister doesn't?" Nicole laughed. She gave Jeremy's arm a squeeze to reassure him. He wasn't entirely convinced that she was telling the truth, but decided to let the subject go. His mind was still preoccupied with the beating he was sure to receive later that night.

"I think my mom's in the living room. C'mon." Nicole pulled him by the hand. She led him to the living room where her mother was watching the evening news through glossy eyes.

"Hi, mom."

The sudden voice startled her mother. She jumped slightly, and then slowly turned to look at Nicole. As she did so, she discreetly sat an empty martini glass on the table.

"Oh, Nicky. Chad came by earlier. And who's this nice looking young man with you?" Mrs. O'Leary asked with a look at Jeremy.

"Mom, Chad and I broke up earlier today. This is Jeremy." Nicole nudged Jeremy forward. He awkwardly stuck his hand out, not sure of the proper greeting to use.

"Nice to meet you, ma'am." He squeaked. His palms were suddenly clammy and burning.

"Nice to meet you, too." Mrs. O'Leary reached forward and shook Jeremy's hand, hiding her drunken stupor as best she could. "It's nice that Nicole picks the ones with manners."

Nicole noticed the slight slur to her mother's words, and decided the meeting should be over now.

"Well," She started. "We're going out with Natalie tonight, so I have to go get ready."

Jeremy moved to take a seat on the empty love seat. Nicole pulled him close to her.

"We'll be in my room if you need anything."

"Okay." Mrs. O'Leary agreed, not realizing that she didn't have a choice in the matter.

"And you might want to tell Jackson and his school of delinquents to stop getting wasted on the front porch." Nicole had little faith that her mother would listen.

"Nicky, you know what your father says."

"Jackson is an adult who pays rent. He can do as he pleases." Nicole mimicked her father's voice. "That's such bullshit, mom. He pays 50-dollars a month in 'rent', but he borrows twice as much from you guys half the time."

"Nicole," her mother became somewhat serious and somewhat sober. "I don't want to discuss this without your father. And I really do not want to go over this in front of your company. That's rude."

"Whatever, mom." Nicole took Jeremy's hand in a firm grasp and stormed off to her room. Her mother took a sip from the empty glass, and was surprised to find it in that condition. She fumbled in the couch cushions while muttering curses. Her hands clamped around a bottle of gin. She pulled it out, and attempted to pour a glass. She was sure her hands were steady, but she was a dripping wet drunk. The gin filled the glass in a rush. It overflowed and drenched a copy of Glamour magazine. The TV Guide and World Weekly News narrowly averted disaster. Mrs. O'Leary passed out halfway into her first sip. The glass fell to the floor as the FOX newscaster scolded the secular media.

"Why did you talk to her like that?" Jeremy asked as they entered Nicole's room.

"She's a hypocritical drunk with no backbone." Nicole slammed her door.

"But you should still respect her. That's your mother." Jeremy counseled her.

"Jeremy, I want the mother that I had before everything fell apart. She used to have a backbone. She used to be someone I could look up to and depend on." Nicole put her hand to her head in frustration.

"It doesn't matter what she's done, Nicole." Jeremy kept his voice calm and neutral. "She's not just your family, she's your elder. She's your mother. She gave birth to you. You should always treat her with respect. Maybe she isn't who she used to be, but we all can't be strong all the time, Nicole. She's supported you for how long? Maybe now it's time for you to support her some."

"Jeremy, you know nothing of the betrayals that have transgressed behind the walls of this home." Nicole's tone took on that of a warning.

"I don't need to." Jeremy quickly countered. "You don't always need the whole story to know what the right thing to do is."

Nicole admired his sudden courage. He was taking a stand with her, and doing so in hopes of making her a better person.

"You're not going to let this go, are you?" Nicole sighed.

"I don't think I, in good conscience, can let this go." He smiled at her with the warmth of a spring sunset.

"Fine." Nicole gave in not to make Jeremy feel better, but because he was right. "I'll try to change that, okay?"

"Okay." Jeremy agreed.

"Now, what to wear?" Nicole quickly changed gears. She turned to her walk-in closet. This closet was a powerful area. It was revered within the ranks of the school they attended. This closet is where the ideas for what was acceptable and hot and new and cool "You can watch my TV or whatever." She said as she disappeared into the den of her fashions. "We've got the platinum deal on our cable, so all the channels you could ever want are there. Plus there's my DVD player if you want to watch a movie."

I think I'd rather watch you, Jeremy thought.

"Okay." He answered, turning on the television to satisfy her. The channel on display was an MTV derivative that actually played videos. Currently on show was an up and coming independent band that the followers of underground music had known of for years, but as of now MTV was "breaking" the news about them.

"Oh, I love these guys. I just downloaded their CD a couple days ago." Nicole popped out of the closet. "Turn that down a second, please."

Jeremy did as he was told. Nicole slipped a CD of her own making into her stereo and cranked up the volume. The same band that had been playing on the television was now blasting out of her stereo. Jeremy felt the entire house shake as synth beats and ringing guitars rained down. Nicole, dancing and snapping her fingers returned to her closet. Jeremy listened as she sang along. Several items of clothing began to fly from the closet, landing on the bed where Jeremy now sat. A T-shirt hit him in the face, and he wasn't entirely sure it wasn't done on purpose. A pair of pants landed at his feet and suddenly Nicole reappeared.

"Now, to put together the perfect outfit." Nicole began laying out the clothing she had retrieved in several possible combinations. She held each up to Jeremy and asked his opinion. His responses indicated that he liked everything. In the end, she went with her own sense of style, knowing Jeremy was woefully uneducated in the world of fashion. She selected hip high jeans and a bare mid-riff shirt that had a neckline so low it could have doubled as a bikini top.

Nicole began to undress where she stood, still dancing to the current soundtrack of her life. She disappeared once to replace the unused clothes in her closet. Jeremy could almost hear the hangars clanking as she put them away. He was filling with a warm sense of fear. She made him feel so good just by being with him, and it could all end the second she decided. He was afraid to be without her. This is love, he realized.

Nicole once again reappeared, her skimpy top now hiding poorly beneath a semi-transparent long sleeve, black spandex top that ended in frills at the cuffs similar to a dark, gothic rose. She allowed Jeremy to look her over, and then turned to her vanity desk and mirror. She squirted a handful of hair product into her hand moved toward Jeremy with a playful determination.

"What's up," he backed away some. Nicole was fast though. She mashed the gel into Jeremy's hair, and styled it to her liking. Jeremy relaxed and allowed her the freedom to work over his image.

"There," Nicole said after a few seconds. She backed away, and gave a satisfied look. "The good old 'mussed up with gel' look. The girls are gonna love it. One rule from here on out for the night: Do not touch your hair, or let anyone else. Leave the rest to me."

"Okay, sure." Jeremy had no idea that his hair looked 'cool'. To him, the reflection in her mirror that he could see looked how his hair did every morning, if he didn't comb it.

"Now, I just have to do make-up and we can go. Natalie should be here by then." Nicole smiled.

"Didn't you already do that this morning?" Jeremy asked.

"That was make-up for shopping. Now I have to do make-up for going to a party at Veronica's house. Those are two very different occasions, young man."

She giggled. Jeremy shook his head. All of this pomp and circumstance would have been a joke to him before he met her. Now it struck him as somewhat tragic. How could these beautiful young women think that they weren't beautiful enough with the genetics god gave them?

Nicole moved away from Jeremy. She concentrated on removing the face she had applied earlier and focused on creating the Nicole that would appear tonight. Although Jeremy was disheartened by Nicole's need to "make-up" a face, he wouldn't let it get in the way of him wanting her. He watched in amazement as the girl he had looked upon all morning vanished with a vigorous alcohol pad scrubbing. Nicole meticulously scrubbed her face and applied her make-up. For the split second that her face was devoid of any product, Jeremy could actually see that she had freckles. They were a very light brown, but they were there.

Natalie and Elizabeth arrived half an hour after Nicole began her makeover. The two entered Nicole's room unannounced.

"Hey guys." Nicole didn't bother to look at them. "This is Jeremy. Jeremy, these are my best friends, Natalie and Elizabeth." Nicole made informal introductions that left much unsaid. Natalie held her hand out.

"It's nice to meet you Jeremy." Natalie pretended their previous chat had never happened. Jeremy not wanting to stir any pot of snakes did the same. Elizabeth waved to him with a small smile. He mirrored her greeting as he did Natalie's.

"So, you're the one who's got Nicky causing all this trouble." Elizabeth leaned on the chair Nicole sat in.

"No," Nicole turned to interrupt her. She would defend Jeremy, even from her friends. It was imperative that he understood what he meant to her. It was also a priority that everyone understand who was in control. "Jeremy didn't cause any of this. I did. I decided it was time for a change."

"A long overdue change." Natalie gave Jeremy a smile in a show of approval. Jeremy wasn't sure what to say. His encounter with Natalie in the woods was still fresh in his mind. He wondered if Nicole was playing with him, and if so, had he passed an opportunity with Natalie that any man would have been an idiot to look past? He had no idea, so he sat with a simplistic fool's grin holding his face together.

"You two need to stop sounding so grim." Nicole warned. "I didn't assassinate anyone. I cheated on Chad and just have to appear to let everyone know that I have formally left him."

"Nicole, you're assassinating Chad, honey." Natalie clarified. "You know what this will mean for him. And to have you do it at Veronica's house with the entire school watching, well, that's outright social murder. From freshmen to seniors, you will have a full audience."

"God, this is stupid." Nicole stopped her make-up application process.

"What do you mean?" Elizabeth asked, as she knew Nicole wanted her to.

"It's just so immature." Nicole stood. "How did I let myself get bogged down in all of this crap for so long?"

"Did you forget that I told you the same thing every day for the past four years?" Natalie wanted some recognition. She had more backbone than Elizabeth and would mildly challenge Nicole at times.

"I know." Nicole conceded unexpectedly with a smile. "I just don't know why I never listened."

"So don't go tonight." Elizabeth advised. They all knew this was unacceptable though. Nicole had lived her life to be that girl that everyone else wanted to be. To just stop performing as expected would end her social life, just as she intended to end Chad's.

"We can just go to a movie or something." Natalie suggested with a hollow tone.

"No," Nicole muted the idea. "The people want to see the noble's at each other's throats. We can't let them down, can we?"

"That's the dumbest thing I have ever heard." Natalie rolled her eyes. "Tell her, Jeremy. Tell her how dumb it is." Natalie nudged his shoulder.

"That's not why she's doing it. She likes the rush of the unknown." He and Nicole shared a silent smirk. The room fell quiet. Natalie and Elizabeth were uneasy with the nonverbal communication between Nicole and Jeremy. Nicole walked over to him. Her eyes were tearing. She softly kissed his lips and swallowed her delight.

"It's a little early in the relationship and the afternoon for psychoanalyzing." Nicole smiled.

"But I was right, huh?" Jeremy let a glimpse of his pride sneak into his words.

"Jeremy, you're new here, so you probably don't know this: The room's only big enough for one of us to be right." She turned to face her friends. "So, let's get to this party."

Natalie and Elizabeth had been caught off guard by the intensity of the emotional exchange between Jeremy and Nicole. They had never expected to see her like this. It was as if they too could feel that hollow place inside of her slowly filling with each moment she was with him.

"If you say so. We've got to pick up something to get us primed still." Natalie stood straighter.

" And I have to meet Jeremy's mom. It's on our way, kinda. Let's go." Nicole took Jeremy's hand and dragged him behind her.

"Meet his mom?" Natalie asked.

"Yep." Nicole turned. "She said she wanted to meet me and he told her I was pretty."

"Is that so?" Natalie looked to Jeremy. "Maybe Nicole really did pick a decent one this time."

As the group exited the house, Nicole stopped at the front door.

"I'll be right there. I have to do something." She told Natalie, who was already opening her car door. Jeremy, who was at the front door with Nicole, stopped as well.

"Everything alright?" he asked. "They were right, you know. We don't have to go." Now that he had given Elizabeth's idea more thought, and the time of their arrival was nearing he was eager to avoid any physical violence against his person.

"I'm going to take your advice." Nicole smiled. "Instead of talking at my mother, I'm going to start talking *to* her again. I'll be right out."

"Okay." Jeremy replied after a moment of hesitation. He turned his back and walked to the car as Nicole re-entered the home. She walked into the living room where her mother lay passed out. Nicole sat next to her. With the caress of a butterfly, Nicole brushed her mother's hair from her eyes. Mrs. O'Leary slowly awoke and peered out.

"Nicole, sweetie, is everything okay?" Her mother asked with hardly any voice.

"Everything's fine, mom."

"You're all dressed up."

"We're going to a party. Me, Natalie, Lizzie-"

"And that boy?"

"Jeremy, yeah."

"He seems very nice. Wholesome."

"I like him."

"That's good, dear. I'm glad you're happy."

"When will you be happy, mom?"

Her mother glanced around.

"Has your father come home yet?"

"No. He must've stayed late, again."

"Then I'm happy right now, dear."

Nicole didn't have anything to say. Sometimes, heartbreak can't be voiced. She heard Natalie start the car outside. Without saying a word, Nicole rose to her feet, and turned to leave.

"It'll all work out, Nicky, I promise." Her mother grabbed at her hand.

Nicole stood her ground, not turning to face her mother, but not walking away either. "Is that supposed to mean something? You and dad made promises to each other once, remember?" Nicole took a step away.

"I don't think either of us meant it, dear." Her mother whispered. Nicole waited an instant. She squeezed her mother's hand and then pulled free.

"I love you, mom."

"I love you, too, Nicky. Be careful." Mrs. O'Leary yawned.

"I will." Nicole assured her and made her exit.

"Took you long enough." Natalie said as Nicole shut the front door behind her. Natalie, Jeremy, and Elizabeth sat on the hood of the running car. "We took turns molesting your man while you were busy."

Jeremy shifted uncomfortably; unsure as to whether Natalie had told Nicole anything of their... encounter in Tahronghy Canyon.

"He's too wholesome for that." Nicole smiled.

"Not if he stays with you." Elizabeth opened the passenger door. Nicole laughed and hopped in the backseat. Elizabeth nodded for Jeremy to follow. Within minutes the quartet was on their way. Elizabeth and Natalie were somewhat perturbed at having to wait to meet Jeremy's parents before starting to drink, but they understood. Very few people had parents who thought you were okay if you were plastered. The drive was spent reminiscing over homecoming parties of years past. Natalie parked in the driveway Jeremy pointed out when they came to his block.

"So, this is it, huh?" Nicole eyed the small, single family home.

"Yeah, I know it's not much."

"But it's a home." Nicole finished his cliched line.

"Whose old car is that?" Natalie inquired about the topless, black, 1965 Cadillac El Dorado that was parked on the sidewalk in front of the house. It was a mean car; An old piece of muscle that refused to die. No one wanted to see that car driving in motion or sitting still. It was hell on wheels, literally. Everyone in the car was uncomfortable after Natalie forced them to acknowledge its existence, including Jeremy. He gulped hard, before speaking.

"That's my Uncle Dane's car. He, uh, must've gotten out again." Jeremy answered vaguely. No one was sure where this Dane had "gotten out" of, but they had a good idea. Since she started the conversation, Natalie continued.

"Gotten out of where? Prison?" She asked.

"Yeah. He's been in and out of there for his whole life. He comes by when he gets out, stays a few nights, borrows some money, and ends up robbing a 7-11 or something. Then the police come ask us about him, and we say we don't know where he is and they eventually find him at some hole in Nevada or Arizona or Texas. But he's my mother's brother, and she loves him." Jeremy explained in a rush.

"And you don't?" Nicole questioned his loyalty.

"No, that's not what I meant. I mean, we never really talk about him... about his history and all that. When he comes by, it's just like 'oh, Dane's by to visit again.' And my mom makes dinner and we all sit around and play cards or something, before he goes out to the bar with my dad. It's weird."

"Not really." Nicole said softly. "But it doesn't bother your dad at all?"

"No. He and Uncle Dane are good friends, so they get along alright. Dane introduced mom to dad back in high school, I guess. Mom got dad to clean up his act, but Uncle Dane stayed the same."

"Huh. Shall we go?" Nicole was in a hurry to change the subject and get a drink.

"Okay, but I am not sure how clean it is, let me just warn you." Jeremy said. The girls laughed.

"Do you really think I am that superficial?" Nicole rolled her eyes, feigning outrage.

"No." Jeremy rushed to apologize. Nicole cut him off with a laugh and a finger jab to the ribs.

"I'm kidding. Let's go. We're wasting keg time." She turned to Natalie who had opened her door.

"You two wait here. It might be best if I handle this alone with Jeremy."

"Fine, but hurry please." Natalie sighed.

Nicole exited the car, and Jeremy followed. He led her up to the short walkway to the door. Before he opened it, he stopped.

"Thank you." He said sincerely.

"For what?" Nicole asked.

"Treating me like this. Like I matter. No one's ever really done that." He revealed.

"And that's a tragedy. You're so special, and it took me this long to realize it. You should be angry, and upset, but you're not. You're a beautiful person, Jeremy." She took his hand in hers, and placed it on the door knob. With her help, he turned it, and pushed the door open. Jeremy found his father sitting in the living room, which the front door opened directly into. His father wore a pair of well used jeans and an exclusive t-shirt that only those with 400 cigarette carton UPC's could obtain. He was a short man with leathery skin and broken fingernails. A cigarette burnt nearly to the butt rested in his fingers. His hair was dark brown and straight. It had been combed at one point in the day, but was now mussed and wet from the shower he took when he arrived home. Upon seeing Jeremy, he mashed the cigarette into the top of a beer can, and threw the cigarette inside. He turned the television down, which was broadcasting the Cubs game.

"Hey stranger. Finally decided to come home, did ya? And this must be the reason we've seen so little of you lately." Jeremy's father stood and extended a hand in Nicole's direction. She accepted and they shook briskly. She could feel the hard, sharp calluses on his palm biting into hers. This was a man who worked for a living and had the scars to prove it.

"Avery Bloom." He introduced himself. His tone implied that he'd like to know her name.

"This is Nicole, dad." Jeremy inched closer to her.

"Nicole...?" He prompted her for her last name.

"O'Leary." Nicole answered.

"Well, the first girl Jeremy's ever brought home, and you must be the prettiest one in school." Jeremy's mother appeared from the adjoining kitchen. She wore an apron and had a dark sauce of some sort splattered on her chest. She wore an ear to ear grin.

"Thank you." Nicole blushed.

A toilet flushed down a small hallway ahead of them. A tall man appeared. He had dirty blond hair that had been cut severely short. His skin was leathery and covered in tattoos. A hand rolled cigarette hung from his lips, which were covered in burns and black tobacco stains where they weren't cracked and chapped. His eyes were permanently bloodshot, weathered, cold, and hard. He wore a faded and torn t-shirt from the late seventies. An original KISS concert t-shirt. His pants were dark black leather. He could have doubled for a grimy 70's rock star or biker. His muscles were tight and toned, though not overly large. Nicole guessed this was the infamous Uncle Dane.

"Did you say O'Leary?" Uncle Dane asked.

"Yeah." Nicole answered, finding herself intimidated for the first time in her life.

"Why?" Avery Bloom asked Uncle Dane.

"Your parents from Chicago?" Dane inquired further, inhaling from his cigarette. Smoke drenched his face, and hid his features.

"Yeah, both my parents have lived here all their lives." Nicole was getting uncomfortable.

"Any relation to Harold O'Leary?" Taking a long drag on his cigarette, Dane narrowed down his search parameters, along with his eyes.

"That's my dad." Nicole held up a hand as if to stand her out of the crowd. Avery Bloom and Dane shared a look. Avery finally understood why Dane had so many questions.

"Really?" Avery said. "Tell him Avery says hello. Me, him and Dane went to school together. In fact, your dad and I both pitched on the same team way back in pee wee baseball."

"Avery, a girl could care less about your glory days. Can't you see they're getting ready to go out. She even got Jeremy to wear a nice shirt and fix his hair." Mrs. Bloom fingered the collar of Jeremy's shirt.

"Yeah, there's a big homecoming celebration tonight." Nicole informed them. She looked at his parents, but her eyes kept darting to the imposing figure of Uncle Dane, who never took his eyes off of hers. He stood silently smoking his cigarette, and breathing deeply.

"Really? Where?" Avery Bloom asked.

"Veronica Barbarossa's parents are allowing her to have a little get together." Nicole was careful not to use the word 'party'.

"Oh. The Barbarossa's, huh." Avery Bloom knew of them by the sound of his voice. He realized just how far out of his class this girl was. "Didn't she win something recently or last year, maybe."

"Miss Teen Illinois." Nicole beamed, as if she were an admirer.

"I don't know." Avery said. "How long do you kids plan on staying out?"

"Dad, I'm 18." Jeremy was embarrassed beyond belief.

"Don't argue with your parents." Nicole pinched Jeremy's arm and wormed her way into his parent's trust. "But in all honesty Mr. Bloom, the celebration will probably go pretty late."

"Celebration... uh-huh." Avery wasn't fooled by her verbiage, and let her know it with a wry smile. "Well, I guess it's okay. I mean Dane would like to see you Jeremy, but this is your senior year and all. And you are 18, as you said. Nicole, would you mind waiting outside a moment while we talk with Jeremy?"

"Of course not. Take your time." Nicole was scared and intimidated by Dane, but she knew how to charm people like an old street hustler. She gracefully bowed out of the scene and closed the door behind her. Her skin prickled and crawled with the feeling that Dane could still see her through the door. The way he watched her was unsettling to say the least.

"She really seems like a very nice girl." Jeremy's mother told him.

"Yeah, she's great." Jeremy agreed with a smile.

"Homecoming party at the rich girl's house. How did you ever land that?" Dane asked.

"Dane!" Jeremy's mother hit her brother's arm. Avery laughed.

"Okay, okay. Here." Avery handed Jeremy a crumpled 20$ bill from his wallet. "Get her dinner or get flowers or something."

"That's not gonna cover a night with a girl like that." Dane laughed. He pulled a wad of 50$ bills that no freshly released prisoner should ever have from his pocket. He gave Jeremy two of them. "It's homecoming weekend. Go out. Have fun. I'll see you later. Don't worry about when to come home, just make sure that whatever you do, you're safe and not driving."

Jeremy looked to his dad for approval of Dane's instructions. Avery Bloom nodded with a smile.

"Thanks Uncle Dane, Mom, Dad."

"Have fun, sweetie. And be a gentleman." His mother put her arms around Avery's waist.

"Okay, thanks. I'll see you guys later." Jeremy was a bit confused. He never expected his parents to go for any of Nicole's plan. He left the house and found the porch empty. Nicole had returned to the car. Jeremy stood alone for a moment in wonder. He didn't know the three people in that house. They had never been as laid back and agreeable with him doing much of anything social. Now, it didn't seem like they cared, as long as he kept the pretty rich girl on his arm. Jeremy stopped focusing on the circumstances of permission and walked to the car.

Inside the house, Avery turned to Dane.

"Why'd you give that girl such a grilling?" Avery asked.

"She's trouble. The O'Leary's have always been trouble." Dane sighed.

"I like her." Jeremy's mother silenced any more foul talk of Nicole. The two men looked at each other, and resumed their watching of the baseball game.

That was the weirdest thing I have ever seen." Jeremy said as he loaded himself into the car.

"They seemed nice enough." Nicole smiled.

"They seemed like different people, all because I brought a girl home." Jeremy sighed.

"They thought you were gay." Nicole concluded.

"What?!" Jeremy wasn't expecting that.

"Sure," Nicole stood firm in her diagnosis. "They've never seen you bring a girl home."

Natalie snickered. Elizabeth slapped her arm. Nicole smiled and continued her theory.

"Anyhow," She put a hand on Jeremy's arm to soften the blow. "They've never really seen you showing a healthy interest in women. Most of your time is spent at school or at work, or with guy friends, right?"

"Right, I guess." Jeremy muttered.

"And you work at the GAP of all places." Nicole continued. "So they thought you might be gay. Now that they suspect you might get laid by what your mother referred to as the 'prettiest girl in school', they're ecstatic and only want to help you achieve that goal."

"You really think that's true?" Jeremy's heart sank.

"Sorry," Natalie interrupted, putting a hand on his knee. "But we've all seen the Gay Son Syndrome before."

Jeremy's head bowed.

"How much lamer could I be." He sighed. The girls laughed.

"If it's any consolation," Nicole said as Natalie pulled the car away from his house. "You probably will get laid tonight."

Mrs. Bloom watched them leave through the front door. Nicole had been right in her thinking. Now that his parents were sure of his heterosexual lifestyle, they were a bit overeager to help him succeed in the endeavor. The Bloom's would celebrate in their own way. Mrs. Bloom would open a box of wine. She and her husband would make love during the seventh inning stretch, and the Cubs would go on to win the game. Dane would leave after midnight and hold up a small convenience store for a mere 200$.

They decided to stop and buy liquor now, as opposed to later. Jeremy, Elizabeth, and Natalie waited in the car, which was awkward for him. They discussed the intricate story of how exactly Nicole and Natalie were but weren't related.

Nicole entered the store alone, at her own request. Jackson was stacking 12-packs of beer in a Budweiser display. He looked up as the bell over the door rang.

"Hey, Nicky. Where's the stud?" He asked.

"Where's your cheering section?" Did you leave them on someone else's porch for once?" Nicole spat.

"Nope. Turns out there's a big party over at the Barbarossa place." Jackson said matter-of-factly, as if Nicole wouldn't already know that.

"And being a 24-year old male, you have nothing better to do than go to a high school party. You think because you dropped out as a senior that you're still counted as a classmate?" Nicole asked.

"Like there won't be guys over 18 there." Jackson attempted to justify himself.

"Maybe, but they'll all be useful people, actually attending college. I'm curious, Jackson: Does the term, 'statutory rape' mean anything to you? I mean, are your friends asking these girls before they grope them?"

"Nicky, if the grass is green, some one's got to mow it." Jackson smiled.

"You're disgusting."

"Does that mean Elizabeth will be with you when you show up?" Jackson asked.

Nicole walked over to her brother and stood inches from him.

"If you ever touch her, Jackson, whether she says she wants it or not, I'll fucking kill you." Nicole jabbed a finger into his chest hard enough to bury her nail through his shirt and into his skin. Jackson stumbled back and gave a laugh. It was a hollow retort. The pain on his face let her know that he had been physically hurt. Nicole made a 180-degree turn and marched to an aisle filled with hard liquor. She selected a bottle of gin and then grabbed a six-pack of a popular German beer.

"So, I'm assuming you're going to show up no matter what I say." Nicole spoke to her brother as she made her way to the counter. Jackson, seeing her ready to make a purchase, walked around the counter and stood behind the register.

"You know it." He rubbed his chest where a small dot of red had stained his ancient Beastie Boys t-shirt. "Plus, the Ill Feted are going to be playing there."

The Ill Feted were a local alternative/punk group that had been trying to get a record deal for years. They were not much older than Nicole, maybe 3-4 years at most. She had even dated the lead singer for a bit on one of her and Chad's many "breaks". They played the same 10-song set at every gig they managed to slither into, and 6 of the 10 were cover songs ranging from KISS to the Sex Pistols.

"Great. Nothing like more mid-20's dropouts playing poorly stylized pop-emo-punk." Nicole threw a 50$ bill on the counter.

"So mom and dad gave my rent money to you, huh?" Jackson was trying to rile her up again.

"Keep the change, dick." Nicole snatched a pack of cigarettes from the counter display. She stormed out of the store with the bottle in her hand and the box tucked under her arm.

"See you later!" Jackson called after her. "And Elizabeth too, I hope!"

Nicole plowed her bottom into the backseat of Natalie's car, next to Jeremy. She thrust the beer into his lap and held the bottle of gin between her knees. With the vigor of a southern mother giving her child the switch, Nicole began to pack her carcinogen sticks. Jeremy was confused as to her sudden change of character, but didn't say anything. Natalie and Lizzie knew exactly what had happened. Jeremy wasn't aware of just how volatile the relationship between Nicole and her brother was. He thought their banter was just that, because he had no idea what lay beneath it all. Natalie and Elizabeth were unaware of the basis for the hatred as well, but they knew exactly how any amount of time spent with Nicole and Jackson together affected their friend. Nicole never interacted with Jackson and came away happy.

"Nicole," Natalie broke the silence. "Jeremy offered to kick in money for the booze while you were gone. Lizzie and I didn't know what to do." Natalie knew what to do, but wanted to take this opportunity to cheer Nicole up.

It worked. Nicole smiled.

"Jeremy, I don't need you to buy anything for me." Nicole informed him.

"I just thought it was the right thing to do." He explained.

"It would be, but I'm not broke, sweetheart." Nicole put three cigarettes in her mouth and lit them all. She passed one to Lizzie and one to Natalie. Nicole raised her eyebrows at Jeremy. He silently declined and the group went on their way.

By the time they reached Veronica's house, 2/3 of the bottle of gin had been consumed, along with half of the six-pack. Jeremy himself had only taken in one of the beers. His experimentation with liquor had been minimal prior to meeting Nicole, and he was well aware of his limitations. Even now, his head was light and his bladder felt full. He planned to refuse any more offers for a drink the rest of the night. Being Nicole's passed-out, lightweight date wasn't on the agenda, even if an ass-kicking was.

The Barbarossa home was large, even by the standards of Nicole's echelon. Nicole knew it had 6 bedrooms, and 4 ½ bathrooms, just like everyone else did. Veronica failed to miss an opportunity to brag about her family's financial status. Natalie, Nicole and Elizabeth had also been to the house at prior social gatherings. Most times, they managed to get along with the hostess well enough to avoid any major incidents. Jeremy was one of the social misfits. Previously, he had only dreamt of being invited to one of the legendary parties at Veronica's house. He was aghast at the sheer size and glory of the home.

The house itself sat within it's own brick fence upon a small hill. The hill was more of a lump in the ground, but a big enough lump to foist the house a few feet higher than its neighbors. Lights formed parallel landing strips up the drive way. Tonight, the large cast-iron gates with the fabricated letter B on each side had been left open. Cars lined the drive-way all with way to the front door. The drive-way itself was nearly a hundred feet long and ended in a circle around a marble fountain of a mermaid allowing her babe to suckle. Drunken teenagers and young adults littered the lawn. Their numbers grew the nearer one got to the house itself. The sound of music could be heard from outside the perimeter fence. Lights and silhouettes were in every window on all three floors of the home.

As people noticed Natalie's car they began to migrate towards the house. Even these lower castes of high school society knew that there was to be a momentous confrontation tonight. The queen had been caught with the stable boy and the king had chosen another. Everyone loves a tragedy. Tonight they were anticipating the equivalent of a school bus running into the nursery at a hospital while on fire. The stage had been set earlier when Chad changed his Facebook status to single. Tonight the tip-top of the social ladder was to undergo a vast restructuring with a possible, but unlikely, complete collapse. All came to watch. Some came to choose sides when it was over. Some came because it was one of those rare occasions where even the most common of the commoners would be allowed access to this arena. Through Jeremy, they saw a chance for themselves. They saw a way into the popular cliques with what they perceived to be little or no selling out. They weren't aware of how much Jeremy would be required to sacrifice for his flirtation with nobility.

Natalie pulled her car past all of the others; The SUV's and the foreign imports that stood as symbols of wealth wasted on the fancy of youth. She stopped nearly at the front door. Ignoring any responsibility in parking, she shut down her vehicle parallel to the Jaguar that everyone knew to be Veronica's. A very large crowd had gathered. They stood as media at a movie premier, making a walkway for the stars. They waited to catch the fodder for gossip of weeks to come: the first visage of Nicole and her cinderfella as they exited their carriage.

Natalie actually exited first. She more than anyone was used to playing Nicole's second. She knew her role in this dramatic event, as did Elizabeth. Both women had long ago come to terms with their standing concerning Nicole. They understood and accepted this as a blessing, not a curse. As such, Natalie filled the role of a bodyguard, whereas Elizabeth was more of a personal assistant only because secretary was no longer a politically correct term.

Natalie immediately cut off two juniors who were trying to actually open the door for Nicole. Elizabeth busied herself telling a group of semi-popular and gossip hungry sophomores where exactly it was that Nicole had found such a fabulous shirt.

"I feel like a rock star or something." Jeremy's hands were drenched with sweat. He dried them on his pant legs.

"Tonight," Nicole straightened his collar. "You are. It's kind of a rush, isn't it?"

"Yeah." Jeremy didn't know which gave him the bigger rush: the fear or the excitement.

"It's called popularity. It has no monetary value, but people fight and kill over it. Don't let it go to your head. That's the secret. Or you might not only forget where you came from, but who you are." Nicole's words were strangely calming. The noise of the crowd outside the car was frantic, but Nicole wasn't. At least she didn't show it. She squeezed one of his hands.

"Now be a dear, Jeremy, and carry the beer. I think I'll carry the bottle." Nicole snatched the liquor off of the floor and exited the car. The crowd of 10-15 people was silent for a fraction of a second. To Nicole, it was a lifetime. This was that moment. This was what being the most popular girl in school was all about; This one second when everyone stopped to give her their undivided attention.

Whispers and mumbles erupted as Jeremy appeared at her side. They had all seen him in the car, so they knew he was indeed there, but to see him actually in the flesh emerge validated their hopes and dreams. Jeremy himself felt awkward and uncomfortable. He had always been a mere shadow, unnoticed. Now he was the essential prince charming who still felt like the inconsequential frog. It was as if

Nicole had told them, "Behold! All it takes is one day and I can create the most beautiful of the beautiful people!," only because they saw what she wanted them to see. Jeremy himself felt the truth. He was merely a bolt in a cog in a machine much larger than he.

"What are you all doing out here? Isn't the party inside?" Nicole began taking a drink while walking to the front door. Jeremy followed suit with the grace of a rusty puppet whose joints were lubricated with super glue. It was only luck that he didn't fall and injure himself as he twisted the cap off of a bottle of beer and put it to his mouth. He was mimicking her, even though he had thought earlier that drinking further was a bad idea. Now it seemed that a drink was the antidote to the sickness to his stomach. Nicole watched him take a sip. As he pulled the bottle away from his lips, Nicole tilted the base of it to keep it pouring. Jeremy struggled to stop a cataclysmic spill. He puckered and swallowed every drop like a newborn at the nipple. The crowd that had now tripled in size began to chant: "Chug, chug, chug."

Chug Jeremy did. When Nicole first touched the bottle, he had assumed she was trying to embarrass him. Now he understood that she was endearing him to this world of excess and fervor. People who had never known his name before today were cheering him now. He finished the beer and the crowd erupted. It was a baptism of fire before the congregation to alleviate any doubts about his rights to be on the arm of the Grand Queen. He answered the people with a belch into the night sky as a coyote howls at the moon. With his trepidation awash in a sea of liquid courage, Jeremy allowed Nicole's enchantment to carry him over the threshold of Veronica's house.

Inside, people milled about, red plastic cups glued to their hands. These were the people who doubted that Nicole would show up or thought that the rumors about her and Jeremy were untrue. Jeremy himself was amazed at the house. It opened into a large foyer that led directly to a remarkable winding staircase as wide as a small sofa. Large double oak doors were opened on either side of the staircase. People were everywhere. Jeremy didn't see how anyone could breathe in the congestion, let alone move about. As Nicole led Jeremy through the house, voices went silent, and the people parted. After they passed, murmurs slithered about. Nicole gave nods and compliments to those that she knew/had decided to acknowledge. Jeremy nodded and smiled uneasily as random people patted him on the back. Elizabeth, who had followed them with Natalie, busied herself with dispelling gossip overheard as they passed. It was damage control before any damage could be done.

Jeremy noticed the deeper they moved into the viper's den, the more notorious the faces he saw. The house itself seemed to be layered based on the social level of the people, much like the bonfire had been. They nobles weren't keeping the peasant's away from them, as much as they were keeping themselves away from the peasants. The cliques and groups that frequented these parties were xenophobes. They feared those that they didn't know, and were even intimidated by them. Jeremy didn't know what facets of their society they represented. All he could discern was that there were identifiable pods of people within the differing social sects. He was suddenly saddened. He didn't understand how or why people lived like this. He had been average and normal his entire life. He couldn't fathom living this way and he hoped Nicole didn't expect him to.

Nicole had taken him left through one set of the large oak doors into a room that was set with couches covered in what appeared to be velvet. Paintings of enormous value from dead Greenwich Village artists hung on the walls. The room itself was the size of half his entire house. They continued through this room and through a sliding glass door. They exited the house onto a patio area. Jeremy was able to take in the majesty of a backyard that could have been a small public park. The band had set up what little equipment they had next to the pool. Here the Ill Feted butchered their own songs. A crowd danced around the pool like a group of village idiots. Every few seconds someone was thrown into the water, causing the crowd to roar. Nicole scanned the area and found one segment of cobblestone patio that stood out due to its relative lack of activity. Bordering the end of the oblong shaped pool was a hot tub. The swim team surrounded the cheerleading team here. They sat on reclining wrought iron pool chairs. One pool chair was separated from the others. Here the demon queen fulfilled her succubus role with Chad. Nicole glanced toward the band before she continued to walk. The lead singer had been singing while looking directly at her. She acknowledged him with a flimsy nod. They had some good times together in their short fling, and they both recognized that without sharing it publicly.

The swim team began grumbling as Nicole and Jeremy approached. Nicole had to pull Jeremy with her. He had stood still when she began moving, his feet unable to willfully take him to his doom. Chad pushed Veronica aside and waited for Nicole to get within earshot. He wanted to speak first, but Nicole beat him to it.

"So I see you heard I'd moved on." Nicole stood a few foot from the lounge chair with hands on her hips, a bottle of gin dangling from her right.

"Finally." Natalie muttered louder than usual on purpose from behind Nicole.

"Yeah, I bet you're happy, dike." Eric B. snapped his head toward Natalie, fulfilling his wingman role.

Nicole ignored this banter and focused on the real threat at hand.

"I just want you to know, Chad, that we can resolve this like the young adults we are." Nicole waited, wagging the bottle in her hand. The band onstage had noticed that they were losing the crowd. Bradlee Van Graham, the lead singer of the Ill Feted had thought this might happen, when news of the local goings on had reached him. He himself was only two years older than Nicole and her class, and knew of her power over the people. The band lowered its tune and watched with the rest of the gathering.

"You know better than that, Nicole." Chad stood, inching his way toward them with visible menace. "You embarrassed me, and you embarrassed yourself with this crap you pulled. You went behind my back, again, and made this loser some kind of lover. You made me look like a fool, after everything I did for you." Chad tried to play a victim of some sort.

"Like that's never happened before." Natalie played on Chad's last statement. The crowd near enough to hear laughed. Chad disregarded her. He began balling his fists.

"I made you, Nicole." He pointed at her, fingers digging into his palms. "I gave you everything, and this is how you repay me."

"Repay you?! Made me?! Are you truly trying to convince anyone that this is the first time you and Veronica have been together, because you sure look comfortable with one another. Are we not counting the time she had her lips on your scrotum and a thumb up your bum?" Nicole stopped denying the truth, allowing everyone who had seen it to publicly talk about it now. No longer would she protect him and his ego, while punishing those who spoke the truth on the matter.

"That's bullshit!" Eric shouted. Chad was in shock. He stopped, not sure how to respond. Veronica's continuous smile didn't help any defense he intended to mount.

"Is it now, Eric?" Nicole continued. "Then how exactly did Chad get those anal fissures that kept him out of those 3 swim meets that year?"

"That was a pulled hamstring, Nicole. Don't you start any lies." Chad stood now within arm's reach of Nicole and Jeremy.

"Was it?" Nicole asked the question on everyone's mind, moving close enough so that only Chad could hear her. "Don't make me take this any further, for your sake." She warned with the truth of a gunslinger.

Chad gritted his teeth loud enough for her to hear them squeal.

"I ain't no faggot." Chad pushed Nicole aside and cocked back his fist. Jeremy took a step back, intending to try and roll with the crushing blow coming his way. As Chad stepped forward there was a sharp intake of breath from the crowd. Jeremy closed his eyes. He never saw Nicole regain her balance. He never saw her lash out with the fury of a tigress. He never saw the bottle of gin refuse to break as it crashed into Chad's cheek. Chad stuttered back a step, and Nicole hit him again, this time breaking the bottle cleanly on his forehead, gashing it open. Jeremy's eyes snapped open at the sound. He did see Nicole preparing to deliver another blow as Chad fell to the ground. The band had stopped playing entirely.

"She fuckin' killed him!" Eric shouted with the pain of an abandoned lover. Chad let loose a loud snore, shattering Eric's accusations of murder.

"Hey Nicole!"

She turned to Bradlee Van Graham.

"Bradlee," She smiled. "The drama's over. I think the people are ready to hear some music again." She waved the busted bottle at him. Bradlee nodded, and counted off. His band followed him into an average pop-punk ballad. The people continued to talk about Chad, but did so while milling away from the scene of the crime. The event had come and gone in a matter of seconds. The king (Chad) was dead. Long live the king (Jeremy). Nicole turned back to Veronica who was pressing a towel into Chad's forehead, helping Eric to try and wake him. Nicole pushed them aside.

"Move." She commanded them. "I've done this more than once." She told them. Eric knew it to be true. Veronica just didn't want her date to be knocked out all night.

Nicole took a beer from Jeremy, and stood over Chad. She opened it, and poured the contents on his face, washing away the small trail of blood. Nothing happened at first. Chad's chest heaved after a moment, and he began to cough. His eyes opened slowly. He shook the blanket of unconsciousness away and sat up.

"So here we are." Nicole stepped back.

"Look." Veronica finally spoke, her demure smile now gone.

"No," Nicole stopped her. "This is how it's going to be. I've moved on. I'm not going to be made a fool of by you two anymore. You do as you please, and no one touches Jeremy, understand?"

"No way." Eric B. Spoke for Chad. Chad slapped an arm into Eric's gut. Veronica and Eric helped him to his feet.

"Fine." Chad spoke at last. "I was done with you anyway." He shrugged Veronica off and turned to Eric. "This party sucks. Let's go see what else we can find."

Natalie refrained from making another poke at Chad's homosexuality. The swim team trickled out. Not one of them had the stones to look Nicole in the eyes as they passed. Eric B. attempted to jump at Jeremy in order to make the latter flinch. Jeremy, who wasn't paying attention, looked like quite the tough guy for not moving an inch. Natalie slapped Eric in the back of the head. Some of those at the party were still paying attention in case Nicole and Veronica began battling. Veronica stood alone now. Even the cheerleaders who had been at her side had shifted away. They were back near Nicole, where they had been when Veronica first joined the team. The more things changed, the more they stayed the same.

"It doesn't have to be this way." Nicole offered simply.

"Oh, shut up," Veronica snapped. "You wouldn't be happy if you couldn't ruin everything for me." She scowled. Nicole took Jeremy by the arm and walked back toward the house amid soft cheers and a few whistles. Elizabeth melted off into the crowd, chatting with anyone who hadn't seen the action to let them know exactly what happened. Veronica hung her head. Black tears, stained with mascara and pain fell to the concrete at her feet.

"Sweetie," Natalie put a hand on Veronica's arm. "If you really think any of this was about you, then you are further gone than anyone thought." Veronica began to openly weep to the snickers of the crowd. Natalie reluctantly offered a shoulder. She walked Veronica into the house and to her room. It was here and now that the disassembling of Nicole's surrogate family would begin.

"So that was interesting." Jeremy took a drink of cheap, light, keg beer. He and Nicole had found some privacy in a secluded gazebo off of the main house. The area was one that had oddly been neglected by gardeners. Nicole knew the reason. Veronica's stepmother had requested it left alone after her miscarriage. She didn't tell Jeremy of this. It was somewhat morbid. Vines grew out of control, swarming the stone monument that had been erected to a life that had never been given the chance to live. They were akin to ants on a mound of sugar: relentlessly devouring and inescapable. The thing that struck Jeremy as odd was the small bench in the gazebo. It was a stone bench bookended by lion heads. The strange thing was the lack of any foliage. The stone was well worn, as if used frequently. Nicole knew why, but if Jeremy wasn't asking, she wasn't telling. Every morning, Veronica's mother would come to this gazebo after taking her morning Prozac. She would sit here sipping exquisite, imported green tea from china cups that had long ago moved beyond reasonable prices.

"'The Universe will not end with a bang, but with a whimper'... But you had fun, right? And you ended up okay, just like I promised." Nicole sought validation of a sort.

"Yeah." Jeremy obliged. "It was exciting, but a little anticlimactic. It's nice to have a girlfriend who kicks ass."

Nicole's face jerked at the title he had bestowed upon her.

"I mean... that just slipped out. The girlfriend part." Jeremy attempted a recovery.

"It's okay." Nicole smiled. "I think I'd like to be your girlfriend."

She gently kissed his cheek.

"I don't always get you." Jeremy admitted, turning to face her.

"On the contrary. You've entered the stratosphere of popularity now, because you did manage to get me." Nicole played with words.

"No, I mean," Jeremy sighed. His emotions were intense, and it was becoming harder for him to clearly state his feelings. "It's like I never know what you're going to do next. Like one minute we're... making love... and the next you're chopping squirrels up or beating someone with a bottle. I don't know how to help you find a healthy outlet for all this rage you have, Nicole. More importantly, I don't know how to keep you happy. And that scares me."

"Sweetie, I'm a big girl. You let me worry about me."

"I can't, Nicole. I think I love you. When you love someone, you can't just let them go it alone." Jeremy put himself out there, not caring about the consequences.

"You love me?" Nicole blinked away a tear.

"Yeah." Jeremy said with self-realization. "I've never felt like this before. My body trembles when you touch me. My eyes and attention are drawn to your voice. I can't stand not being with you. I can't imagine going on without you."

"Let's go. I want to show you something." Nicole grabbed him by the arm.

She led Jeremy back toward the brothel of debauchery that was Veronica's house. As they neared, the sounds of the party began to overtake them again. Nicole narrowly avoided a rain of vomit from a third floor window. She leapt away with the litheness of a cat and immediately scanned her shoes and pants for any chunks that may have splashed onto her. She and Jeremy looked up to find the offender. A woman, not a girl, but a grown woman with waist length onyx hair was leaning out of the window. Spittle stained her cheeks. Drool hung from her lips to the second story. She was topless, and shaking violently. One would think it was tremors if not for the bestial rhythm of her movement, and the loud grunting coming from the room she resided halfway in. A young man was visible standing behind her. He was emphasizing each of his thrusts with a low, drunken growl. As he gyrated his pelvis, he was sure that he was giving her the best intercourse of her life. The idea that he was woefully inadequate couldn't enter his mind due to the male cheering section behind him.

"Who's that?" Jeremy asked after seeing no look of surprise on Nicole's face. He was ready to jump into action to save the woman from what was obvious to him as a rape in progress.

"Slow down." Nicole held him back. "That's Veronica's stepmother. It's not an aberration. Why do you think Veronica's so popular with the boys? People don't learn to be whores all by themselves."

"That's kinda harsh." Jeremy muttered.

"But it's true."

"It sure looks like a sexual assault."

"You can't rape the willing." The vile declaration rolled from Nicole's mouth. "I hate that statement, but it's brutally honest in this instance."

"So we aren't going to do anything?" Jeremy couldn't believe that this went on with no intervention.

"What do you want to do? Rush up there with our 'Captain-Save-a-Hoe' capes on and interrupt a perfectly consensual gang bang? For what? Your ego? Are you in the mood to be told by thirty or so people to go fuck yourself?"

"Okay, calm down."

"You've got to learn that you can't save the world, Jeremy. The majority of us can't save ourselves, and what are human beings successful at more often than self–destruction?"

"And the minority of us?" Jeremy asked, challenging her.

"What?" She raised an eyebrow.

"The minority. If the majority can't save themselves, then shouldn't the minority do something to help them?"

Nicole smiled.

"You'll never stop trying to be a hero, will you?" She said after the moment had passed. She mashed her lips together, readying her argument. "The minority get tricked. They are persuaded to fight people in the same predicaments, all but guaranteeing no sort of victory. Why do you think that the white population, though in the minority, is still able to control 99% of the country and world? The minority, be it race, creed, nationality, are tricked into fighting amongst one another. So those who could truly help are trapped fighting each other, while those who can't help themselves continue to take all they can and trash it."

"So you believe that a large portion of the world, if not almost everyone, is insanely ignorant?" Jeremy was aghast.

"You don't? Look at all the protests in this country. Instead of doing something, people promoting peace stand in the road holding signs, while their opponents aim rifles at them. Our ruling class allowed and for a time encouraged the military to actively seek high school dropouts and miscreants, instead of honor roll students. And once we got them in uniform, we paid them less, and gave them less benefits in exchange for their lives. These are people that are asked to die for us, Jeremy. I'd say they deserve a little better.

"Take a look at businesses. Did you know that Wal-Mart forces their clients to continually lower prices. Say a small food company gets an item in Wal-Mart, thus securing a victory over their competitors. Now this client has to keep lowering their prices. So yes, they have the largest national retailer on their side, but they are constantly losing more and more profit to do so. And this continues until they cannot afford the cost of doing business with Wal-Mart. At this point Wal-Mart can force the small company lower their prices again, or make an offer to one of the small company's competitors. So while the two food companies fight it out, the world's largest retailer makes billions, and wins either way.

"Those who are destroying all that they can trick the little ones who could be doing something into fighting one another. And the worst part is that they destroy it all in the name of family values and morality. That's the trick. Tell people it's good for them, and they will let you get away with anything." Nicole continued onward. Several globules of undigested food trickling down from above emphasized her point. Jeremy took one last look before shuffling behind Nicole in defeat.

Inside the house, they encountered a long line of gentleman winding up the staircase. Jeremy figured it was for the bathroom. Then he remembered the scene he had just left. At the end of the line was none other than Jackson O'Leary.

"Waiting for your turn?" Nicole sighed at her older brother.

"Hey, Nicki, I'm not the only one." Jackson swept an arm in the direction of the line before him.

"No, but you are the last one. How disgusting is that?" Nicole asked.

"Whatever, I'll take what I can get. Where's Elizabeth, while we're talking about it."

Nicole's face went blank.

"This is the last time I am telling you, Jackson. If you touch her, I. Will. Kill. You. Where you stand."

"My sis," Jackson nodded at Jeremy. "Always the serious one."

Nicole tired of this eternal cycle of arguments. Her brother was the last person she wanted to deal with tonight. There would be plenty of time for that later...

With a flick of her wrist and middle finger, Jackson ceased to exist in her current reality. Nicole moved through the crowded home with her "try-me" swagger, continuing to search for Natalie or Elizabeth. It was Jeremy who spotted one of the two. Elizabeth was nestled in the center of a crowd, retelling the night's events to late-comers. They showed the proper respect by moving before having to be asked.

"Gossipmonger." Nicole gave Elizabeth a hug.

"They asked, so I just had to tell them. It's not exactly everyday that Chad's ex-girl pimp-smacks him with a fifth of gin." Elizabeth's take on things drew the requisite chuckles from those listening. "But you two sure have been absent for awhile."

Nicole nodded to her left at Jeremy.

"Yeah, we're actually going to head out now. I was just looking for Natalie to make sure you two got home safe."

"Oh, Nicky. She is so bad." Elizabeth shook her head and grinned while referring to their absent friend. "Her and Veronica have been connected at the lips for the past half hour. The last I saw, they had quarantined the hot tub for themselves."

"Sluts." Nicole smiled. "It's always a party once we show up, isn't it?"

"Yeah." Elizabeth agreed. "This one is never going to be forgotten."

"Yes, it will." Nicole thought out loud.

"Call me tomorrow, Elizabeth. Okay? And be safe. And don't talk to my brother or the bottom-feeder patrol he came with, alright?" Nicole played the concerned mother.

"I will, and I won't." Elizabeth promised. "You want me to call a cab for you now?" Elizabeth opened her cell-phone.

"Please do." Nicole accepted the offer. Elizabeth dialed away. Nicole and her prize possession continued to the back yard. The party was quieter than before. The band had finished playing and now a savage, bass-heavy dance track played on the speakers.

"Isn't this a little weird?" Jeremy asked.

"What? My cousin and my hated enemy making out? Or two teenaged glamazons putting on a burlesque show in the water?" Nicole eyed Natalie and Veronica, both fully clothed and submerged up to their shoulders in the hot tub. They had a small crowd of their own as they made a juvenile attempt at drunken passion. Natalie knew she was using Veronica for the same reason Chad had; it was the closest she could get to truly having Nicole. Veronica, though not brilliant, understood that she was being used and didn't care. Even if it was false, a hollow infatuation made her feel wanted.

"Well," Jeremy elaborated. "Don't you hate Veronica?"

"Yeah, for the most part." Nicole admitted.

"So then how are you okay with this?"

"She'll never choose Veronica over me. And maybe... Maybe, Natalie can train her to not be such a bitch."

"And Natalie can't get burned by this in any way?"

"Jeremy, after seeing what you have tonight, you should now two things: 1) you have to risk to gain. 2) We don't get burned, we do the burning."

With that the argument was settled. Jeremy had no rebuttal. Nicole said a short good-bye and congratulations to Natalie. Natalie reciprocated and Nicole left. The cab that Elizabeth had called was waiting at the ornate gate entrance to Veronica's home. On the ride, Nicole told Jeremy the most embarrassing stories about those who had attended the party tonight.

When they arrived at her house, she allowed him to pay the cab driver. He insisted that no gentleman should ever let a lady pay for a cab ride. Drinks and dinner may be okay, but he wouldn't settle for her paying the taxi fare.

Nicole's house was dark inside, save for the running television. A TV salesman pitched a set of "truly incredible, downright innovative" knives to her darkened home. Her mother was knocked out on the couch, where Nicole had last seen her. Her father slept soundly alone in his bed. Nicole could hear him snoring through the bedroom door. Jeremy waited patiently in the entryway to the house. Nicole instructed him to meet her in his room. As he trotted off, she went into the kitchen. She took 3 bottles of water from the refrigerator.

Nicole strutted into the living room where her mother struggled to survive the rigorous dreams of depression and intoxication. Nicole set one bottle of water down, and opened it. She took a Kleenex tissue from the box on the table and with the touch of a cherub she began wiping the crusted drool from her mother's face. Finding it hard to wash away, Nicole folded a corner of the tissue, and dipped it in the bottle of water. Once more, she worked on cleansing her mother. Nicole was careful not to wake her. Once finished, she scooped up the unopened bottles of water and her mother's bottle of liquor. She dumped the liquor down the sink in the bathroom. Afterward, she vowed to get rid of the remaining liquor in the house when she woke the next day. She wouldn't let her mother give up on herself so easily.

Interlude: Anatomy of Infidelity:
The Ballad of Harold O'Leary

He was smart. He was successful. He was respected. He was useful. Harold O'Leary held all these truths of himself to be self-evident. What he wasn't: happy. His life had been slowly rolling down a hill of mediocrity into a sea of despair. He felt hollow and alone. His wife wanted nothing to do with him. His daughter had hated him for longer than he could remember. His son was an utter failure. All of his varied and impressive achievements in biochemistry were overshadowed in his mind by his deepening sense of gloom. On the morning that his daughter drunkenly marched into the GAP to accost Jeremy, Harold was watching his assistant/intern Rebecca leave his desk. It was at this moment that he decided his marriage was over. He decided to take something for himself.

Harold waited for Rebecca to disappear from view. Immediately, he turned to his computer monitor, and looked at his reflection. He fixed his middle-aged hair as best he could. He told himself that he was a good-looking man. Why shouldn't a girl of her age want to try something with him? He knew she wanted to impress the company, and Harold was well embedded in the workings of Hallibush labs. He could use that to his advantage. He knew it was manipulative and cruel, but he didn't care. This wasn't about Rebecca's feelings or self-respect. This was about his pants. Harold hadn't had sex with anyone other than himself in the bathroom panting over a magazine in over 2 years. Rebecca seemed interested in him. She always gave him that wry smile. She often asked him to come out for drinks, albeit she was inviting him to come out with the rest of the staff after work as well, but still, she always extended the invitation to him, whereas no one else did. She wanted him, and if she didn't, she would.

Harold sat back in his chair, and unaware that he was even doing it, turned the picture of his family face down. As he began reading slowly through his long list of e-mails, Rebecca reappeared with a two fresh cups of coffee from the coffee stand in the main lobby, and a pile of papers under her arm. She knew what Harold liked, from months of fetching his standard order: One cappuccino double shot with whipped cream, no sugar. She held a cup of her own that was an exotic blend that included chocolate and whipped cream topped with caramel.

"Here you go, Mr. O'Leary." She set his cup on the cup holder on his desk. He pulled up a chair from behind his desk and motioned for her to sit. It was a courtesy he had never shown before. Rebecca was somewhat taken aback by his sudden show of interest. Harold smiled at her.

"How long have you been working here?" He asked.

"Well, uh, 7 months now. Not really working. I'm still an intern. There's no openings yet and even then, there's the waiting list." Rebecca grinned weakly. She had waited for this day for some time. She had been grinding away for free while going to school on loans that would take her years to repay just to get noticed by someone at this company. Her assignment to Harold hadn't been her choice, but she had welcomed it. She knew from the moment she saw him that he was susceptible to temptation. If screwing Harold O'Leary for a few months got her the job she needed, Rebecca was ready to accept that duty. It was her bold determination and acceptance that would put her in control of this relationship. Harold O'Leary never stood a chance.

"And you've called me Mr. O'Leary every day, no matter how much we've worked together." Harold flashed his teeth. "I don't think we have been properly introduced, and that is my fault, I must admit." This simple statement could have gone a long way to fixing his breaking home, had Harold ever used it there with the sincerity he had with Rebecca.

"I'm Harold." He extended a hand.

"Rebecca." She gave him a dainty shake. As he pulled his hand away, she held for just a second longer. It wasn't a large signal. In fact, it could just be misconstrued as a reflexive action. But she had put it out there. Now that he was noticing her, it was time to go to work. Rebecca had been listening in on many of Harold's personal calls here at the office. She worked in the small cubicle next to him every day; it wasn't snooping so much as it was paying attention to her surroundings. She knew he was having trouble at home, and would use that to her advantage.

"Well, please, call me Harold."

"Okay, Harold." She smiled.

"Now, those results." He motioned for her to give him the bundle of papers under her arm.

"Oh, yeah." She pretended to be lost in his charm.

Harold took the papers from her and began to swiftly sift through them. With an abrupt jerk, he set the papers on his lap and looked at her.

"You know, I was kind of in a rush this morning, and ran out without bothering to grab a bite to eat."

"Oh, do you want me to go get you something?" She offered.

"I was thinking of going myself. Would you like to come?" He had to test the waters. His offer was not out of line, or inappropriate. Co-workers in all facets of life went to eat together. He was one of those who would attempt to use this relationship to begin an illicit affair. Rebecca paused at his offer, not wanting to seem too eager.

"Well, technically, I'm supposed to stay on the grounds for my entire 8 hour day, as my internship contract states." She frowned.

"Actually, it says that you must remain on company task for those 8 hours, and if we're reviewing results while we eat, that's a company task. Besides, I have a little pull at this place, remember? If I say you can leave the building, you can leave the building." Harold flaunted his position of power.

"Well, breakfast does sound good. To tell you the truth, I skimped this morning myself and crammed in half a pop-tart on the drive here." Rebecca admitted.

"Great." Harold clapped his hands together. "I know a diner that makes these great Belgian waffles." And he did. Because his wife had shown it to him when they were dating.

The diner that Harold spoke of was a family owned, self-proclaimed "greasy spoon". It was a small affair, with 8 booths, and short counter that had 6 small stools crammed up next to it. You know the place. No one besides the locals ever stops in, unless it's the last choice on a road trip where cash has run so low that even Denny's is out of the question. The grand old American mom and pop breakfast/lunch shop. The place where everything seems to have the flavor of the morning's bacon because everything is cooked right in the very same bacon grease, and finding the cook's cigarette ashes peppering your scrambled eggs is a distinct possibility. The diner was a throwback to a time when people really could take a pocketful of cash and relocate to start fresh in America. It was a testament to hard work and daily hustling and bustling to keep the bills paid.

The stools were taken by the usual retirees who drank black coffee, read the morning paper, smoked and ordered the same bland meals every day in order to make sure they stayed regular. If there are two things retired men know well, it's the weather, and their bowel habits. Only one of the booths had a patron. He was an elderly gentleman reading yesterday's paper. At his age, yesterday's news could be tomorrow's news. Over the years, it had all blurred into one big mess. Things were always going down the proverbial tubes in one part of the world or another, and if they didn't love us (U.S.?), then they hated us.

Harold hoped that the nostalgic effect of the building would help loosen Rebecca's thighs a bit. He also assumed that no one he knew would come here, including his wife. Hell, she was probably drunk off of her ass on the couch right now. He also didn't want to foot too large of a bill just in case his plans didn't come to fruition. Rebecca was indeed somewhat impressed by the diner. It was nice, in a 50's kind of way. The atmosphere of a restaurant is something that cannot be replicated or falsified. The authenticity of this building stirred something in everyone who entered it's doors. It had been opened and run by the same family for over half of a century, and in today's come and go franchised world, that's saying something.

The diner used no type of host/hostess. Harold simply led Rebecca to a corner booth. It wasn't completely away from the windows, but it was as close as he could get. The booth was half covered by a window, and he offered this seat to Rebecca.

"Oh, wait." She said standing back up as he sat. "We forgot the papers from last night's results in the car."

"Don't bother." Harold grabbed her wrist a bit too eagerly. He hurriedly retracted his hand. "I mean, I didn't really want to get out of there to read the reports. I just needed a break and a bite to eat. Please."

"Okay." Rebecca conceded. This was her chance to get to know him and figure out how to exploit him. "Are you feeling alright, Harold? Is something bothering you?"

Harold O'Leary was far from alright. He was feeling downright insane at the moment. What was he doing? Was his marriage really in such a state of shambles that he had resorted to attempting to tempt an intern? Yes. Yes, it was. Harold held a hand over his lips and looked out of Rebecca's age-stained window. He blew out his breath in a hearty gust and then rubbed his hand across his face to refresh himself.

"I don't know, Rebecca. I don't know. I think I'm going to be getting a divorce. I think I messed up a long time ago, with one critical decision. I singlehandedly destroyed my family, and the one thing I could do to fix it, I can't. Even now, it would be too late, and here I am." Harold continued looking out of the window. A waitress appeared at their table. She was in her mid-forties, and every day wished that she had finished high school and not had two kids before she was in her twenties. Now she just worked, and worked hard to keep what little food she could afford on the table. Some nights, when money was low, she turned tricks at the local truck stop. Although, with all the competition in their teens, most men didn't want a well traveled woman whose breasts and labia had begun to sag.

"Can I get you two something to drink?" She offered with a smile that had been presented to each and every patron of this establishment for the past 15 years.

"Um, just a coffee for now." Harold didn't look at her.

"I'll have an orange juice, and a coffee as well." Rebecca smiled as the waitress left, not bothering to jot the small, routine order down. When the woman was out of earshot, Rebecca turned back to Harold. "Harold, is there something you want to talk about? I mean *if* you want to talk about something."

"This isn't right." Harold blurted. He had lost the backbone to go through with his plan.

"No," Rebecca put a hand on his. She wasn't letting her future get away when it was within her grasp. "Really. It's okay. I can be more than a co-worker." The double entendre was lost on neither of them. "I mean," She smiled, as if covering up a mistake. "I mean, we can be friends, right? You can talk to me. I mean it. It will make you feel better."

Harold thought a minute and then decided *what the hell*. Why not tell her? What could it hurt? That's how he came to tell her everything. Rebecca was repulsed, but didn't let it show. She could swallow the story down, for now, and pretend to see him as the victim. Harold O'Leary talked and shared and allowed himself to express what he had kept inside. This simple act of communicating was all that he had needed to do for all the years he had been married. It was all he had needed to do to have his wife and children understand him. And if he had listened to them in turn, everything would have been different. But now was too late. Now his words would have rung hollow with them. Now they were merely a tool that Rebecca would use.

"Oh, Harold. That's so sad. I don't know what I can do to help." Rebecca held his hands in hers. She could see that Harold was choking back tears. As the waitress set their drinks on the table, Rebecca felt herself not pretending to care, but actually caring about Harold. She felt a pain for him, that she didn't think was possible. It was pure pity. What she had intended to be a cold manipulation was causing emotions in her that would make the relationship real.

"So, you two ready to order?" The waitress noticed that the laminated table menu that also served as a placeholder hadn't been moved.

"Sure, just give us two of the special." Rebecca ordered. She didn't know if there was actually a special, but she figured what diner didn't have a daily special?

"Alright. Two of the special." The waitress repeated, again not bothering to write it on her small notepad. She whisked away and left the two alone again.

"Ah, it's nothing." Harold lied, taking his hands back. "I'm sorry. I shouldn't have burdened you with all of that."

"No, it was nice." Rebecca smiled.

"No, it wasn't. You probably think I'm the scum of the earth. I think I'm the scum of the earth. Even though it was so long ago."

"Exactly." Rebecca saw her opening to capitalize. "That's not you anymore, is it, Harold? That's not the you I see every day. You've changed. You may be right, it might be too late to save your marriage or reconcile with your family. That just means you'll have to start over again, I guess. But your life's not as over as you make it sound."

"Maybe." Harold conceded to her argument. Her voice was soothing, and fresh in a stagnant world. "Enough about my dysfunction, though. Tell me about you, Rebecca."

Rebecca did tell Harold about herself. Over the entire breakfast, she told him about her journey from a lower class trailer park to a scholarship to now working on her master's degree in biochemistry. She

246

told him about her family, her lost loves, and her dreams for the future. She told him of her dream to actually get a salaried position within Hallibush labs. She worked like a snake charmer, teasing him and luring him in. With each sentence, she made him want her more. Slowly, but surely, she seduced him with language.

"Well, that was refreshing." Harold slid a fifty dollar bill onto the table and stood. Rebecca followed suit.

"Yes, thank you, Harold." She slid his arm through his. It was a friendly gesture, but the electricity between them as they touched was unmistakable. They walked out of the restaurant and to his car. He opened the door for her, and she smiled. They drove back to their place of work talking now about the results of the last night's work. As Harold parked in his reserved parking space, Rebecca put a hand on his.

"I meant what I said, Harold. Thank you." She paused, looking intently at him. Harold fought the urge to kiss her there. His entire body shouted at him to take this young, supple, willing woman and ravage her.

"Yes, ahem, well." He stammered. "Maybe we could do it again some time."

"Maybe next time we could have dinner at my place." She gave a slight raise to the corners of her mouth, and exited the car. She had him.

They spent the entire day working together on making his dream a reality at the office. The new experiments had yielded some truly promising results. Harold did his best to work as near Rebecca as he could. They each shot each other passing looks as the day progressed. When 5:00 p.m. rolled around, Harold still declined to go drinking with his co-workers. He did promise to join them sometime in the future. Rebecca and Harold snuck out of the parking lot separately. He followed her in his car to her apartment. Once inside, their inhibitions were lost and they became drunk with a carnal sense of pleasure. And that's how affairs begin.

Life is Hell and Suburbia is a Lie

Chapter Eight: Things Must Get Better Before They Can Get Worse
<u>Part 2 of 3</u>

"I don't know, dear... I suppose it will feel like warmth on the wind." That was the response Mrs. O'Leary gave her daughter when pressed for information on what freedom would feel like. Three months had passed since the incident at Veronica's house. Jeremy and Nicole were still going strong, but her relations with Natalie and Elizabeth were strained at best. Nicole was spending more time alone with Jeremy and alone with herself. In public, the girls kept up the pretense of friendship, but publicly, they were growing further apart with each passing moment.

Now, three months after Nicole relieved Chad of any respect by knocking him out with a bottle, she was talking with her mother. Nicole had questioned Mrs. O'Leary's definition of freedom because that's the reasoning her mother had used when filing for divorce. Their home was alcohol free now, and it had immensely helped her mother. The alcohol-free rule only applied to her mother however. Nicole's hypocrisy ran deep. She herself still drank to deal with personal issues, and her father was imbibing a bit more regularly as well. Mrs. O'Leary had once again become the woman that Nicole remembered admiring.

Nicole and Mrs. O'Leary began attending church together again. Nicole suffered through the services knowing that the time together helped her mother. It hadn't stopped the divorce from coming, though. Nicole found herself torn because of this. She wanted her mother to be happy, yet she wanted her family to stay together. Coming from a broken home had never been a part of her plan in life.

So, today, as they spent the Sunday afternoon gazing through the windows of a shopping district, Nicole had asked her about the decision. It was an old area of town; the type that was popular before the era of strip and mega-malls. Back when "going downtown", meant actually going downtown and walking along the city streets as you shopped as opposed to the current model of "going downtown" where shoppers headed to the nearest mall or box store that sat on the edge of the city, conveniently near a highway exit. No, this was an area of storefronts that all had been built with brick and mortar instead of plywood and plaster. Houses and old city buildings converted to condominiums surrounded the area. These were the areas of the city that were often targeted for urban renewal (after the minority neighborhoods were revamped and residents evicted, of course). That urban renewal consisted of a McDonald's and the omnipresent Starbucks. Chicago itself was a special city as far as urban renewal, due to the University of Chicago's long relationship with the renewal projects. The University had for years used it's influence to secure renewal projects near the University itself. These transactions began in private, but soon became rather public.

"Freedom, Nicky. Freedom is the best answer I can give you." Mrs. O'Leary said simply.

"Freedom?" Nicole was aghast. She brushed her now shoulder length and dyed black hair from her eyes as a gust of wind bullied it. "Freedom? You're not a slave, mom. You could take the time to try and work this out; Change it into what you want it to be."

"It's not that simple." Her mother answered. Mrs. O'Leary pointed at a green dress in a window as they passed. "How about that one?"

The question was a direct attack on all fashion; the dress was revolting. While Mrs. O'Leary may have been more clear headed, her sense of fashion was still decades behind. Nicole pushed her mother along, shaking her head.

"No, mom. That thing's hideous. Tell me this: How will you know when you're free? Really free?" Nicole was still curious. She was wondering if she herself was trapped.

"I don't know, dear. I suppose it will feel like warmth on the wind." Mrs. O'Leary slyly ducked into a chocolate shop before Nicole could question her further. It was a quaint building, set in a strip of stores. The Chocolate Shoppe was the smallest of its neighbors, a clothing store and an electronics repair store. There was a custom wrought iron frame above the door, holding a wooden sign that had the words "Chocolate Shoppe" burnt in a cursive script. The windows themselves were littered with chocolate on display in a stadium fashion, with each new level holding a different delight. Chocolate roses sat in a central vase on the stadium's base level. Each rose was a complete chocolate construct with dark chocolate stems, milk chocolate leaves, and white chocolate petals capped with a strawberry creme. Milk chocolate molasses chips filled the first row of the stadium, oozing their way into the best seats. The middle section was home to milk chocolate covered pecan buds. The cheap seats were reserved for the best product actually, as they sat near eye level. In these seats were the rum-filled chocolate truffles; Expensive delights that would knock you on your ass after a full dozen. Gold lettering bordered the windows with the store's title in case anyone missed the product or the wood-burnt sign. The smell of the sweets didn't move far from the store, but they were potent none the less. Once Mrs. O'Leary opened the door, a wave of olfactory sensation gushed forward over both women. The fresh smell of churning fudge and savory chocolate thrust itself upon them. Nicole followed her mother, contemplating what her mother had just said.

"Oooooh. They just made a fresh batch of pecan fudge." Mrs. O'Leary stood at the counter with a sample pinched in her fingers.

"That sounds good." Nicole agreed. Her mother ordered a full pound from the attendant.

"So, how are things between you and Jeremy?" Her mother asked while they waited.

"Good, I guess." Nicole smiled.

"You guess?" Her mother wanted to hear more.

"Yeah. He makes me laugh. We talk about nearly everything. He argues with me a lot; Questions what I say and believe." Nicole smiled.

"Really?" Her mother feigned shock. "Someone dares to disagree with the queen?"

"Princess, mom. The princess," Nicole playfully pinched her mother's arm. The attendant handed over a bag of fudge. Mrs. O'Leary handed him a credit card.

"The funny thing is, mom," Nicole continued as her mother signed a receipt. "I like it when he does that. I like everything about him. I like just having him in the room with me. I like the way one of his ears moves a little higher than the other when he smiles."

"Your 'likes' sound a lot like what I remember love to be." Nicole's mom teased as they left the store. Nicole didn't argue because she couldn't. She had tossed the "L" word around in her head a few times, wondering if that was what she was feeling. She had never been in love before, and so she wasn't sure what it should feel like.

"So," Nicole finally spoke again. "Did you ever feel that way about dad? Did you ever like everything about him, even some of the things you thought you hated?"

Her mother was silent. Mrs. O'Leary removed her car keys from her purse, noticing her new SUV just ahead. She fingered the car keys in contemplation, remembering... She thought of her wedding day, and then of her honeymoon. She allowed her mind to drift back to the time when she and Harold were just dating, although back then they still referred to it as courting. Mrs. O'Leary let her thoughts drift back to walks in the park and petting sessions at the movie theater.

"Yes... There was." She revealed, coming back to reality. "I don't hate your father, Nicole. He's just not the man I married anymore. All those 'likes' that you described, they're not there anymore."

Mrs. O'Leary gave Nicole some time to digest this, while she unlocked the door. The lights flashed signaling activation of the keyless entry system.

"So, what do you think about biscuits and gravy for dinner?"

"Sounds fine, mom."

When they arrived home, Nicole crept to her room. She called Natalie's cell phone as she tossed her jacket on the back of a chair. As the phone neared it's third ring, Nicole became slightly annoyed. She didn't see herself as an egocentric person, but she did expect her friends to be there for her when she needed them. As Natalie's familiar voicemail greeting began, Nicole hung up without saying a word.

This was how things seemed to go now. Natalie and Veronica had truly hit it off. Turns out, Nicole's worst enemy was her best friend's version of Jeremy. For years, Nicole forced Natalie to put up with Chad, and now the situation had reversed. Natalie spent as much time as she could manage with Veronica. This in turn meant that Nicole had to spend more time with her as well. At first it was extremely uncomfortable, like a man with a hook for a hand giving a rectal exam. Over time, the situation had somehow devolved into something even more awkward. Today wasn't a day Nicole felt like sharing with Veronica, so she abandoned Natalie. Elizabeth, unlike Natalie, answered before the first ring was finished.

"Hello?" The sounds of a large crowd were hovering behind Elizabeth's voice.

"Hey, Lizzie, it's me." Nicole tried to ascertain where exactly Elizabeth was, but she couldn't place the sounds.

"Oh, hey, Nicky. What's up?"

"Nothing much. Just got back from church with my mom."

"Aw, you're still doing that? Is she doing better?"

"Yeah. It's worth it."

"Cool. Well, we're just getting ice cream over at the Dairy Queen." Elizabeth felt the intensity of the conversation grow with one word: "we're".

"You and Natalie?" Nicole spoke quietly and deliberately, to clarify the situation.

"Nicky, it's all three of us." Elizabeth sighed. As things between Natalie and Veronica became more serious, Elizabeth consistently found herself caught in the middle.

"Figures." Nicole's tone grew cold. "Tell her, if she finds the time, to give me a call. I won't hold you all back from your dessert any longer."

"Nicky, don't be that way." Elizabeth pleaded. "Here, Natalie wants to talk."

"Hello, Nicky?" Natalie's voice suddenly burst over the phone. Nicole heard a deep sigh in the background.

"Natalie..." Nicole wanted to pour her heart out, but her anger was unyielding.

"Nicky, what's up?" Natalie asked.

"You didn't answer my call, Natalie." Nicole sighed.

"Oh, I left my cell at Veronica's when we left. Sorry."

"At Veronica's." Nicole spoke quietly. "Of course."

"Nicky, come down and get some ice cream with us, and we'll talk." Natalie invited her.

"Hmph." Nicole sighed. "No, I don't think that's gonna work. I'll call you later, I guess."

"Wait." Natalie let her heart show, and the urgency came through in her voice. "I can come over right now, Nicky. Are you at home?"

"Don't worry about it." Nicole wanted to punish Natalie for what she felt was betrayal, and at the same time, she wanted to let Natalie go, before...

"No, I'm on my way." Natalie assured her.

"Of course you are." Veronica could be heard sighing in the background.

"No, no." Nicole ordered her. "Just, just do what you were doing. I have to meet Jeremy soon, anyhow."

Nicole lied. They both knew it was a lie, but they left it at that. It was easier that way. If they didn't have the confrontation, feelings wouldn't be hurt any more than they were already.

"You sure?" Natalie asked.

"Yeah. Jeremy will be here soon. That's what friends are for." Nicole said shortly, disconnecting the call, and alienating herself from her friends a bit more. Her phone immediately rang in her hand. The screen told her it was Elizabeth's phone calling. Nicole debated answering but decided that would just be a waste of time. The phone rang until her voicemail kicked in at 12 rings. There was quiet for a few minutes, and then the ringing began again. Once again someone using Elizabeth's cell phone was trying to get back in touch with her. When her cell phone quit ringing for good, it notified her of available voicemail messages. Nicole wafted between pros and cons of checking these messages when the house phone in her room began to ring. She reached toward the receiver, but abruptly withdrew her hand. The phone rang until the answering machine picked up.

"Hey, it's Nicky, and you better have a good reason for not just text messaging me or calling my cell!" Nicole's recorded voice beamed.

"Nicole," Natalie spoke quietly after the beep. "I know you're there. I don't know what to do, Nicole. All of me wants to come to you, and part of me wants to stay here. And I think that little part of me is right. Please pick up. Please. I don't know what's happened, but I can help. I can at least be a shoulder. If it's about your parents, Chad, Jeremy, us, or whatever, I can be there. Please pick up. Or at least call me back later. I promise I'll have my cell all night from here on out. Call me. Please."

Natalie stopped begging, just as the machine cut her off. To Nicole, everything seemed to be going wrong that possibly could be. Her best friend was becoming a best friend and lover to someone Nicole hated. Her parents... well, her parents were what started this spiral, and they weren't going to patch anything up soon. Even though she hated her father, she wanted her family. She needed to have her family. Drowning her sorrows in a bucket of ice cream would be perfect, but she couldn't do it. She had already eaten enough carbs for the day with her indulgence of fudge earlier. The poor diet and non-stop drinking had caused Nicole to gain four pounds in the last three months. She knew that everyone noticed what normal people would call a healthy bit of meat on her abdomen. Nicole saw a pouch and hated herself for it. No one had to say anything about it; the way their eyes drifted to her midsection said enough. Determined, and frustrated, Nicole donned a pair of spandex shorts and a sports bra. She marched into the basement and began to trounce the elliptical trainer. Nicole didn't intend to stop working until someone made her, which is exactly what her mother did four hours later.

Mrs. O'Leary came downstairs to find Nicole as she usually did on the exercise equipment. Nicole was dedicated to keeping her figure. She exercised and lifted weights according to a strict regimen that any sane personal trainer would call cruel and unusual punishment. People who thought she just got lucky genetically were dead wrong. Nicole had her enviable physique because she worked to get it. She didn't tell anyone this, though. It'd make them envy her a little less.

"Dinner's almost ready." Her mother called to her from the stairs. Nicole nodded vigorously in acknowledgment. Her mother waited a few moments, but Nicole refused to directly exit the machine. Mrs. O'Leary thought about saying something about Nicole's incessant need to be perfect. She thought about telling her daughter that her figure was perfect already. That Nicole would be fine with a few more pounds on her frame. Mrs. O'Leary thought about saying a lot of things, but didn't follow through with that urge. She disappeared back up the stairs without saying a word.

After her mother's visage faded from the corner of her eyes, Nicole powered down the piece of equipment. She marched upstairs to her room and stripped down. In the full-length mirror that adorned the back of her bedroom door, she admired her physique. Four pounds heavier or not, she still looked damn good, and that's all that mattered. Her body was a dream that many young girls would abuse themselves to achieve. Some of them would die trying to reach that goal. Many would starve themselves and somewhere along the line, their perceptions would be forever altered. No matter how they saw themselves, they would only see the worst possible. As they sat wasting away, no more than a true sack of skin and bones, they would see bulges of fat and unsightly blubber. Nicole would never go that far. Her mind was a bit shattered at the moment, but anorexia wasn't an option to her. She saw it as disgusting and a form of failure. Nicole O'Leary did not fail.

Satisfied that she would be back in top form soon, Nicole jumped in the shower. She scrubbed in a steaming assault and then rinsed in an ice-cold rain. Neither of which managed to dull that pain that was beginning to ache inside of her.

Chapter Nine: Winner, Winner, Chicken Dinner!

Her parents were seated at the dining room table when she entered the room. She had rushed and still had a purple, $60, designer Egyptian cotton towel wrapped around her head. Harold O'Leary was slumped in his chair very low. So low, in fact, that his back was actually resting on the seat of the chair. He fiddled with his silverware idly. No sight exudes pity more than a broken man.

Mrs. O'Leary waited for Nicole patiently. She had her hands clasped, ready to have someone say grace. The outfit she had worn to church still adorned her. It was a simple flower print, common for spring dress. Nicole hadn't noticed before, but she was sure her mother hadn't worn that dress in a long time. The smile her mother wore was as ecstatic as her father's frown was depressed. Nicole pitied him. She truly did. But that pity was not enough to outweigh her hate. Her father was finally beginning to acknowledge his feelings. It was too bad he chose to do so far beyond a time that would have been considered "too late".

The passing weeks and months had not been kind to Harold. His eyes were red and baggy. Mr. O'Leary had been drinking more lately. Unlike her support of her mother, Nicole let him travel that slippery slope of alcoholism. He might think he could drown his troubles away, but Nicole herself, using his same form of treatment, knew better. The alcohol was causing him to have massive mood swings. He spent his time down at the Elk's Lodge, or locked in his bedroom. Nicole wasn't sure what he did at either place. She had heard him crying in his bedroom once. In fact, Mr. O'Leary was spending his days alone, for the most part. His affair with Rebecca was failing due to his drinking. She had a prestigious position now, within Halliburton, thanks to Harold's letters of recommendation. Harold's position within the company was itself in jeopardy, again due to his alcoholism. Rebecca and he still met some nights, when he would call her late from the lodge for a ride. She would pick him up and take him to her place where they would attempt sexual relations. Harold, by that time was normally too drunk to function or even form an erection. When he could force himself to become aroused he would lay his chunky flesh upon hers, exhaling strong spirits in her face, his body ferociously trying to sweat out the alcohol, and he would grind away. She found no pleasure in the situation, but he was still her boss, and for all she did have, she had no sort of companionship. So Rebecca figured she would allow him to use her as much as she would use him, until she could find better. They rarely talked anymore, because talking led Harold to crying, which Rebecca couldn't stand. He wasn't the powerful man she thought, or had previously met. He was a despicable miscreant.

The O'Leary table had been graced by homemade biscuits, gravy and scrambled eggs. It was the old, "breakfast for dinner" routine. Nicole's mother had placed the syrup and ketchup near Nicole's plate, unsure of which her daughter would prefer on her eggs tonight. Nicole seated herself. She bowed her head, gently clasping her hands before her.

"Lord," Mrs. O'Leary began. "Thank you for this meal we have been blessed with tonight. Please sanctify our food and let it fill us. Thank you, Father. Amen."

"Amen." Nicole repeated.

Her father said nothing. As Mrs. O'Leary closed the prayer, Harold began heaping spoonfuls of eggs onto his plate. With complete disregard for everyone present, he slammed the bowl of eggs on the table. Yellow puffs of aborted chicken flew about, littering the previously pristine table setting. Nicole moved to speak, but her mother shushed her with a serious look that shocked Nicole.

Harold plowed his hands into the biscuits. They were a family favorite, from a recipe that Harold's mother had passed on to her daughter-in-law the day of her wedding. It had been learned by daughter from mother for generations, dating back to the first in Harold's line to cook the recipe. This one had been taught from one of the slave girls on a plantation long lost in the Civil war. Five generation of O'Leary women had been granted access to that recipe, at the very least. It had aged well, still tasting better than any mass produced item on the market.

As Mr. O'Leary threw biscuits on his plate, he mashed a few of them. Some in the bowl were left with his vengeful fingerprints. Still others he managed to gouge chunks from. Again, Nicole moved to speak, but her mother gave her the stern look that said simply, "Shut it." Only when Mr. O'Leary began spooning gravy about his plate did the maternal unit bother to speak up.

"What are you doing, Harold?" her tone was incredibly flat. Her face showed concern, but her voice held neither concern nor condemnation.

"Eatin' dinner. What the hell does it look like?" He grumbled.

"You're drunk, and throwing a tantrum." Mrs. O'Leary now let a scolding tone creep in to her voice.

"Oh!" Harold cried. "As if being a drunk in this house has suddenly become a crime. How many nights have I come home to find you passed out on the couch?" Harold was right. He had lived months with his wife a stumbling drunk.

"I may not have always been perfect," Mrs. O'Leary shot back, clearing her throat. She was stung by his accusation, even if he was right. "But I did put my family first, Harold. God knows I never threw myself into the depths of a bottle and came to the dinner table."

"Yeah, well, God knows a lot of things." Harold gave a response that wouldn't make sense at any other table. But this home was on the edge of the map. And on the edge of the map, here, there be secrets.

"Oh, you are right about that." Mrs. O'Leary snapped. Her voice threatened to unearth a dark truth. One that Harold himself wasn't ready for. Nicole didn't know if she could stand to hear any more. It wasn't that she didn't know what they were talking about. Her fear came from having to hear her parents say it out loud in front of her, even though that's what she wanted most, secretly. Perhaps, had they brought the secret to light that night, and dealt with it, things would have been different. They wouldn't have ended the way they did.

But that dark dungeon of clandestine truths that rested in the heart of those present was not opened. Not on this day.

"Caring about your family, does not include getting a divorce." Harold sat up straighter, changing the subject. It was a subtle hint to Mrs. O'Leary to leave that dirty truth she had threatened behind. Anything else was fair game, but that fact was to stay buried. *For now*.

"After all this time, don't tell me how you care for this family." Elaine O'Leary was not going to budge. "Caring for this family isn't fooling around with that little tart from your office. Do you even know what sexual harassment is, Harold?"

Elaine O'Leary hardly moved as Harold slapped her.

"Daddy!" Nicole could hold her tongue no longer. She grabbed Harold by the arm. He shrugged her off so hard Nicole flew into her chair. She toppled over the chair, struggling to regain some sort of balance, but to no avail. Nicole fell to the floor, the chair landing next to her. As she looked up at her father, she found that he had moved to stand over her. He was pointing at her face, wildly waving an index finger that tickled the air before her nose.

"And you!" He seethed while looking at Nicole. "Don't think I don't know about you whoring around town, spending my money and ruining my family name. You think it hasn't gotten all the way back to me? I hear my staff snickering behind my back. You and all your little slut friends careening about town: drunk and giving it to anyone who'll take it."

He had insulted and assaulted Nicole. He had belittled and embarrassed her. That was unacceptable. Nicole now had nothing to hold her back from letting him have it. She followed her instinct to strike back.

"Maybe you're just mad that none of my friends ever tried giving it to you."

Harold O'Leary's face slowly morphed through a slew of emotions after Nicole's verbal dart. At first his jaw dropped, shocked at hearing her speak the truth about his desires. His mind reeled. His eyes bulged as he gasped for air. Slowly, he recovered. His mouth closed and his eyebrows became heavy. They sunk deep into his face as his rage continued to build. His teeth were grinding together, producing an eerie soundtrack for the moment. Nicole feared the worst as he raised a balled fist. She could see his white knuckles glowing like beacons of pain. As he reached to steady Nicole by grasping her throat, Mrs. O'Leary stood and gently grabbed his arm.

"That's enough, Harold." She whispered. She felt disgraced for not being able to stop him before he pushed Nicole down. Harold let his body relax. He allowed his wife to escort him from the room, but never took his eyes away from Nicole. His expression became blank, but Nicole could see the hatred in the back of his mind seeping out.

Elaine O'Leary took Harold to their bedroom. She sat him on the bed. He laid back and curled into the fetal position. Harold was alone in his despair, staring off into the darkness. Elaine moved the half-empty bottle of whiskey from the nightstand to within his reach. She noticed several of her sleeping pills had been strewn about the floor. She hadn't taken them since she and Nicole began attending church again. Elaine had forgotten about the medicine that she had used to help dull her mind each night. With care, and discretion, Elaine replaced the pills in their nearby bottles. These she took with her as she left the room. She would let him drink as he pleased, as he had allowed her. She would not let him commit suicide with her medication. That was out of the question. The pill bottles went directly into the kitchen trash.

Nicole, now seated in her chair again, waited patiently at the kitchen table as her father was put to sleep. She was dumbstruck by the night's events. Never in all of her nightmares and dreams had her father acted the way he had tonight. The filthy sound of his hand crossing her mother's face played over and over in her mind. He had been ready to do worse to her. That terrified her. Nicole didn't know what would have happened if her mother had not intervened. Mrs. O'Leary had tolerated the abuse herself, as a sort of self-penance, but would not allow that same abuse to be endured by Nicole.

"Are you okay?" Nicole asked as her mother entered the kitchen and threw the pills in the trash.

"Fine dear." Her mother smiled, looking at the antidepressants in the trash. "Damn doctor's aren't satisfied unless you're a slobbering and stupid." Mrs. O'Leary commented. It was her way of affirming the new-old her. She was moving on, no longer needing to be pharmaceutically regulated.

"Now, where were we?" Elaine O'Leary sat again at the table. She began filling her plate with zest. Nicole decided to follow suit. She was still uncomfortable, but felt safe. Her mother was here, and even 18-year old independent women need that sometimes, she told herself. There was something still troubling Nicole, though. She worked up the courage to ask her mother about it, as she served herself a scoop of eggs.

"Why did you let him do that?" Nicole asked, referring to the slap heard 'round the table.

"Do what?" Elaine gazed about the table looking for the salt and pepper. Realizing she had forgotten to place them to begin with, she stood and walked to the curio cabinet that held her crystal collection and the matching salt and pepper shaker.

"He hit you, mom." Nicole said simply, feeling that something was awry.

"You think that's the first time?" Elaine laughed, seating herself. She gingerly peppered her plate.

"He has hit you before?" Nicole was amazed. She was sure she knew everything about her family.

"Sweetheart, real couples have real problems." Elaine shrugged. "Your father and I have gone through our fair share. You learn to put up with a person's faults when you love them."

It was a poor, antiquated excuse. Nicole couldn't stand it. She'd never put up with abuse. Nicole didn't realize that those words were what every abused woman said, before it happened to her. Too often, we will sell out our beliefs and principles just to feel loved.

"But you're not putting up with it anymore?" Nicole questioned uneasily. She feared the conversation might move to an area that would dash all of her hopes upon the jagged rocks of truth.

"I suppose I'm not." Elaine sounded as if she'd just come to the realization herself.

"Because you don't love him anymore." Nicole continued.

"I suppose I don't."

They were silent for several minutes. Her mother was the first to speak again.

"Could you pass the gravy, dear?" Mrs. O'Leary asked.

They ate dinner whilst having a conversation. They discussed current world events, happenings in their lives and the day at church. Nicole's mouth stayed on topic, even while her heart was broken. Events through the day had cemented the truth for her: her parents would not, nay, *could not* stay together. After her father's meltdown, she didn't expect her mother to have any feeling left for the man.

After they finished dinner, Nicole and her mother washed the dishes together. They often had in the past, and it seemed with the transformation of her mother that it was appropriate to begin the practice again. Nicole had learned a great deal about running a household from her mother. That knowledge is all that kept the family afloat during her mother's slow-speed come apart.

"Nicole," Her mother asked while drying a glass that Nicole had just finished washing. Nicole hated drying the dishes. She could never get all of the streaks off of the clear glass. Her mother was a professional, and took this duty. Nicole was content washing. "Are you okay?" Elaine asked. "Do you need to talk about all that's happened some more?"

Elaine O'Leary was genuinely concerned for her daughter's well-being. Any mother can tell when their child's upset. Elaine knew, from maternal instinct, that something had settled inside Nicole's stomach and was knotting her insides. There was a pain there and Elaine wanted to help. This environment, their house and home, was becoming the last place to raise children, even those who are grown. Nicole might be of legal age, but she'd always be her daughter. Mrs. O'Leary would always have something to teach her little girl, until her dying day. That's the way mothers are.

"I'm fine, mom. Really." Nicole lied, shaking her head. "I'm just so glad to see you happy again. I would never expect you to stay with someone who put their hands on you."

The fact that she was lying was clear to both of them. It was a weak attempt, and to the mother paying attention, a useless endeavor.

"Nicole... please don't think ill of your father. He's in a very tough place right now. He's a patriarch who feels powerless and betrayed." Elaine pleaded while giving an explanation. She was correct in her diagnosis. Harold O'Leary was indeed powerless and betrayed.

"Not by Jackson, I'm sure." Nicole referenced the low standard her father held her brother to with a sigh.

"No, probably not." Her mother agreed with a sigh of her own. "But I don't want any of this to make you kids take sides. That's the last thing we need."

"Mom, your personal life is yours. I'll leave that alone." Nicole agreed "But as for me, the man tried, and would have hit me to tonight. I don't care about him anymore. For months, I have been waiting and praying and hoping that you two would work things out. Now... Now I could care less what happens to him. I just don't care anymore. After how he acted, how can you ask me to?"

"You're right." Her mother agreed promptly. Nicole had expected an argument. "You know that you have always been so mature for your age, even now?" Her mother placed a hand on Nicole's back. They finished the dishes in silence.

Her mother left the kitchen to check on Harold and Nicole plundered the trash can for it's narcotic treasures. Even then, she thought to herself that she, of course, was no addict. Her actions were those of a woman possessed, though; Possessed by a drive to satiate an internal hunger for nervous system depression.

Nicole marched up to her room, her fist's bursting with pill bottles. As soon as she closed the door behind her, she opened a bottle and took two pills. She didn't bother to check which ones she was taking. She took two and that should work just fine for now. The only other thing she could think of that she needed was a good dose of Jeremy and a beer. He'd make her smile and the beer would amplify the medication.

The pill bottles joined their brethren in the top, right corner of the drawer in her dresser where she kept her unmentionables. Nicole had been consistently stealing her mother's medication for years now. Seeing her mother happy was a great thing for Nicole. Losing her drug supply was going to be a downer, but she'd find a way to make it through. With her connections, Nicole could find a new supplier, but then she'd have to pay for them. She promised herself not to worry about that bridge until she crossed it six and one-third bottles from now.

Jeremy, she reminded herself, was who she needed to call at this moment. Searching for her cellular or cordless phone, she discovered that Natalie had called both lines. Her answering machine indicated that there was a new message, as did the voice mail icon on her cellular phone. The little red light on her cordless phone dock blinked at her, calling out as it was designed to do. Nicole didn't want to deal with her dissolving friendships at the moment. She deleted both messages without listening to either of them. Natalie had made her bed. Now she could lie in it and wait.

Nicole used the speed dial feature to contact Jeremy. As the phone rang, she glanced at the television, which she'd left on since last night. A known felon and rap artist was taking the time in a public service announcement on MTV to try and influence her vote. The election had ended over a month ago. Nicole kept watching because her favorite reality television show was on at this time, and should return after the commercial break. The show followed the normal formula: cameras follow a celebrity couple long enough for the viewer to realize that the elite are generally ignorant and wholly untalented.

"Hello?" Jeremy's mother answered the call.

"Hi, Mrs. Bloom, it's Nicole. Is Jeremy around?" Nicole unlocked the automatic sweetheart voice that she had charmed so many with.

"Oh, Nicole!" Mrs. Bloom showed a genuine pleasant sense of surprise. "Jeremy said that you both got an A on that trigonometry test you were studying for. Good job!"

It was true. She and Jeremy had spent several hours in the past two weeks studying. During that time he realized how dedicated to success Nicole actually was. Failure and mediocrity were not options for her, drying clear glass dishes being the exception to this rule. Nicole had given up on that long ago. Should Nicole encounter failure or mediocrity in any other facet of her life, her world would surely begin to collapse. She practiced hard, studied harder and partied hardest.

"Yeah," Nicole displayed a false humility. "We really busted our butts to get that one."

"I'm just so glad Jeremy is with such a nice, smart girl. Oh! Here he is. I'll talk to you later." This was a white lie, and they both knew it. Like "good to see you," or "it's been fun," those greetings that come out of your mouth before you even know what you are saying.

"I can't wait, Mrs. Bloom." Nicole had no idea what else to say. Somehow, *put your god damned son on the phone already*, seemed wholly inappropriate.

"'Bye now."

"Goodbye." Nicole silently wondered how long the insipid woman would carry on with these pleasantries. She herself was running out of inane things to say. She could hear Jeremy discouraging his mother from talking to Nicole. It embarrassed him. He still felt unworthy of his girlfriend. His family's middle class was his shame. Nicole had told him several times she envied his family life. That jealously was at its highest today. Jeremy never believed her when she said things of that nature. Her family had everything his did and more. He could see nothing in the Blooms that the O'Learys should covet.

"Nicole?" He finally encouraged his mother to leave him alone for the time being and answered Nicole's call himself.

"Hey, Jeremy." Her voice warmed, as did her heart, just hearing him. "You busy?"

"Not really. We just finished dinner. What's up?" He asked.

"Think you could come over for awhile?" The sunshine in her voice began to set. Jeremy picked up on this immediately.

"What's wrong?" His concern was genuine.

"I just, I need you here. To talk. Please?" Nicole scarcely avoided crying. The knot in her stomach was growing. She didn't want to have to talk anymore on the phone. She needed him there with her to hug and hold her up as she broke down.

"Okay, yeah. I'm on my way." Jeremy sensed the urgency in her voice.

"'Kay. Bye." Nicole bit her upper lip and ended the call abruptly on that note. It was a rude act, meant only to show her desperation. She had spent her entire life perfecting the damsel-in-distress bit. Only this time, it was real.

Chapter Ten: Living the Dream

Nicole attempted to get drunk while waiting for Jeremy, but it just didn't feel right. She dug into her dresser drawer and removed a pill bottle. Even this though, she decided to wait on. The night was young, and she had several other ideas of how to work off her rage.

Nicole decided to dress while waiting. She picked out a black cheerleader outfit. It consisted of a small designer top that hugged her frame and a black skirt with white pleats. The front of the shirt had the skull of a cat on it. She searched her closet and came up with a softball bat from her younger years. She wasn't sure why, but she took it and the bottle of whiskey nearby, which was the object she was originally searching for. Dressed for success, with the necessary tools in hand, she waited outside her house for Jeremy.

Sitting alone as the sun set, Nicole was visited by a familiar sight in the neighborhood. Walter Betha, local paperboy, was riding his bicycle down the block. He came to a skidding halt in front of Nicole. His face appeared smudged with dirt. Upon closer inspection, Nicole realized the blemish was actually smeared chocolate. It ran down his face and onto his jean coveralls. His white and blue striped long-sleeve shirt had the stains on it as well. Nicole could see that these were all caused by the chocolate covered nougat candy bar in Wally's hand.

"Nicole!" Wally beamed. Talking to Nicole was always the highlight of his day when he was able to achieve such a feat. Nicole was always nice to him. And she was pretty.

"Hey, Wally. How's it going?" Nicole asked with a smile. She liked Wally. He was so... innocent.

"Good. I got a candy bar." Wally offered the bar to Nicole. "Wanna bite?"

Nicole stood and grinned.

"Maybe just a little one. I don't want to get too fat."

Nicole bent forward and took a small bite of the candy bar. She wasn't really hungry, but she knew how people tended to treat Wally. She didn't ever want to be one of those people.

"Aww, you're not fat, Nicole O'Leary. You're very pretty."

"Why thank you, Wally!" Nicole placed a small kiss on Wally's cheek. Oh how she longed to be so ignorant of the complexity of life. Wally blushed and shied his face away as Nicole returned to her seat.

"Watcha drinkin'?" Wally asked her, spying the whiskey bottle at her ankles. "Can I have some. I gave you some of my chocolate."

"Uh, it's medicine." Nicole lied quickly. The last thing she wanted was to hurt his feelings.

"Oh, medicine. Can I have some?" He blindly asked.

"Oh, no, Wally." Nicole exaggerated her face into a serious look. "This is special medicine and I have to take it all. But I tell you what, next time I see you at the mall or the store, I'll buy you a soda, on me, okay?"

"Oh boy! Can it be a frozen lemonade if we are in the mall. Frozen lemonade is the best!" Wally became excited just thinking about the afternoon delight he enjoyed the most.

"You bet. Now you better get going, Wally. It's getting dark, and I know your parents like you home before dark."

"Yeah." Wally looked at the sky. "You're right, Nicole O'Leary. See you later, Nicole O'Leary!" Wally shouted and began to speed off on his bike. In doing so, he dropped his candy bar, which caused a mini-crisis in his life. He stopped the bike and bent sideways to pick up his treat. With his lack of psychomotor skills, he fell over, and began to cry. Nicole shuffled toward him and picked up his candy bar. She dusted the small pebbles from its surface and handed it back to Wally. As she rubbed his shoulders, he stopped crying and returned to his feet with her help and soothing coaxing.

"There you go, all better." Nicole kissed him on the cheek again. His salty tears were warm and endearing.

"Thank you Nicole O'Leary. See you later! You owe me a frozen lemonade!" Walter Betha sped off into the distance, coming dangerously close to wrecking his bicycle into a parked SUV on the street.

Nicole returned to her seat. The pills were beginning to take effect. Her body was feeling lighter than air. She took a drink of the whiskey, and lit a cigarette. She set the softball bat across her lap and waited.

This is how Jeremy found her as he arrived. The bat was the first thing he noticed, and it begged a question. He could tell she had given in to the alcohol bug by her breath and the now half-empty bottle of whiskey at her feet. It shocked him to see her so openly rebellious. He carefully sat next to her after exiting his car. She handed him the bottle without looking at him. He took a short, obligatory drink. Jeremy had learned a great many things from Nicole in their short time together. The worst was how to smoke. He was now smoking 1/2 of a pack of cigarettes a day. 10 cigarettes divided equally somehow in the 16-20 hours a day he was awake. He removed his own pack from the gray slacks that Nicole had purchased for him. He wore a matching gray cardigan that she also purchased. The sleeved were rolled up to his arms. He slowly lit his own cigarette and looked into the sky, as Nicole was.

"That's the great bear." Nicole referenced the stars. "See it." She pointed out each star slowly. Jeremy placed his face next to her finger, sending shivers through her. She traced the outline of the constellation.

"The Greeks said this was Callisto. Callisto was chosen to be the companion of Artemis. She pledged herself to virtue, as Artemis required. But, Zeus, in his infinite infidelity, loved to seduce young maidens. And he seduced Callisto. When Artemis learned of Callisto's pregnancy, she turned Callisto into a bear, hoping that a hunter would slay her. Artemis was a cruel goddess. She once changed a man into a stag after he saw her bathing and set his own dogs on him. They tore him to shreds."

Nicole paused before continuing.

"But Callisto was lucky. Zeus took pity on her. For it was his fault that she had been put in this predicament. So he sent her to the heavens, still in her bear form. There she's rested for millennia."

Nicole finished.

"Long day?" Jeremy asked after several minutes had passed. He flicked his ashes on the ground.

"Couldja tell?" Nicole grinned so faintly, it appeared more as a nervous tic.

"What's the bat for?" Jeremy got to the pressing question on his mind. He felt it was time to address the elephant in the room.

"Got some aggression to work out." She replied matter-of-factly, as if he should have known already.

"I see." Jeremy began to tread carefully. He hadn't forgotten the squirrel at the cabin. "And just how will you or we do that?" He had to know exactly which wild ride she would be taking him on tonight.

"We'll take my car. But you'll have to drive." Nicole declared. Her feet parted. He noticed her small purse with her car keys hanging out of it between her ankles. Inconspicuously, like children passing notes in grade school, she pushed the purse toward him with her Nike clad feet. Jeremy scooped up the bag. It was clear he would have to wait for her to reveal her plans.

They walked to her car in silence. The only semblance of communication was them passing the bottle of whiskey back and forth. Jeremy glanced nervously at the softball bat several times. Whatever Nicole had in mind was obviously violent. Jeremy opened her door for her, as a gentleman should. After he shut it and began walking to the driver's side, his mind was in turmoil. Every atom of his being told him not to drive her anywhere. But her pouting lips and tear streamed mascara forced him to discard reason and take his chance.

"So, where to?" He asked, adjusting her driver's seat to his height.

` "Just drive. I have to get away from here. But stay in the residential areas." Nicole advised. Jeremy offered no further questions, even about that last little instruction. He drove as told through nearby streets in absolute quiet. Nicole was giving the day's events a re-examination in her mind. She came to the conclusion that God, if there was one, hated her. If God hated her, well, there was no point in trying to impress him anymore. She thought about her parents and what they were putting her through. *Why have children if you don't plan to care for them*, she wondered. Her cheeks flushed as she felt a sudden rush of blood to her head.

They continued this way for forty minutes. The sound of Nicole rolling down her window was more like a rolling thunder. Jeremy's head snapped to her as he drove.

"You okay?" He asked. She was petting the softball bat.

"Speed up." Nicole instructed him. Jeremy eased his foot a little harder on the accelerator. The speedometer crept up from 30 mph to 40 mph. Nicole began to breathe deeply; Long breaths in through the nose, long breaths out through the mouth. She tried her hardest to rid herself of the burning in her chest. Never before was there a greater dance with futility. She couldn't stop what was inside her, because it was all she had become. Hatred that burned this deep couldn't be contained through modified Lamaze breathing techniques. It was too late to try and hold it back. With complete disregard for personal safety, Nicole extended herself out of the window, up to her waist. Even the cool night air blazing past her face couldn't stop the inferno within. Jeremy, caught off guard by her actions, swerved, almost wrecking into a parked car.

"Nicole!" He shouted. Jeremy had thought she was going to jump from the moving vehicle.

"Just keep the wheel steady." She shouted back at him. Jeremy wanted to argue, but decided keeping his attention on driving was the best action to take. Any sane person would have just stopped the vehicle. Jeremy wasn't sane though. Not when it came to Nicole. Jeremy was in love.

Nicole herself had given up the internal struggle. She allowed the embers of anger to grow into a firestorm. The flames licked up from her heart, and through her arms. She gathered her strength and cocked back the softball bat. The very next parked car they passed (an import, because suburbanites know American vehicles have next to no trade-in value), she swung the bat and crashed in the passenger window.

The sound of exploding glass rattled Jeremy. He had guessed by then what her plan was though, so he was somewhat prepared. His only concern was being spotted. The broken window had allowed the car alarm on the assaulted vehicle to perform its duty. Jeremy spied for observers and sped up. The rush of speed only encouraged Nicole.

She swung away at every opportunity. She shattered rear, driver and passenger windows. Rear-view mirrors felt her wrath as well. Even one poor little rear turn signal met an aluminum end. Nicole was indiscriminate in her vandalism. She went after trucks, cars, and two motorcycles. She swung the bat until something more attractive caught her eye.

"Stop the car." Nicole plopped back into her seat. "Park it."

"What?" Jeremy didn't understand, but slowed down.

"There." Nicole's hand nudged the steering wheel toward an open parking space on the nearby curb. Jeremy wasn't ready for her to do so, and lost control of the vehicle for a moment. As he regained authority over the steering wheel, he slowed to a stop at the point Nicole had commanded. Nicole's nudge had almost caused him to rear-end a Cadillac SUV. She paid no attention to this small matter. Nicole was surveying the area for possible on-lookers as Jeremy parallel parked. It was late now, and the only people awake were those who's residences were blocks behind them and had felt Nicole's wrath already.

"What's up? You see a cop or something?" Jeremy asked. Nicole put a hand on his leg.

"Nope, even better. Let's go do the SPCA a favor." She hinted, cryptically.

"What are you talking about?" Jeremy still hadn't caught on.

"C'mon." Nicole decided not to let him in on anymore of her plan at the moment. She jumped out of the car, bat in hand. Sirens from their earlier visits scarred the night's serenity.

Nicole walked up the street slapping the barrel of the bat into her open palm. Jeremy locked the car and jogged to her side.

"Do you remember Mrs. Johnsen, from school?" Nicole asked as they stood on the sidewalk.

"From last year?" Jeremy implied having some knowledge of the person in question.

"Yeah." Nicole acknowledged his answer.

"Didn't she get fired for inappropriate relations with a student or something?" Jeremy gave a short recount of the tragedy that was Mrs. Johnsen's teaching career at their school.

"More or less." Nicole said. "She was one of the female physical education instructors and the head volleyball coach. She started teaching at our school just that year. It was a shock to many that she was given the coaching position right out of the gate after Mrs. Delmar retired, because Mrs. Kroger was the assistant coach, and next in line. Mrs. Johnsen was a fresh grad from the University of Chicago. Graduated with honors, top of her class. She was a nice lady, who looked her young age. She could have probably been a model. Remember her blond hair, always pulled back in a ponytail? Her figure was the only I've ever been envious of. And she had those otherworldly blue eyes. Not hard to see why a young girl, struggling with her sexuality would be attracted to Mrs. Johnsen."

"That's what happened. Sandy Mickelson, one of the best on the volleyball team falls for the gorgeous coach. Sandy, though, is 18 years old. She's a senior with a promising scholarship to some PAC-10 school, I don't recall which one.

"Anyhow, Sandy and Mrs. Johnsen start this illicit relationship, seeing each other on the sneak. Natalie, who happens to be ten times the player Sandy was, gets benched in favor of Mrs. Johnsen's new lover. We tried talking to the coach, but she wasn't listening, or didn't want to. I had no choice but to report Sandy and Mrs. Johnsen. It wasn't right. Natalie was going to let it slide, but I couldn't. Natalie is, or was my best friend, I guess. They couldn't get away with what they were doing to her. There was a hearing with the school board. The media jumped all over the story. Not only was it a sensational story of a teacher/student love affair, but it was a lesbian love affair at that. News feeds around the country ate the story up. A senator in North Carolina actually used it as an example on his anti-gay platform. One little phone call from me ruined lives. Sad, I guess, but what could I do? Natalie didn't deserve that.

"Long story short, there was a hearing, Mrs. Johnsen was fired. Sandy loses her scholarship and drops out of school. They move in together. Natalie gets her roster spot back and later gains a scholarship of her own. And my cat, Chuckles, (you never met him), is never heard from again." Nicole finished her narration of the legend of Mrs. Johnsen. Her voice was flat the entire time. Her face was a perfect match for that look. Jeremy saw no emotion the entire time, save for a small smirk near the end. The bat still smacked in Nicole's palm.

"So, you think they killed your cat?" Jeremy clarified, when he did not need to. It was obvious that was what Nicole thought. He was scared that she was planning a murder at this moment. He didn't know if his feelings for her could overwhelm the morals inside him, should it come to that.

"I know it." Nicole assured him. "I saw Sandy in the grocery store one night. I was running in to grab a chaser. Me and the girls were late for a party in the canyon. Sandy all but admitted it to me as I was debating between 7-UP or Sprite." Nicole walked into a yard and stopped suddenly as she was talking.

"So what did you do?" Jeremy was scared to hear the answer, but he knew he had to. His mind flashed back to the way Nicole had so efficiently, and coldly dispatched the squirrel at her cabin.

"Nothing." Nicole shrugged. "My dad bought me a new cat. It was a Persian purebred. It pissed all over my clothes and shredded my prom dress. I hated that fucking cat."

"So, not to be rude, but where's all this going? I don't get it." Jeremy asked bluntly. Jeremy had decided that he could stand with Nicole through a crime of passion. However, he wasn't sure if they would be able to cover it up well enough not to get caught. He wasn't sure Nicole was telling him the entire truth, either. Nicole's previous actions had shown him that she was a vindictive beast who often acted with no sense of responsibility. She was born of a generation who had rode the dot-com wave until it crashed, ruining retirement accounts worldwide. That lack of empathy and sympathy carried over to Nicole. As much as she hated her father, she was more like him than she could ever admit. She didn't know of any offense that her father's money, influence and stock options couldn't get her out of. There was no way Jeremy could imagine that someone killed Nicole's cat and the girl just let it go.

Jeremy also knew better than to question Nicole at certain times. He could pry more into the story, once she calmed down, but he wouldn't. He really didn't care about the truth of Mrs. Johnsen, Sandy and Nicole's cat. Nicole would probably just lie about it anyhow. He cared about what she was going to do now.

"Where it's going," Nicole answered, pointing the bat at a nearby tree in the yard next to them. "Is right there."

Jeremy juggled his vision in the direction she had indicated. He saw only a tree. He realized that couldn't be the focus of her attention. Squinting, he pulled back a portion of the curtain of night. The base of the tree seemed to move in response. *Trees don't move*, he thought. He focused with more intensity, and saw that it wasn't the tree at all. It was a large cat, probably twenty pounds and black as twilight.

"Nicole, mailboxes were one thing-" He began to try and reason with her.

"Shhhh." Nicole tapped the bat softly on his lips. "Silence."

She began to stalk the cat as it would its own prey. Her body seemed to lose all weight. Jeremy watched her float on her toes across the grass and over a shrub. The cat began to purr as Nicole circled it. It was acutely aware of her, and welcomed any attention she was going to offer.

The cat's name was Aspen. He had been a gift from Sandy to Mrs. Johnsen, when Sandy was still a student. Sandy had sent it after Mrs. Johnsen had come to visit her in the hospital. As Jeremy suspected, Nicole had done more than just report the teacher and student relationship. Nicole and Natalie had taken the same bat Nicole now held, and they waited patiently. They watched quietly three houses away from the very one Nicole now crept in front of. When the opportunity arose, they beat Sandy into a coma. Mrs. Johnsen, well accepted by Sandy's family, sat with Sandy for 47 days. 47 days Sandy lay acutely aware of the outside world, in a dream state. She could hear her family and doctor's talking about her. She could hear the nurses talking about how she wasn't going to make it. She lived in a daydream where she relived the attack over and over. It was a hell Nicole didn't know she had inflicted upon the poor girl. Sandy, once awake, had to undergo weeks of physical therapy before she could even go home. Her muscles had greatly atrophied and she had developed a bed sore on her backside. That scar would last forever. Later, she had gotten a tattoo to cover the wound, but she'd always know it was there. That dull ache in her lower back that cried out with when cold weather rolled in would never release. While Sandy rehabilitated, she had her mother pick out Aspen from the many "free cat", ads in the local newspaper. No matter the time of year, there's always a free cat in every city. Sandy wanted to let Mrs. Johnsen know that she had indeed felt her love holding her hand every day through the ordeal. She had felt the loving bed baths and the lotion rubs. She could remember each changing of the dressings on her wounds. Sandy remembered it all, and wanted to show Mrs. Johnsen that she was more than appreciated: she was loved.

Aspen had previously belonged to a family of four: a father, mother and twin daughters. He had been raised with the 6-year old twins. Aspen was great with kids and people in general. He greeted everyone with a purr and a lick of the fingers. He presented himself to all comers with an air of humility and playfulness. It was baby number 3 that was Aspen's undoing. Baby number 3 was unexpected and allergic to cats. Aspen was evicted promptly, but lovingly. He made the perfect pet for Sandy and her lover. He played and moonbathed in the front yard at night. He never clawed the furniture or peed on the carpet. He usually came in to eat when Sandy came out to gather up the morning paper.

As Nicole circled him, Jeremy looked on. Her eyes glossed over. The muscles in her arms twitched under the cold moonlight. Aspen rose to his feet, expecting a warm caress from this stranger. Nicole raised the bat above her head. The aluminum allowed a dull thud as she brought it down on Aspen's skull. Aspen didn't make a sound. He wanted to. He wanted with all of his feline heart to cry out for help. The initial blow had demolished much of his brain tissue. He had lost all control of his body, and was a bag of meat waiting to die. Were his brain not partially crushed, it wouldn't matter. The cat's mouth and throat had been rendered useless. With his skull broken and brain smashed, Aspen could only reflexively twitch his paws. Nicole hit him. She hit him again. And again. And again. Her arms flew within a flurry of fury. Each swing was a bit harder than the last. Through her ferocity, Jeremy could hear her uttering her father's name. Her face was pulled and stretched by hatred and anger. She was an untamed beast, let loose from a dark pit in the hearts of all men. This is what men were meant to be. No matter how they changed their looks and pretended to aspire for better: man was and is a destructive beast with no regard for anything but himself.

Jeremy watched with a mix of emotions. Fear coursed through him. Not only might they get caught, but he wasn't sure how safe he was from her rage. Animal attraction thrived in his loins. He would feel sick about it later, but right now he was aroused at seeing this powerful, uncontrollable thing that Nicole had become. Jeremy kept his eyes on survey-mode, to make sure that no one saw them, glancing away from the carnage every few seconds. Nicole's actions were disturbing. Jeremy was relieved that she had only taken action against the cat, and not against a person. Her raw strength and passion still drew him to her.

Ten minutes passed. Nicole's blows began to slow. Her chest burned, heaving in and out with monstrous breaths. Her arms began to lose their super-human strength and endurance. She fell to her knees, while continuing to swing the bat. The cat was nothing more than a flat pelt, drenched in blood and bone. Miniscule chunks of flesh were strewn about the area. Nicole stopped swinging the bat finally. It wasn't that she wanted to finish; She couldn't raise her arms another time.

Jeremy, sensing it was now safe, rushed to her side. He brushed a tooth fragment from her cheek. It left a path of blood smeared through trails of tears on her cheeks. He used his sleeve to wipe clean her face and exposed neck. As he sat with an arm around her, he began to pick particles of Aspen from her clothing.

"We better get going." Jeremy advised. Nicole sniffled, and slowly nodded in agreement. Jeremy reached with trepidation toward the bat. When Nicole didn't jerk it away, he began to pry her steel fingers from the handle, one at a time. Her hands shook slightly, once relieved of the weapon, like leaves in a breeze. The shaking was due to the massive tension still visible in her arm muscles. Jeremy encouraged her to stand with his assistance. He shuffled her back to the car. She accepted his help into the front seat. Jeremy placed the weapon of cat destruction in the trunk. When he returned to the driver's seat, he found her with a lit cigarette hanging from her lips.

"I'm sorry you had to see that." Nicole muttered, looking out of her window.

"It's okay." He said with reassurance. "You want to talk about it?" Jeremy referenced the source of her anger, not the recent events.

"Not yet." Nicole refused to look at him.

"Okay." Jeremy didn't want to pressure her.

"I'm hungry." Nicole said simply. "Let's find a gas station or something." She looked now through the windshield. Droplets of rain appeared as a fine mist.

"Yeah, okay." He started the car and left the street of the crime. His sense of direction had always been admirable. The boy knew his east from his west. Three blocks away was a small convenience store. Jeremy headed there, figuring that it was the best choice; the store also sold liquor and they could both use a drink. What was left of Nicole's whiskey wasn't going to cut it.

Neither of them spoke as he drove. She sat in her silence, wringing out her hands. They hurt on every level. The pain began at her wrists and intermittently shot sharp darts to her fingertips. Underneath the pain was a lingering soreness. It all helped her to feel better. She had vented until her body couldn't carry the activity on any longer. The hurt and betrayal that had brought it all on hadn't gone away, but it was muffled now.

Jeremy parked in front of the store, and looked at her. There were no other vehicles in the parking lot.

"What do you want?" Jeremy asked. "I'll grab it."

"No." Nicole turned toward him. "We're out of whiskey." She confirmed his earlier thoughts about their current need for alcoholic beverages.

"I know. I'll try and-" Jeremy eagerly began. Nicole put a crimson stained hand behind his neck and pulled his face close to hers. She kissed his lips softly to silence him. With his protests abated, she rested her forehead on his and looked in his eyes.

"I'll distract the clerk, you pocket a pint or two, okay? Then we buy some sodas or something and get out of there. Alright?" Nicole laid out the plan.

"Sure. Yeah." Jeremy waited for Nicole to fully exit the car and close the door before he even opened his. Nicole's promise to "distract" the clerk left Jeremy with reservations. He exited the vehicle slowly. Nicole had used a palm full of water scooped from the car's hood to wipe off her face and hands. Black mascara dribbled down her face, accenting the gothic look she had dressed with. Jeremy was encouraged to hurry up by Nicole's flat palm banging on the car hood. He jumped and stumbled toward her.

A small Asian man sat behind the counter of the store as they entered. He was watching a Spanish soap opera. Nicole gauged his age to be in his late twenties. His hair was cut short and stuck up from his head in small spikes thanks to generous amounts of designer hair gel. Nicole noted the subtle blond highlights near the tips were evenly and apparently professionally applied. He wore trendy Old Navy khaki shorts and a t-shirt sporting the latest catch phrase that marketers thought was hot, even though it was so welcome-to-last-month. He was fresh meat in the water and didn't know that in these waters, there now be a shark. Nicole flexed her dorsal fin and swam toward the clerk. Jeremy dogpaddled toward the cooler that contained juice and sodas.

Nicole let her body lean easily on the counter, bolstering her already bulging distractions.

"Excuse me." She asked the young man. He was already looking at her chest.

"Yeah?" He glanced from her face to Jeremy and back to her cleavage.

"I'm kinda new here." Nicole lied, twirling her hair in her hands. "My little brother's dropping me off at a party."

"Okay..." The clerk's eyes flicked over toward Jeremy, who was removing a bottle of soda from the freezer. Nicole tightened her arms against her side, forcing her breasts forward; Any more pressure and they were sure to come bursting out. The ploy worked. The clerk fixed his eyes on her chest again.

"Well, we're looking for a party, on..." Nicole thought of the area. She needed a place opposite of Jeremy's direction. This way, when the clerk gave directions, he'd be tempted to face that way. "Windsor Hill." Nicole decided.

"Windsor Hill?" The clerk searched his memory. "Oh, that's just up the street here." The clerk, eager to help Nicole fell into the trap. He turned, as Nicole had planned. With the clerk's back to him, Jeremy took this time to dart into the alcohol section where he pocketed two random pints of alcohol.

"You make a right at this light on the corner." The clerk explained to Nicole. "Then you make a left on Bradbury. Keep going until you hit Trent Avenue and make another right. That'll put you at the entrance to Windsor Hill."

Nicole noticed Jeremy back at the water cooler, just as the clerk turned back to look at her.

"Thanks." She smiled.

"No problem." The clerk took a second to glance at Jeremy who pretended to be uncertain of which beverage to select next.

"Hey, Bart." Nicole called to Jeremy. "Let's go."

"They don't have any Diet Cherry Coke." Jeremy yelled back to her.

"Just grab me a regular one, then. Hurry up." Nicole pretended to be disgusted. Jeremy reacted with a sigh, snatching the prescribed cola. He shuffled over to the counter and laid his two Coca-Cola's out. Nicole paid and they left.

"I can't believe that worked." Jeremy laughed when they were safely in the car.

"Why not?" Nicole was a less elated. "It was my plan, wasn't it? How much longer are you going to doubt me, sweetheart?"

"But, I've just never done that." Jeremy wouldn't let her bring him down.

"No, I guess you haven't." Nicole admitted.

"So, where to?" Jeremy asked as Nicole looked over his selections: one Canadian whiskey and one cheap Vodka.

"Do you remember when I took you to Bartlett Park that night and you tried your first Xanax?" Nicole referenced her introduction of the prescription pills to the young novice.

"Yeah. What's there?" Jeremy half expected her to want to go to a petting zoo to mutilate some more rodents.

"Calm, Serenity." Nicole answered ambiguously.

"Alright. Okay." Jeremy followed along, not that he had much choice. She would go with or without him. He was unsure of what could possibly come next on this night. He drove with careful determination. With each street they passed, he anticipated a police car roaring in behind them. Jeremy was sure that the someone had to have seen their crimes and reported them. Nicole, not anxious at all, fiddled with the stereo. She changed the station each and every time a song came on that was remotely upbeat. She was down in the dumps, so to speak, and determined to stay there for the time being. It's one of those strange discrepancies of humanity: the sadder we are, the more we want our surroundings to reflect it. Nicole's mounting depression had been building for some time, accompanying her sense of hopelessness. Her actions in the car only served to prove that no matter where you go, there's a sad song on the radio somewhere.

Bartlett Park was a small area of grass planned and designed with the covenant-protected community that had been built alongside it. Several benches and a playground floated in an ocean of wood chips. Sand brought cat shit and any community worth their homeowner's association fees wouldn't be caught dead with cat shit in the park. No, sand in the playground was a lost delicacy, along with swing sets and cloth nets on the basketball hoops.

The park sat on the edge of a man-made lake; Although, the lake would be better described as a small pond. A trail paved with blacktop circled the park and lake. Several fitness stations littered the trail, encouraging runners, walkers, and all other visitors to participate in various exercises. The entire park and lake were surrounded by the new and upscale housing development known collectively as Bartlett View. The park was fully lit with small lamps that protruded a foot from the ground. Bartlett View security was present on the roads in the area, but rarely patrolled the park, despite warnings on signs posted every 30 feet or so on the trail. Bartlett park had become a favorite of Nicole and her friends during her Freshman year. Jeremy had come here only the one time with Nicole.

Nicole led Jeremy to the small playground after he parked on the street. The glass bottles of stolen liquor clanked against the car keys in his pocket. The night breeze was cool. The wind was soft enough that it caused Nicole's longer hair to tremor, but not sway. Nicole navigated past the maze of pipes the developers called a playground and directed herself toward the merry-go-round. Though recently constructed, the merry-go-round had lost much of it's paint. It had several sections that had been colored in red, blue, green and yellow. It stood out in the area, because the other playground equipment was constructed of dull brown and tan metals. The merry-go-round was a symbol of the lost art in childhood recreation. Play, after all, is the work of children. The merry-go-round was a simpler device from a simpler time. Compared to the twisting slide that connected to the zip-line that ended next to the cavernous Plexiglass bubble covered fort (which all sat nearby), the merry go round was an ancient device. However, it was the most used device in the area, as evidenced by it's heavy wear.

Nicole sat here, on the merry-go-round, in the yellow section. She grabbed the support bars on her sides and waited. Jeremy mimicked her position on the red section next to her. She reached into his pocket and retrieved one of the bottles there. He sat silent, unsure of what to say. Often, it was difficult to know or tell which Nicole would be present at any given moment. He was beginning to feel the quiet that preceded Nicole's storms. There was always this slow downtime; A sort of physical crash before the burn of emotions.

As she drank from the bottle, Jeremy expected her usual, calculated sipping. Instead, she gulped down a quarter of the bottle in a matter of seconds. When the bottle finished kissing her lips, Jeremy hurriedly thrust one of the sodas they had purchased towards her. Nicole traded the whiskey for the soda. She took a miniscule sip of Coca-Cola while Jeremy took the whiskey. Nicole didn't want to diminish the blaze of the Tennessee sour mash. Jeremy allowed himself a short sip of alcohol. Lord knows, after the events of the night so far, he needed a drink. His drink was so small, in fact, that he didn't need a chaser drink for himself. Nicole produced the pills she had stowed away earlier. She took one and offered another to Jeremy. He accepted, but didn't take it. Instead, he discreetly crumbled it between his thumb and the steel beneath him. The alcohol had begun to work it's magic on Nicole's sinuses. She sniffled up a large ball of phlegm and spit like a baseball player. Jeremy took the opportunity to brush away the remnants of the pill she'd given him.

Nicole began to slowly kick the ground as she lit a cigarette. Her action set the merry-go-round in motion. The device began to turn, and Nicole's force of push increased. Jeremy helped her move the gadget along.

"Pretty crazy night, huh." Nicole said with an unenthusiastic laugh.

"Yeah, I guess." Jeremy didn't prompt her to continue. He was going to let her move along at her own pace. The last thing he wanted right now was for her to feel pressured. Over the past few weeks, Jeremy had learned that pressuring Nicole to talk made her defensive and, often times, downright mean.

"I don't know what's going on, Jeremy." Nicole confessed in a quiet voice.

"What do you mean?" Now that she seemed to be silently asking for a cause to talk, he gave her one.

"Everything's just crazy, Jeremy. It's like I'm not myself anymore. Everything I used to know, isn't what it used to be. Everyone's changing and I just don't get it." Nicole's feelings began to pour out.

"Well, people change, Nicole." Now, as Nicole began to open up, Jeremy began to take a more direct approach with his conversational contributions.

"Yeah, but sometimes, you just don't expect it. Some things you expect to stay the same. Forever." Nicole exhaled deeply.

"But they never do. Nothing stays the same forever. You just have to adapt and go with the flow or find a different river to swim in." Jeremy rationalized.

"I'm tired of swimming, Jeremy. I just want a nice little device to float along on. Maybe one of those inflatable, pool/lawn chairs that you see in the movies all the time. I could just lay back and let the current take me."

"Where's the fun in that." Jeremy quashed the idea.

"I've had enough fun, I think." Nicole declared.

"What's gotten into you, today?" Jeremy hunted for the root of her current distemper.

"Natalie and Veronica are still carrying on. I know Natalie's happy, but I honestly thought this thing with them was going to last only a few days or a week maybe." Nicole confided.

"And there's no way for you and Veronica to co-exist, huh?" Jeremy asked.

"No." Nicole's answer was lightning fast and firm. "There's just way too much history for me to let it all go. Betrayal always cuts the deepest. And those deep cuts rarely ever heal right. Is it really so much to expect a little loyalty from your best friend?"

"You keep talking about your expectations, but not about others. Don't you think Natalie expected you to stand by her?" Jeremy dared to present a differing perspective. Nicole didn't continue arguing. She drank slowly from the whiskey bottle, allowing Jeremy to turn the merry-go-round.

"Fine." Nicole sat up. "Let's go." She ordered.

"Where?" Jeremy rolled to his feet as Nicole began the short march back to the car.

"To test your theory." Nicole pulled out her cell phone. She dialed Elizabeth first. Jeremy trotted up to Nicole's side, still unsure of what she was planning. Her moods and behaviors were so manic, he never knew what to expect. One moment, she was here or there and the next she was neither.

The telephone rang twice before Elizabeth answered. Nicole couldn't believe she had been made to wait for the second ring.

"Hello? Nicky?" Elizabeth maintained her perky attitude. Nicole could hear sounds in the background that were obviously those of a large social gathering. One Nicole had not been invited to. Loud music was accompanied by the chitter-chatter of a grand crowd.

"Lizzie." Nicole had meant to emulate her friend's cheeriness, but that proved difficult. "What's going on?"

"Oh." Elizabeth hesitated. She knew by Nicole's tone and question that the conversation was entering a rather dangerous territory. She could lie, but Nicole would know, and then Lizzie would face her wrath the same as everyone else. "We're just all hanging out at Veronica's place. What are you up to?" Elizabeth wasn't untruthful, but neither was she clear on the situation. The "we" she spoke of was undefined.

The bit of hesitation in Elizabeth's voice threw Nicole. It wasn't like Elizabeth to treat her this way. *Had Lizzie debated lying to her*?! The rage within Nicole began to fester and burn once more, at this slight hint of possible treachery. The thought of Lizzie lying to her pushed Nicole back into a dark place. *Perhaps Elizabeth needed reminding of her position in the world*, Nicole thought.

"Elizabeth. Sweetie. You know better than to lie to me." Nicole's words darted out, startling Jeremy. The coldness to her tone was absolute. Cooler than a polar bear's toe nail, some might say. "It's obvious you're at a party. And I wasn't invited. That's very rude, dear."

"Nicky-" Elizabeth took a backpedaling step to ready an explanation.

"Shut it." Nicole silenced her. "You remember who I am, don't you? You remember everything that I've done for you. You remember how I stuck up for you, took you, and made you someone."

"Nicole, I just thought-" Elizabeth shuffled away from the loud sounds of the party. Nicole heard a door shut in the background, and suddenly, the party died. "Nicole, I was just thinking-"

"No." Nicole stopped her. "You weren't thinking. You hardly ever do, and that's why I'm left to clean up your messes. And this is the thanks I get. You can't even tell me the simple truth about a party anymore. Maybe next time you get plastered and then gang-raped at a party, I'll let the truth be told, and leave you to deal with it alone."

Sniffles answered Nicole from Elizabeth's end of the line. Nicole waited to see if they were tears of regret, or tears of anger.

"I'm sorry." Elizabeth stammered. "I just, I guess I wasn't thinking. You're right."

Nicole smiled. It was the slippery smile of something unnatural, but oh so human. She was a mean manipulator, and Elizabeth had never stood a chance. Nicole would wreck the girl, if she had to.

"It's okay, sweetie. I'm sorry I had to speak to you in such a manner, but can you see now what Natalie's little fling has done to us?"

"Yeah." Elizabeth, broken and trained, agreed weakly.

"I want you to dry your cheeks, fix your face and pretend that I just talked to you about regular gossip. I'll be there in a half an hour or so, and we'll get this all sorted out, okay?" Nicole instructed.

"Okay." Elizabeth tried not to trip over the tail tucked between her legs.

"Okay. Love ya! Bye!" Nicole hung up without waiting for a response. Jeremy, who had been watching only one side of the conversation, was aghast. By this time, he had seen many of Nicole's personalities. Never had one scared him so. The vindictive, hateful Nicole before him was a predatory beast that would devour all put before it. Jeremy had never expected her to turn her fangs directly on Natalie or Elizabeth.

"Is everything alright?" Jeremy asked, feigning ignorance.

"It will be." Nicole answered with an icy tone, staring past Jeremy. "*It will be.*"

"So, what's the plan then?" He asked.

"There's a party at Veronica's, apparently. And we just got invited." Nicole opened up the passenger door. "I've got business to handle. Seems that the court has decided to have a gala without the queen."

Jeremy felt the searing determination entering Nicole's voice. She began to change once more. The vulnerable girl who she truly was hid as the tyrant she pretended to be took control. Jeremy knew what that meant, and he worried. He tried to stall her.

"Nicole, why even go over there tonight? Let's find another party or something." He attempted to redirect her. Nicole's mindset since he had first met her and especially tonight, was severely unstable. After seeing what she had done to the cat, he was terrified of what act Nicole may be tempted to commit once they arrived at Veronica's house.

"Jeremy, my life is dictated by a delicate balance of dedication, determination and an unwavering sense of duty. I have to go to this party. Do you think I want to do this?" Nicole asked rhetorically.

"If you don't want to do it, you don't have to." Jeremy answered, still unsure of what exactly "it" was going to be. Even though she had been slowly changing him, he had on his own been attempting to alter her skewed ideals as well. He hadn't succeeded as often as he'd failed.

"Jeremy," again, Nicole stressed his name, as a mother does when reprimanding a child. "You can't just do what you want all the time. There are times when you must do the things you hate, because it's the only appropriate response that a given situation may allow. I'm not going to Veronica's because I want to. I'm going to Veronica's party because that's how certain people have forced me to act. Or react rather."

Nicole was an expert at the blame game. Even without the drugs, she'd be able to sleep at night after spewing all that bullshit. She'd been making excuses for her petty need for public adoration so long that she'd almost begun to believe it herself. Jeremy still retained some of the common sense he had been given before he met her and wasn't falling for her reasoning.

"We can do whatever we want, Nicole. Let's go hang out on those water towers on Fremen Road again. Or let's go see how much free food we can scam out of McDonald's. Or let's just go back to the park and enjoy tonight." Jeremy began to wildly throw out suggestions based on past nights that they had shared.

"Please." He resorted to begging.

Nicole reached in his pockets, and snatched out the car keys. She shifted in the passenger seat and reached to the steering wheel. She started the car and looked at him.

"Someday, you'll learn to *hate*, Jeremy. Just like me." She said, unsure if that was a promise or a curse.

Before he could respond, she shut the door and looked forward. Jeremy knew this meant the discussion was over. She would go to the party with or without him. He gave up, deciding it would be best to try and control Nicole once they arrived. He knew that in reality, he would never be able to control her. Attempting to control Nicole in any fashion for prolonged periods of time would lead to Jeremy's destruction. She was a wild thing. The more you try to love a wild thing, the harder they try to pull away, a woman in a movie had once said.

Jeremy gave in and they sped off into the night. The pair rode with no conversation. Jeremy was busy trying to figure out in his head just what Nicole could be planning. Nicole had no plan. She was occupied with thoughts of treason and revenge. All Nicole knew for sure was that certain people had forgotten their roles, and it was high time that they were admonished.

Chapter Eleven: Life of the Party

Veronica's house looked as it always did with her parties. People milled about, a river of bodies spilling from the front door and onto the lawn. Red, plastic cups that had once been full at the site of the kegs were strewn about, almost as decorations. Loud music vibrated through the ground and the noise of conversation bubbled about like a mad scientist's serum steaming on a table in some dark laboratory. The crowd had been separated into its usual castes. The have's and the have-not's were locked in the continual struggle of adolescence and young adulthood.

The outer edge of the "Oh-so-closes" gawked at Jeremy parking Nicole's immediately recognizable automobile. He had become something of an urban legend within the school. He was the nobody who somehow broke into the ranks of the privileged few. They had watched his transformation over the last few months with a sense of envy and awe. Not only had the relationship catapulted Jeremy clear into a new social stratosphere, it had elevated Nicole within every circle of popularity. The "Oh-so-closes" and those below them had renewed faith that they too could someday join the ranks of the nobles. Because the popular kids rarely dated outside their own ranks, they practiced a disciplined sort of inbreeding. With Nicole not only choosing, but elevating Jeremy, she had proven that the lovin' didn't always need to be kept in the family. Those who wished to be popular now showered those who were with more praise and gifts (monetary and sexual), with the hopes of being the next Jeremy. This had gained Nicole the adoration of her own high society peers.

Nicole led Jeremy, even though they walked side by side. They silently made their way past the riff-raff and into the house. Chad and the rest of his swim team had been relegated to a lower position near the front door of the home. After his embarrassing beat down, and the loss of his mistress to another woman, his reputation had been irreparably tarnished. He tried to play down the demotion as being by choice, but everyone knew that he had fallen a few notches on the totem pole. Nicole had effectively neutered the stud. Chad sneered at Jeremy as they walked past. Nicole tossed her hair and sighed. It was a subtle signal to all in attendance that Chad was still not to be allowed his former post.

"Are they outside?" Jeremy asked Nicole as they stood in the entryway.

"Always. Veronica thinks that a hot tub is some sort of status symbol." Nicole answered him.

"You don't?" Jeremy asked.

"I think people spread syphilis, chlamydia, and pink-eye in hot tubs." Nicole said. A few people who had been listening in on them laughed. Nicole grinned back at them. A small treat of recognition from the female sovereign.

"So then, we're just going-" Jeremy began.

"To the basement" Nicole cut him off.

"But I thought-"

"There's a bar in the basement. We'll have a couple shots and a beer and see what happens. They know we're here. They'll come on down in their own time." Nicole explained, licking and smacking her lips.

"I still don't understand what we're doing here." Jeremy sighed.

Nicole led him to a door just off the entryway, that led to the basement.

"You will." She kept her voice coy and low. Jeremy had known Nicole intimately for a few months at this point and still she was a mystery to him. Her next move was never something he could deduce, even with his devoted thinking on the drive over. The main reason for this was his thinking. Jeremy was one of the popular kids now, but he didn't understand everything that the title of popular required to be maintained. He thought in the now. Nicole had learned long ago that in order to sustain the style of life she deserved, she had to think two to three steps ahead.

The basement of Veronica's manse was not merely a finished room with a wet-bar. The walls were a well-finished oak. The floor was covered in a glossy black tile with ornate, gold, Victorian trim. The main lights were dim, with stained glass shades. They hung low from the ceiling. The stained glass held images of bartenders and drinks done in an early Victorian style. Veronica's father had purchased the custom ordered pieces from an Irish immigrant in Philadelphia who specialized in glass making. The alternative light sources in the room were the numerous neon signs advertising different brands of ale and spirits that adorned the walls between the painted pictures of Old Chicago, before the fire. The signs were all authentic from real distributors, not auctions or novelty stores. In the corner of the room sat a jukebox. The Seeburg HF100G 100, first produced in September of 1953. It played 100 selections on both sides of 50 individual 45 speed vinyl albums. The catalog currently within the machine was a vast library of doo-wop bands such as The Marcels with their Blue Moon and the old style crooners like Harry Belafonte. Each of the albums in the chrome beast were collector's items themselves. They were all original presses that Veronica's father had scoured the country for. He was a sucker for delicious vinyl.

The mood of the basement held a different tone than the rest of the home. The room's life echoed it's decor. It was relaxed and secretive, much like the baroque wood carvings that decorated the oak bar stools with images of masons and forefathers past. This was a room where people too young in mind and experience acted grown, or as close to their slanted version of "grown" that they could get.

Dark booths ran along the wall opposite the bar. In these booths, young suburbanites who had been infused with a false sense of coolness by the MTV hip-hop culture dealt capsules of heroin and forms of cocaine. The addicts acted unashamed of their extravagant habits, snorting freely. Those who had graduated to injecting drugs still tried to keep their desires discreet. The dealers themselves wore gold and silver chains with button up shirts and variant ballcaps from professional sports and the Negro leagues. Their language reflected a black community they had never known beyond the black dealers who sold them product at sharply inflated prices and, of course, music videos.

In the late 80's, a fledgling music style from the 70's began to infuse a dead society. Rap and hip-hop, first populated by stars intending to emulate costumed bands like Parliament Funkadelic, was a land of tights and sequined clothing. They sported leather jackets with chains and cheesy, neon stage getups. They sang party songs and odes to their DJ's. As the culture changed, so did the music. As the music did, so did the dress. The music began to reflect the drug and gang culture, and by the late 80's, the music was getting coverage from mainstream media. What was once called a "fad" in the late 70's was now a threat to conservative American ideals. Groups like N.W.A. (Niggaz With Attitude), spat in the face of Nancy Reagan's Just Say No campaign. While some still labeled the music a passing sensation, others tried to outlaw it. Popular culture began to embrace rap music and thus, it began a slow infection of white America. Rap music and hip-hop were ideas that young, white America was beginning to embrace with a fervor.

By the turn of the 90's, the drug trade was booming. Rap music, proving it was not a fad, exploded along with all of hip-hop across America. The slang, the clothes, the swagger, and most of all, the music had triumphed. The music that honestly gave a nightly news report of the black community had become chart topping video and radio fodder. With this constant exposure came crude mimicry. By the end of the century and the beginning of the new millennium, young, suburban, white kids had adopted many of the traits and negative aspects of the black community because they were, "cool". Both demographics would have been better served if their youth were move focused on learning and working for change. Now, the "fad" had infiltrated the heart of America. Most parents weren't happy about it, but there was no stopping what could not be stopped.

Society in general wasn't much of a help, either. Being proud to be white had been laced with the racist, redneck, and Nazi stigma. Everyone else in the country was pushed into being proud of their heritage, except young white kids. It didn't help that those who were proud to be white generally exercised little restraint in voicing neo-Nazi or white supremacist thoughts. There was no positive outlet for those young suburbanites to express pride in themselves, their history, and their heritage. They latched on to something it was okay to be proud of.

Nicole had never fallen too far into the hip-hop culture. She listened to the music and wore the clothes associated with the movement, sometimes. She had no false, ghetto accent. She never used Ebonics. Her body language was pure 'white girl', when she wanted it to be; Having a little rhythm was never a bad thing.

Nicole waded through the thin basement crowd. She received nods and shouts from across the room. Jeremy had no idea that Nicole had ever associated with anyone in these circles. He felt stupid for not thinking of this possibility earlier. Nicole was obviously well versed in the ways of the world. Of course, she had dabbled in just about everything.

Here, in the depth of decadence, Nicole changed yet again. She brought forth from within a side of herself that was always there, just not with an extreme emphasis. Her eyes became inviting and playful. Her hips and bust moved with deliberate fluidity. Her head seemed to tilt at various angles drawing attention to her neck. Her smile was coy, yet mischievous.

As Nicole neared the bar, she pulled Jeremy with a commanding gentleness to her side. He expected her to sit in the one bar stool that had been emptied for her. Jeremy, although respected as her boyfriend, hadn't been elevated to the point where he'd be automatically given a seat of his own. That would come in time.

Nicole ignored the offer. As she stood at the bar, she whirled around. With a lightning quick hop, she was sitting on the bar. Jeremy had no time to react. Nicole pulled him close, grinding her groin into his chest, subtly. She leaned back on the bar and untucked her shirt, revealing the abdomen of Aphrodite.

"Hey, barkeep!" She shouted. "Me and my good buddy here would like some belly shots."

The young man pretending to be a professional creator of alcoholic concoctions responded quickly to her demand and the roar of the crowd that it drew. Jeremy began to understand. The entire room was watching them now. Nicole intended to steal the show.

"What to drink?" The bartender stared hungrily at the flat, defined form of Nicole's stomach.

"Salt." Nicole placed a hand to the right of her belly button. "Tequila." She put her left finger directly in the umbilicus. Jeremy, who prior had no idea what a belly shot was before, now knew exactly what to do.

Outside the basement, the arrival of Nicole had not gone unnoticed. Neither had her public snubbing of Natalie and Veronica. Word spread throughout the party that Nicole was in the basement. Elizabeth, ever the gossip, was circulating through the party and heard the news first. She had been moving from group to group chit-chatting when she overheard three sophomores excitedly planning how they would get into the basement to see Nicole. She stopped one, grabbing him by the shoulder.

"What did you say?" Elizabeth asked sternly. Her voice bore no excitement. She knew that Nicole being here meant two things: confrontation and conflict. With Nicole's recent erratic behavior, Elizabeth was scared, not excited.

"Um, Nicole O'Leary is here and doing body shots in the basement. Don't you two hang out?" The young man answered Elizabeth unsteadily. He was sure he had secured an escort off of the grounds by even garnering Elizabeth's attention.

"Nicole? Here." Elizabeth pointed at the ground. "You saw her?"

"Well, no, not in the basement. I saw her come in, though." The boy tried to lean away. Elizabeth, done with him, shoved him away. The boy rubbed his shoulder and winced. Elizabeth turned and walked with purpose towards the swimming pool and hot tub.

Natalie and Veronica were sharing a laugh with the other girls in the hot tub, when Elizabeth arrived. Natalie sat with her arms wrapped around Veronica, who sat in her lap. Veronica lightly rubbed Natalie's arm as Elizabeth approached. Veronica, not too close with Elizabeth noticed nothing. Natalie could read Elizabeth's body language well enough to know that something was up. Natalie even suspected slightly what the issue was.

"Lizzie?" Natalie kept a playful mood for the crowd. "What's up?"

"Nicole's here." Elizabeth used the pretense of excitement so as not to alarm anyone to the underlying issues.

"Oh." Natalie also kept up the joyous charade. "Is she coming in, or what?"

"No." Elizabeth slipped, and the concern came through in her voice. "She's here. She's in the basement, doing body shots."

Natalie was angered at Elizabeth's lapse in control. The effect on those nearby was immediate. They all shuffled away in a rush to view Nicole's outrageous behavior. The three girls were now alone on the patio. The entire party was pushing and shoving at the patio doors, attempting to cram into the house to make their way into the basement.

Veronica pulled her hands away from Natalie. Her companion made no move to retrieve them. Veronica's defeat had come before the battle had started. She had hoped that what she and Natalie had was real. Ever since the two first began what was initially a dallying dance with curiosity, Veronica had grown feelings. Natalie was special to Veronica, and vice versa; But no matter how much of herself Veronica offered, she would never be Nicole.

"You're going in, too, aren't you?" Veronica looked at her reflection in the water. Natalie's eyes met hers over Veronica's shoulder, and then Natalie looked away.

"It's not like that, Ronnie." Natalie explained.

"No." Veronica couldn't contain her heart. She didn't attempt to swallow the tears. "It's exactly like that. I'll never be her, Natalie. No matter how much you want me to be, I can't be her."

"Ronnie-" Natalie began another attempt to rationalize her behavior. She was interrupted by an index finger on Veronica's right hand pressing on her lips.

"Stop. Just stop." Veronica spun around to face Natalie. "We're going inside. I'm sure Nicole's eagerly waiting for you. She'll have some fantastic distraction to make sure everyone's still looking at her. And once she's done using you for whatever she needs, I'll still be here, Natalie."

Natalie nodded slightly, hugging Veronica close. It was a silent admission of her feelings.

"But only this once." Veronica whispered. "Only this once."

Natalie nodded again, and slipped out of the hot tub. She and Veronica grabbed their jeans from poolside and dressed.

The three girls had to push and shove their way into the basement. The entire party ignored the normal social protocols. Veronica mentally cataloged the most serious offenders to hand out a suitable punishment later. The politics of young adulthood are vicious and lasting.

A new song was beginning on the jukebox as Natalie was able to get a clear view of the basement. The Isley Brothers were beginning the classic rendition of "Shout, Parts 1 and 2". The album itself was a rare pressing that had cost Veronica's father nearly $5,000. It was the original first edition pressing that had been delivered to the most popular radio station of Los Angeles in it's debut year.

Nicole stood up on the bar as the song began. Natalie noticed Jeremy sitting in awe at the bar, the only male in range who wasn't looking up Nicole's skirt. The sexual tension that Nicole could introduce to a gathering was amazing. Everyone in sight wanted her. It was as if she were surrounded by mutant pheromones that could hijack even the most devoted of partners. Even Veronica couldn't deny a deep attraction within her. Natalie had forgotten their conversation only moments ago. Nicole's dancing and lip-syncing entranced her best friend.

"Weeelllll!" Ronald Isley sang.

Nicole tilted her face skyward, pretending to emit the bellowing voice.

"You know you make me want to shout!"

She snapped to life with a jump.

"Kick my heels up and shout! Throw my hands up and shout! Throw my head back and shout!"

Nicole's lithe body mimicked the narration of the song.

"C'mon now. Don't forget to say you will!"

Nicole turned toward the young man who had been playing bartender.

"Don't forget to say, yeah, yeah, yeah, yeah, yeah!"

Nicole implored a group of 3 sophomore girls, while inciting them to clap their hands, which in turn spread around the room.

"Say it right now, maybe (say you will), C'mon, c'mon! (say you will)"

Nicole brushed tequila salt from her stomach.

"Say that you love me! (Say!)"

Nicole blew a kiss towards Jeremy. It was at this moment that she saw Elizabeth waving.

"Say that you need me! (Say!)"

A wicked grin was turned to Veronica, who flinched.

"Say that you want me! (Say) You want to please me!"

Nicole's eyes found Natalie's. Natalie had been moving steadily closer to the bar Nicole was dancing upon. She seemed severely out of place, dripping wet indoors.

"C'mon now, C'mon now, C'mon now, C'mon now."

Nicole beckoned Natalie to come closer, all the while relishing the pain on Veronica's face.

"I can still remember, when you used to be 9 years old! I was a fool for you, from the bottom of my soul!"

Nicole crouched as Natalie stood next to Jeremy at the bar.

"Now that you've grown up, grown enough to know! You wanna leave me. You wanna let me go!"

Nicole placed a hand on each of Natalie's cheeks.

"I want you to know. I said I want you to know right now!"

Nicole pointed a finger in Natalie's face as the tempo slowed, just brushing her nose.

"You been good to me, baby! Better than I been to myself!"

Nicole twisted her hips hard enough to throw her skirt over Natalie's face.

"Now if you ever leave me, I don't want, nobody else!"

Nicole winked at Jeremy.

"I said I want you to knooowww. I said I want you to know right now!"

Nicole stood-

"You make me want to shout! (yeah) Shout! (yeah) Shout! (all right!) Shout! (all right!) Shout! (c'mon now!) Shout! (c'mon now!) Shout! (yeah!) Shout! (Yea-ay-yeah!) Shout! (Yea-ay-yeah!) Shout! (Yea-ay-yeah!) Shout! (all right!) Shout! (all right!) Shout! (all right!) Shout! (all right!)"

Nicole stomped back and forth across the bar until she reclaimed her original position in front of Natalie and Jeremy.

"Now wait a minute!"

Nicole placed a hand over her heart.

"I feel alll-lll riiiiight. Now that I've got my woman."

Nicole took Natalie's hands in hers.

"I feeelll, all-lll riiiiiiight."

Nicole began to stand.

"Every time I think aboutcha, you been so good to me!"

Nicole let go of Natalie's hands and looked at the crowd.

"You know you make me wanna- Kick my heels up and shout! Throw my head back and shout! Throw my heels up and shout!"

Nicole pranced up and down the bar once again, kicking any drinks that were still in her way, aside.

"Cmon now! Take it easy! Take it easy! Take it easy!"

Nicole pretended to be overwhelmed by the audience's excitement. She placed a hand on her chest.

"A little bit softer now. (shout!) A little bit softer now. (shout!) A little bit softer now. (shout!) A little bit softer now. (shout!) A little bit softer now. (shout!) A little bit softer now. (shout!) A little bit softer now. (shout!) A little bit softer now. (shout!) A little bit softer now. (shout!) A little bit softer now. (shout!) A little bit softer now. (shout!). A little bit softer now. (shout!) A little bit softer now. (shout!) A little bit softer now. (shout!) A little bit softer now. (shout!) A little bit softer now. (shout!) A little bit softer now."

She lowered herself to the bar a little more with each successive chant of the crowd. The crowd followed her instruction and gradually grew quieter with each chant until they were a breeze above silent. Nicole, at the quietest point, was lying on her back, commanding the choir. Eventually, she began to raise her hands slowly.

"A little bit louder now! (Shout!) A little bit louder now! (Shout!) A little bit louder now! (Shout!) A little bit louder now! (Shout!) A little bit louder now! (Shout!) A little bit louder now! (Shout!) A little bit louder now! (Shout!) A little bit louder now! (Shout!) A little bit louder now! (Shout!) A little bit louder now! (Shout!) A little bit louder now! (Shout!) A little bit louder now! (Shout!)"

Nicole raised her hands a bit further with each instruction, until the audience was once again at their peak. Suddenly, Nicole was on her feet again in one swift motion. She leapt into the crowd, landing between Natalie and Jeremy.

"Jump up and shout right now!"

Nicole pulled Jeremy from his stool. He eagerly followed, shouting as ordered.

"Jump up and shout now!"

Nicole placed two hands on Natalie's shoulders. Their eyes locked and in that one instant, countless emotions were exchanged. Veronica looked on, unable to control her anxiety. She felt the rejection when Natalie began to "shout", on cue. Elizabeth, also still shouting with the crowd, put an arm around Veronica's shoulders. She knew the cutting edge of Nicole's wrath. Nicole was still lip-syncing and dancing about as the song ended and the standing ovation began.

Jeremy and Natalie stood with Nicole between them. She placed an arm around each, taking several dramatic bows. While Nicole pretended to look about the room, her attention never truly left Veronica. The gauntlet had never needed throwing. There were to be no battles over Natalie. Veronica was right. She couldn't be Nicole. Not for Natalie. Standing in her own basement, she had once again been reduced to nothing by Nicole O'Leary.

Elizabeth's genuine gestures of comfort provided no measure of such. Veronica, changed by her previous encounter with Nicole, was now genuine. She had been exposed and forced to be true. Now, she was truly hurt, and the one person she wanted comfort from had betrayed her heart. The same heart that had allowed itself to be blinded by the cruelest of emotions: hope. Hope had led Veronica to believe that maybe she meant something to Natalie. Hope had mistakenly caused Veronica to see a possible future where Natalie stood by her side. Hope hadn't caused Veronica to think that Natalie would just abandon Nicole; Hope had caused her to believe there was a worthwhile sense of loyalty between she and Natalie. Hope, that one feeling that will lead us down any road, only to let us down and see us suffer. And once we suffer, what do we cling to? Hope. Hope that the suffering will end. Even when that suffering is epic and legendary.

Veronica shook her head slightly as Nicole laughed. Standing on the stairs, lost in the crowd, she was broken. Veronica realized that all her affluence and show meant nothing. Veronica had nothing left, and Nicole had everything. Veronica had taunted the beast, not realizing she herself wasn't ready for this war. She had no idea how long and painful their dispute would become when she started it. The cost had been high. The stark awareness of Nicole's true person scared her. Nicole was one of the mythical Furies, her vengeance never ending.

As Natalie, laughing with Jeremy, turned to wave Veronica toward them, the shattered young woman instead stormed to her room. Elizabeth followed. Natalie slowly lowered her hand. Her smile began to fade into a slight smirk. Nicole ducked her face around to nearly touch noses with Natalie.

"Everything alright?" Nicole asked, knowing the answer. Her little song and dance had achieved the desired effect.

"Yeah." Natalie hesitated, and then repeated the statement with more confidence. "It's good to see you out and about." Natalie smiled. Just as hope had led Veronica down a false path, so too did this controlling emotion push Natalie to a similar fate. There would never be anything eventful between she and Nicole. Ever. But still, Natalie hoped, even knowing full and well the reality of the situation.

Nicole lit a cigarette, and ordered a round of drinks for the three of them. The "bartender" poured from the tap like a whore singing Christmas Carols: each glass was at least half head. Nicole was disgusted at the aspect of suffering through a half glass of foam, but didn't want to wait any longer for another drink. She licked her index finger, and twirled it in her beer, letting the enzymes from her saliva go to work at clearing the foam.

The noise of the bar had grown considerably. The place was packed now; standing room only. People made mindless conversation about what Nicole had just done, or what she might do next. There was a general consensus that she had livened the place up. Her electric performance had elevated the common gathering and moved it into the realm of a renowned party.

"Go. Mingle." Nicole handed Jeremy his beer. "It's time for some girl talk."

Jeremy looked from Nicole to Natalie, and walked away quietly.

"He looks hot tonight." Natalie drank from her mug gingerly. Nicole smirked.

"Let's not do this, Natalie. Not us. We've been through too much together." Nicole didn't look at her.

"What do you mean?" Natalie recoiled a bit at the request, and the cold tone in Nicole's voice.

"What happened?" Nicole asked, turning to look at her best friend. She licked a bit of white foam from her lips as she awaited a response.

"Well, you tell me. All the sudden you show up-" Natalie was smiling, like all the other admirers, when Nicole cut her off, blowing smoke in Natalie's face.

"I don't mean just tonight, and you know it. I mean with us. We were inseparable. Once. But now... Now I hardly see you outside school. Every time I call it's Veronica this or Veronica that, leave a message!" Nicole ended imitating a voice-mail tone. Natalie was hurt. She had done everything for Nicole over the years to support her best friend. She had spent countless nights with Chad and his pack of mongrels. Natalie had weathered every rumor thrown Nicole's way. She had not only supported, but had encouraged Nicole's relationship with Jeremy. Natalie felt it wasn't much to ask the same in return.

"And it's any different with you?" Natalie brushed her damp hair from her eyes, so Nicole could clearly see the tears forming. "When haven't you been with Jeremy since you two got together?"

"You were one of the one's who told me to date him, remember?" Nicole snapped. "I, however, never suggested you begin or continue with this experiment you have going on."

"Experiment?" Natalie scoffed. She was stunned and offended. "I never asked or needed your fucking permission, Nicole. But that's what it's all about, isn't it? It's not that you missed me. It's that you missed feeling like you were in charge of me. You missed being in control. You missed me running on cue whenever you called."

Nicole was impressed. She had never expected Natalie to break the unwritten rules of aristocracy. Now they were openly fighting and even discussing the truths of their lives. Nicole looked away from Natalie just long enough to dart a smile at a group of eavesdroppers who had been sure they were acting discreetly enough not to be detected.

"Natalie, I never asked you to come down here tonight. Yet you did. Why? Maybe it's that you miss something more than being at my beck and call." Nicole kept the smile. Natalie was audibly grinding her teeth.

"You. Are. So. Hurtful." Natalie allowed a single tear to leave her right eye. "You know why I came down here tonight. You knew. You always knew. I tried my best to keep it a secret, but I know you saw through it. And I thought... No, I didn't think, because I, of all people, know the real you. I knew what could never be, but I loved you, and I let that blind me."

Nicole was the one who felt the pain now.

"Loved?" Nicole questioned the past tense while thumbing the tear from Natalie's face.

"Yeah." Natalie looked away, and then back into Nicole's eyes. "Things change, Nicole. I see now what we were. Things are different now. I don't want what I used to crave, and you aren't who you used to be."

Nicole was on the verge of tears now, herself. The only reason she didn't begin to cry, was that she was cried out, and had no tears left. Often times, we don't realize how much of ourselves we keep within other people. These are the deepest, most honest and pure parts of our soul. This is why we only entrust these parts to a few select individuals over a lifetime. The insight into our own vulnerability comes when one of these people let's go of that part of us. We've entrusted them with a heavy responsibility, and that burden comes with a price not only for them, but for ourselves as well. Much like the words we speak, that part of our whole that we give away, can never be undone or taken back. Once that other person relinquishes that responsibility, that part of us dies. It can never be mended or replaced. This is how one dies, on the inside.

"You're right." Nicole finally conceded, running a hand across Natalie's cheek. "You're right."

Natalie grasped Nicole's hand in hers.

"I've changed. I know that." Nicole opened up. Her eyes never wavered from Natalie's. "I don't know who I am anymore, Natalie. I'm not even sure if I'll survive all this and asking you to come along for the ride was selfish. I do know how you feel... How you *felt*."

Natalie pitied her friend.

"Nicole, I can't imagine what you are going through right now. I can't. I've tried and I can't. But we can still fix this. We can still be friends. I can still be here for you." Natalie offered.

"No." Nicole flatly denied the idea. "All things are good in time and moderation. We, Us, we've had too much time and no moderation. I know you'd still come if I called, but I won't. After all this time, you've finally done something for yourself, and I refuse to interfere in that any longer. It's time we became who we were meant to be, Natalie."

"Nicole-"

"Nope. That's it." Nicole shook away any rebuttals. "Let's not go back to where we were just moments ago. Let's have a clean break. Let me share this one last beer with my best friend."

Nicole held her glass up. Natalie did likewise. They clinked them heartily together.

"To best friends." Natalie toasted.

"We had a good run. Best friends K through 12, who can say that? We'll go off to college and start families and catch up on whatever website has replaced Facebook 30 years from now." Nicole sighed. "I wish you all the happiness in the world, you deserve it, Natalie."

"And you. Besides, we're still family. There will always be Christmas and Thanksgiving, right?"

"Indeed." Nicole agreed. "By the way, I paid Mrs. Johnsen and Sandy a visit earlier. They say, 'hello'."

Chapter Twelve: The End
Part 3 of 3

Today

  Six months after the fateful morning chat with her parents, the divorce was finalized. Nicole's brother, Jackson, had no idea. Jackson would never have noticed they separated if Nicole hadn't told him. Her parents had done it with little to no bickering. Both of them wanted what they felt was best for the kids. A clean break fit that description to both Mr. and Mrs. O'Leary.

  Today, when court adjourned, Nicole followed her father home in her car. Her mother had moved out now, and was living with a friend from church for the time being. Nicole wasn't fond of him, and hated him as much as she hated Rebecca, her father's new girlfriend. Rebecca had been staying over more frequently, and it was driving Nicole crazy. With only these two options until she moved out herself, Nicole chose to stay with her father, only because the house was familiar. She had plans to move out soon anyhow, as soon as she found an apartment or condo suitable for her and Jeremy.

  She parked behind her father in the driveway and stormed past him as he got out of his car. She took note of how far behind he was, and made sure to slam the front door in his face. Harold sighed and followed his daughter into the house.

  Nicole stormed up to her room, and sat at her desk, looking in the mirror. She picked up her cordless phone when her father knocked on her door.

  "Nicole?" He called to her. "Nicole... I'm sorry, for all of it. I'm so sorry. I can't ever fix it, I know that. I know how I failed you, and I can't tell you how sorry I am-"

Nicole cut him off by flinging her phone hard enough that it shattered, leaving pieces wedged into the wood. Her father jumped back. He started to knock again, but withdrew his fist, and went back downstairs.

Nicole looked at her crying face in the mirror. It had all finally come apart. Half a year ago, she thought her world was close enough to perfect. Now, everything was in pieces around her. She thought of Jeremy, and called him on her cellphone. When he answered, she hung up. She crushed the phone under her heel, and decided to stop trying to hold the gates closed. A tempest was coming and she wasn't going to hold it back any longer.

She began to paint her face black with eyeliner. With her entire face painted, she applied the brightest red lipstick she could find. Then she took each of the porcelain masks from her wall, and smashed them on the floor. She took her dresser drawers, and threw them about the room. She changed clothes, and left.

As she walked down the hall, she stopped at her father's bedroom. The door was open, but he wasn't inside. She crept in and retrieved his pistol from the nightstand. She took it, checking to make sure it was loaded. His .380 was lighter than she remembered.

Mr. O'Leary may not have been an intimidating person, but he wasn't a complete coward. Like his father had taught him, he had taught the safe use of firearms to his family as a rite of passage into the O'Leary line. Harold O'Leary had been a law abiding citizen, and every gun control law on the books couldn't stop what came next. Unless the gun control is the complete banning of guns, it won't stop gun violence. Gun bans just stop those who follow laws from *buying* the guns. Criminals, they don't care about bans. Most of them aren't at your local Bass Pro Shop buying a rifle. Most gun control laws just irritate safe gun owners who are following the rules.

Nicole pocketed the gun, and walked into the kitchen. As she did, she saw her father sitting on the couch watching television. She walked out the front door, slamming it. She waited a few minutes, and then rang the doorbell. Harold opened the door, and Nicole shot him in the center of his chest. The force of the blow knocked him back onto the floor. Nicole walked in and shut the door behind her. She pointed the pistol at his head as he gasped.

"Why?" Nicole asked, anticipating his question. "That's why." She put one bullet square in his forehead.

After killing her father, Nicole rooted through the house taking any cash she found and the jewelry. She tore one of her skirts, and a pair of her panties and laid them next to her bed, along with a roll of duct tape. Satisfied that the scene had been set up to be a convincing home invasion, Nicole ran from the house after taking a ski mask from her father's closet. He often kept it near his hunting rifles, so it wasn't hard to find. Nicole marveled at how the tools of her revenge had been here in front of her the entire time she had been disintegrating.

Luckily for her, it was the middle of the day, midweek. Her neighborhood was empty, with everyone at work, or out shopping. No one was around to witness what had just happened. Nicole quickly sped off, mask over her face. She soon came to her destination, and parked.

Nicole walked down to the corner liquor store where Jackson worked in the Gold Mine shopping center. It was a run down, antiquated strip mall. Nicole wore a fuzzy, pink pair of Juicy sweatpants and a matching hooded sweatshirt. The black, hunting, ski-mask covered her face.

Nicole walked here today, because she knew Jackson was working. He had been on the same schedule for nearly three years. As often as Nicole had needed to play the adult in their family, she had known when he would be working and when he wouldn't. Fate just let it happen on "D-Day". She walked up to the counter where Jackson sat reading the letters section of a cheap porno mag. She cleared her throat and he looked up, high as usual. His eyes noticed the gun and he woke the hell up.

"Give me the cash." She said it smoothly, just as she had practiced. His eyes widened as she took the proper shooter's stance. Her feet were shoulder width apart. One hand was on the pistol, the other was underneath the first, cupping it to stabilize the shot and reduce the recoil. Jackson dropped the magazine and opened the register.

"Shit lady, don't shoot me, man," he was begging. "Please." And now he was shaking. Nicole felt sorry for him, but not enough to stop. He set plastic bag on the counter with a small pile of cash in it and backed away.

"Don't forget the stash box under the counter." She reminded him. Nicole had heard Jackson talk of the stash box before. He often fantasized about ripping off his boss when he was stoned. According to him, the owner of the store was too cheap to buy a safe and kept an enormous amount of cash in a hollow section of the floor behind the counter. Today, it would buy her a ticket to go out and see the world. Jackson didn't question how the robber knew. He simply did as he was told. Everything was going according to plan until the little bell over the front door rang. Nicole and Jackson both looked. It was the uber-geek, Jeremy Bloom. He recognized Nicole immediately.

"Nicole?" he questioned. "What's going on?"

Jackson's face lit up. He turned to his sister first in anger and then he laughed.

"Nicole," Jackson sounded like a babbling idiot. "Oh man! Good one, sis! You really had me going there."

"Don't move, Jackson," Nicole said in a deadly still voice. She pointed the gun with one hand and removed the ski mask with the other. She curled the mask so that her face was revealed.

"What do you mean? It's over. I get it. Ha-ha." He gave a dead laugh. Jackson was beginning to get angry now.

"Damn you, Jeremy," Nicole felt her eyes welling up. She held it back. She would not cry. Not here. Not now. Not today. She hadn't cried in the courtroom with her mother. She hadn't cried at the Village Inn where she and Natalie had lunch afterward. She would not cry now. "Why'd you have to show up? Now? Today of all days? Jesus, I'm sorry you had to see this."

"Nicole." Jeremy tried to calm her with a soft tone and passive hand movements.

"Please, shut-up, Jeremy. This is family business. "Nicole nodded at Jackson, then looked at him with her weapon. Jackson put his hands above his head, taking her seriously. "Do you have any idea what happened today, Jackson? Mom and dad got divorced, that's what. Things were never the same between them after what you did." Nicole lost her internal struggle and began to cry.

"Nicky?" Jackson was sure now that she meant to rob and kill him. "Mom, Dad, Wha...? Just put the gun away, please. What did I do?" Jackson's eyes now began to well with tears.

"What did you do?! You knew! And you didn't do anything! And daddy just watched from the fucking window!" Nicole screamed incredulously. She bit her bottom lip until it bled. Silence reigned. Each of them could hear the other breathing. Their hearts all pounded in unison to a beat of fear and danger.

"Remember," Nicole continued. "When I was 12, you and John Mckenzie took me behind the shed out in the back yard to play, 'doctor'? Things were never the same after that. Mom and dad just fell apart. I tried my best to be the best. I did everything right. I got the best grades. I was popular. I wasn't fat. I played sports and activities. I wanted them to know it was alright; That I would be okay. But you..."

Nicole trailed off shaking her head.

"You just couldn't straighten up." The gun never moved as she spoke. "You were a loser all of the time. You. Did. This."

Jackson sensed the wavering in her voice. It was obvious that she was going over the edge.

"Nicole, I-"

"Fuck you." Nicole pulled the trigger. Her brother's head exploded. Jackson fell to the floor with a lively thud. Jeremy cringed, looking away. His mind was disgusted, but his heart was in love. He would do anything for her, but he could not bring himself to look at the body. Not only did the body disgust him, but the chunks of skull and brain that were glued to cigarette cartons behind the counter by plasma and bloody strands of Jackson's shoulder length hair would not go away.

"Oh shit, Nicole." Jeremy stood up straight as Nicole went behind the counter and finished emptying out the stash box. "We gotta get out of here. We gotta get you out of here. Take the money and come with me. We'll think of something."

Jeremy continued to babbling. Nicole stopped listening. She moved to the position she shot from and grabbed the bag of money. She estimated the bag held double digit thousands as she walked toward Jeremy. He moved to embrace her. She shot him in the chest. Twice. He flew back into the glass door. It cracked but did not break. Blood streaked down the window behind him as he slid to a rest on his backside. He began to shake from the massive blood loss. A river of crimson ran down his shirt and onto the floor. Life fluid began to fill his lungs. Nicole was careful to avoid the pooling blood around him. She knelt beside Jeremy and brushed the brown hair from his face. He began to gurgle through his blood. He was trying to talk as he suffocated.

"I'm sorry, Jeremy. I had a slow speed come apart, but I'm better now. You understand, right?"

He didn't answer.

"Oh, but it's okay. Trust me. I love you. Don't worry, there is no God. Life is hell." With that, she kissed his lips. Blood began to sputter and foam from his mouth. She pulled back slightly, licking her lips. She tasted the last bit of life left in his earthly shell. Jeremy was still now. She had felt him leave when she kissed him. Nicole hadn't expected that. She dropped the bag of money and wiped a tear from her face. Pressing her face to his, she kissed him between the eyes.

Nicole walked out of the store, and stood in the sunlight. She felt the rays of heat beating down on her, and soaked them up. She thought of her mother, starting a new life. She pictured Natalie moving on in her own life, growing old without Nicole. She pictured Elizabeth finally branching out on her own when college was too big a place for her to be the queen of all gossip. She pictured Chad, selling life insurance after his college days were over. He'd still land a beautiful girl, Nicole was sure, but she'd never replace Nicole. Chad would always think of her when he slept with his wife.

Nicole stood, putting the pistol in her mouth. She closed her eyes. Somewhere, in the distance at some unknown point, Nicole heard a bang. The thing that was in her... The thing that killed the cat and stole and did all those terrible things... it was gone.

<u>Now</u>
Her mother was right. It felt like warmth on the wind.
She had expected it to hurt somehow.